Praise for Rochelle Distelheim's
SADIE IN LOVE

* * *

"Is it possible that a reader can love every word of a novel? In this case, a resounding yes! I was entranced by this story, its eye and ear, its food, its characters, its wit, and the nostalgic Hester Street thrill of being transported to the Lower East Side of the early 1900's. Brava, Rochelle Distelheim."

— Elinor Lipman, author of *The Inn at Lake Devine* and *On Turpentine Lane*

"Looking for love? Who isn't? Good. You will fall for Sadie Schuster. Hard. And you won't need to spend fifty cents for one of her handcrafted love knots either. You just need to curl up with this delightful story about a woman for whom love is a business, until she discovers she needs some passion in her own life. Who doesn't? For that matter, who doesn't need a little magic now and then? Well, lucky you, because Rochelle Distelheim's luminous first novel contains magic, passion and pure joy. So read it. Live a little."

— Sharon Fiffer, author of *Lucky Stuff* and *Home: American Writers Remember Rooms of Their Own*

"If you don't fall in love with *Sadie in Love* on page one, you may be dead. Or, perhaps you can't read. Because the characters in Rochelle Distelheim's comic novel, set in New York's Lower East Side in 1913, are so delightful, they will snatch your heart before you know what's happened. A Yiddish folktale of magic, love and hope, it is sure to put a spell on every reader."

— Jennie Fields, author of *The Age of Desire*

"I fell in love with the irreverent Sadie Schuster as she takes to heart her horoscope's reading that she must 'learn to live with passion.' She doesn't just 'learn,' she pursues passion and the men who might embody it. Brash, witty and brave, she turns to the obituary column to ask, 'Whose wife was gone?'—even as she takes part in dance contests and the suffragette movement of early twentieth century New York."

— Pamela Painter, author of *Ways to Spend the Night*

Sadie in Love

ROCHELLE DISTELHEIM

Aubade Publishing
Nashua, NH

Edited by Tiffany Jacobs

Cover design and book layout by Cosette Puckett

Portions of *Sadie in Love* are contained in the story "You Can Take Me, You Can Leave Me," copyright © Rochelle Distelheim 2016, JewishFiction.net, ISSUE 17, April 2016

Library of Congress Control Number: 2017964145

ISBN: 978-0-9845494-1-2

Published by Aubade Publishing, Nashua, NH

Printed in the United States of America

Acknowledgements

No book is created by one person alone. I have Fred Shafer to thank, first, for his brilliance as a literary coach, then, for his endless patience as he helped me understand that, if you want to create the hard-to-believe, you must make it seem like the everyday. Then there are The Writers of Glencoe—they know who they are—who listened to three, then four *Sadies*, and, finally, at least ten, helping me to make her more alive each time. There is no publisher more meticulous about logistics than is Joe Puckett, while managing every unexpected glitch with humor and grace. And thanks to Cosette Puckett, the first to welcome Sadie when they met in the submission pile. Then there is my family of three discerning readers, Ellen, Laura, Lisa, cheerleaders extraordinaire, and last, Irv Distelheim, who believed in my writing from our first moments.

This book is for I.H.D.
My Beshert

Chapter One

1913, New York City, the Lower East Side

S adie Schuster sold love knots, hope wrapped in a *schmattah*,
fifty cents. A lot of money in 1913, but hope never came
cheap, especially when it came from Sadie Schuster. "You
think this business makes me rich?" she asked her customers.
"The material alone costs me forty cents; I do it to make people
happy."

She learned her magic tricks in Luvel, Poland, where she and
Fivel lived before coming to New York, two greenhorns, just
married, and talked about love knots as though there really was
magic in this world, and only she, of all the Jews in New York who
came from places like Minsk, Riga, Lublin, Budapest, and Warsaw,
knew how to put them together.

It was a secret, she said, passed from mother to daughter. Her
own daughter, Yivvy, who ran a secondhand antique shop, and
worked the cash register nights at the Cherry Street Cafeteria,
didn't believe in love or magic. Take it or leave it, Sadie Schuster
was the only love knot maker in New York City.

The love knots were works of art. For female customers, Sadie braided strands of the loved one's hair with red thread, added a shirt button, a shoelace, fringe from a prayer shawl, cigar bands, suspender buckles. For men customers, she stole a tooth from the loved one's comb, the lace of a handkerchief, hairpins, boot heels, a snip of corset bone.

Showering scented water over the scraps, she wrapped them in a square of flowered cotton *schmattah*, and tied the four corners together, making a plump little bundle the size of her thumb. If she could get her hands on a little perspiration from the body of the loved one, and rub *that* into the knot, ha! Perfect. Cupping the knot in her palm, she half chanted, half sang, murmuring strange sounds softly; so softly, her customers couldn't recognize the language. That was precisely what Sadie hoped for: her certainty; their bewilderment. It made her seem powerful; it made her customers feel better about parting with fifty cents.

This was the promise: the love knot pulled at the loved one against his/her will, against all reason, against the laws of nature and the Old Testament; against everything, it seemed, except Sadie's say-so. Love always begat love, until two separate people turned into one absolutely and for-all-time happy couple.

Her favorite customers were those who lived in her tenement building on Orchard Street, an eight-flat she and Fivel purchased at auction just before he died. Up and down four flights of stairs, breathing hard, sweating, even in winter, Sadie stirred up love knot business when she collected rent. "Love knots," she crooned, "money for me today; love for you tomorrow. Open up for Sadie."

Unmarried tenants opened up, and asked questions. They were lonely, but not foolish. Fifty cents bought a shave and haircut; a steam bath at Silberstein's Private Water Works; five dances at the Henry Street Saturday Night Social Club; a secondhand derby hat; spats, used; embroidered gloves, the fingers still like new. The list went on and on.

What guarantee did they have, new customers asked, and who could they complain to, if love didn't appear in two, three weeks? "Nobody. God matched Adam to Eve, yes? And it didn't work out. So, who did Adam complain to? Anyway"—Sadie liked to use words from her night school English class, words like *anyway* and *nevertheless*, savoring each syllable as though it were a feast, and she was starving—"leave the details to me; you got plenty to do. Go rent a hall, get ready to make a wedding. I smell success about to happen." What choice did her customers have? Loneliness on the Lower East Side was like an itch waiting to be scratched. Synagogues seated men in front, women in back, behind gauze curtains. Moishe Pipik's Cafe on Lower Broadway was loud talk and cigar smoke, hot blintzes and sour cream, scratchy Gypsy music, but it was no place for romance.

Loneliness hung over Sadie too, now that Fivel was dead, taken by influenza; one week, and—splat! Just like that: dead. Dead, but not gone; Sadie wouldn't let him get away that easily. She talked to him while she worked on her love knots. Sometimes it seemed they talked more now than when he was alive.

"Fivel . . ." Her eyes on the ceiling. "A woman alone, it's no picnic."

Silence.

"I know you didn't want to, but you went before the mortgage did."

Again, silence.

"That secondhand furnace you put in? I said, buy new, remember?"

No sign he'd heard her.

"Well, you can act hurt. Meanwhile, you're up there floating around warm, and I'm down here freezing." Cocking her head, raising her arm: "Remember this watch? For my birthday, just before . . ." Sadie's smile soured. "It keeps terrible time."

Early in June Sadie's business went crazy. Four new customers in one week, enough money to buy white boots with hearts stenciled on the heels, or maybe the used fox scarf with one eye in the window of a secondhand shop near Orchard Street.

By the end of the week, she opened *The Daily Forward*, in search of new, mysterious-sounding words to put into her singsong chants, and, as always, in search of news of the women she'd met in the Canal Street Library—schoolteachers, store clerks, seamstresses, Jewish, Gentile, and all sorts mixed together, for getting the vote. When they marched through the Lower East Side, men booing from the sidewalks, the policemens all over them, they kept on stopping traffic, waving their flags, Sadie along with them, thinking, Thanks God Fivel doesn't see me.

Now, opening the *Forward*, she found not interesting words or suffrage news, but her horoscope: "If you're a June baby, you've got to learn to live with passion."

Sadie looked at the ceiling, toward heaven. "Fivel," she whispered, "hear that? *Passion!* Something we never talked about." Her memories of how passion looked, felt, the way it burned her skin and throat, were older than her marriage. So old, Sadie felt uncertain. Maybe the advice wasn't meant for her. She read the horoscope again: "Learn to live with passion." Suddenly, it sounded like something she'd been waiting to do.

But first, what did she look like? She hadn't been paying attention. Sadie peered into the patch of mirror over her washbasin. The news at forty-one wasn't good: skin wrinkling around the eyes, and sagging under the chin. Elsewhere, what was tight was now loose, and what was once high was slipping. Sadie sucked in her fleshy cheeks, puckered her lips. A woman without a man had to hurry; time was no friend. Growing old on cold sheets was bad for the bones, bad for the skin, terrible for the nerves.

"*Tse-hit-st,*" she whispered, using the Yiddish word for passion, *tsutsing* the *t-s* sounds, grateful she still had all her own teeth. She repeated the word: *tsehitst*. It sang a soft hiss as it rolled off her tongue. A good sign.

Living *tsehitst* was a wonderful idea, but it raised questions without offering answers. Sadie turned to the obituary column. Whose wife was gone now? That month three women her age had left healthy husbands behind. Sadie knew two of them: a house painter with a glass eye that clicked when he laughed or sneezed and a chicken flicker who moved like a freight train. Sadie imagined his immense weight settling into her bed.

That left Herschl Diamond, who peddled blocks of ice, a man she'd seen many times riding through the streets on his wagon, calling out in careful English: "Ice! A cold friend on a hot day!" Nice muscles on that one, she'd thought, good hair, expensive teeth.

Only two, three weeks ago, they'd almost met. She'd been rushing out of her flat and turned, almost tripping over him in the foyer, dressed in a clean white shirt and red suspenders, pressed cotton pants. Never too hurried to admire something admirable,

Sadie watched him vanish up the stairwell and around the curve. So. Now this desirable man was, like her, alone. How terrible. How wonderful.

She lowered the window shades, dimmed the gas jets, closed her eyes, and crooned. She rang a set of six brass bells, snapped her fingers, stomped her feet. The air felt thin, empty. Sometimes the spirits needed coaxing, sometimes they tortured her, accusing her of not believing. Spirits were harder to fool than customers.

Plucking a garlic bulb from the icebox, she hung it on a string around her neck, twirling slowly, then faster. She trimmed her fingernails and dropped the parings into a tiny metal cylinder that contained "The Song of Songs," inscribed on ivory parchment. "Oy," she sang, "I am my beloved's and my beloved is mine."

Aaahhh, they were coming. Sadie felt the spirits crowding into the flat, floating along the edges of the china cupboard, clinging to the sepia photograph of Fivel smiling into the sun, one hand patting his horse.

When they'd settled into silence: "*Him*," she hissed. "Herschl Diamond, that's the one I want." A whirring sound; they were listening. Poking a finger into her chest, she whispered, "For me." Spirits could be spiteful. They could, if they wished, point this adorable man in the direction of one of her customers. "Tell me how much it will cost. I'm willing—*anything*!" A flutter of wings. Sadie thrust her hand out. The air rearranged itself, the faintest feather touch against bare flesh. She shivered. The spirits were like that: friendly one minute; indifferent the next.

Something brushed against her cheek. She heard shrieks, like those heard at midnight in the Catholic graveyard in her Polish village. She'd walked among the tombstones with Ludmilla, the gravedigger's wife, who, in exchange for coins, described passion, and how these spirits were in charge of bringing it—and of taking it away. Sadie, in her American life, could court these spirits, they'd help her get rich, if they grew fond of her.

"Louder, talk to me!" She shuffled across the wooden floor, coaxing. Maybe she'd touch one of the spirits, beg it to sit on her fingernail. They could bargain. The room fell silent.

Of course, how could she forget? She hadn't made her Herschl love knot, filled with Herschl's bits and pieces, then the special chant, the magic words, the rubbing of the knot against her bare skin. They wanted her to do it all, exactly as she did for her customers. "So, I'll make my Herschl love knot," she whispered, "I'll chant like you never heard before. I can wait for your answer. But"—she sipped from a silver cup filled with sweet red wine and spat "*Ptooey, ptooey, ptooey!*" into her cupped palm three times—"don't fool with me too long."

⸎   ⸎   ⸎

Later that night, she talked to Fivel. "You understand why?" It wasn't a question. "An empty bed is a cold place for a hot-blooded woman." In her imagination Fivel was floating seated, so his feet wouldn't hurt. No tie, a ten-cent cigar in his mouth. His feet always hurt, which was why they'd never danced, something Sadie loved even more than she loved the moving pictures. Something she enjoyed even more than she enjoyed her suffragette ladies, and their weekly meetings at the Canal Street Library.

"Stand up," she'd plead, "put out your right foot, follow me." Nothing. Fivel's feet always fumbled, sending Sadie in search of other partners, men she knew from Luvel: the butcher, the carpenter, husbands of neighbors, *anyone*. She adored holding her partner's hand, hugging his shoulders, leaning against his chest, whirling in dizzying whirls to the oom-pa-pa beat. It was the two-ness of it she loved, the sweaty nearness of another body that she loved. Sometimes at weddings or *bar mitzvahs* she'd dance alone, the music lifting her out of the room, out of New York, out of her life.

"Fivel?" He was like this sometimes: stubborn, silent, a mountain of maybes when she wanted reassurance. "The hyenas won't let you live, a woman alone. I need someone to take care." If he'd just send a sign—thunder, a rumbling, a hot flash—to show her he agreed or disagreed. He was probably floating past, smirking, pleased that at last she appreciated what she'd lost. She shook her fist at the ceiling. "Go, find Herschl Diamond's wife, you'll feel better."

That night she dreamed she was a Hollywood star reclining

on a white bearskin rug, dressed in pale chiffon. A banquet of sweets awaited her, honeyed almond pastries spread on purple embroidered satin. Six servants in red velvet with plumed turbans fanned the humid air. Herschl arrived wearing only white trousers, carrying an enormous cake of ice. She beckoned. The ice melted, more ice appeared, melted, until he waded in water to his waist. He swam to her, emerging naked and eager.

"Herschl," she breathed, "I'd know you anywhere." He lowered himself onto the bearskin rug, one hand on her thigh. But it was a cake of ice, not his hand, showering goose bumps over her feverish skin. She heard piano music in the distance, upstairs the Hogan baby was crying, piercing sobs that frightened Herschl off. Sadie awoke, shaken. He was going home to look at his dead wife's picture! No—he was leaving to meet another widow, someone pushy, a woman with no night school education, and no money, who couldn't even dance. She got out of bed, and sipped hot tea. Learning to live with passion at forty-one was hard work.

ᴄᴊᴼᴐ ᴄᴊᴼᴐ ᴄᴊᴼᴐ

One week later, good news stood on Sadie's doorstep in the shape of Herschl Diamond, holding a brown paper bag speckled with water spots, droplets of water running down his pants leg and splashing onto his shoes. Coming up the stairs behind him, Sadie recognized the shoulders, the strong neck, the wild salt-and-pepper hair. Only one week! The spirits must be in a soft mood. Maybe they said, *Ah, that Sadie, she never asks for nothing for herself, such a kind, good person, let's do this for her.*

"You are visiting one of my tenants, perhaps?" She pronounced each word in her careful night school voice. She should have worn her new flowered voile dress, she should have remembered to lose twenty pounds, have her hair waved, fluffed up, sprayed some toilet water under her arms.

Herschl turned, removing his cap, and tipped his head in a gesture Sadie decided was a bow. "The Rosenbergs," he said, jerking his thumb upward, "cousins." He looked very handsome, his eyes, especially; not blue exactly, and not gray, but the best of both colors.

She had planned to wait for him at the corner. Ten thirty every morning, Herschl, his wagon, his horse, cakes of ice mounded behind him like miniature Eskimo houses. She'd buy and, when he dropped change into her palm, she'd close her hand around his fingers, gently, only for a moment.

But this! This was better. Now she could pour a cup of tea, cut up fresh strudel, they'd talk. Two grown-up people who'd suffered, they shared a lot. Her plan was settled in her mind; so settled, in fact, that when he cleared his throat and said he was late for dinner, holding the dripping bag at arm's length, Sadie felt robbed. "Well," she said, following him into the foyer, "since we're on the subject, I'm Sadie Schuster, this is my building." He paused, looking polite. "The owner, not the manager."

"Herschl Diamond," he said, slapping his cap back onto his head, then moving quickly toward the staircase.

"You are welcome, Mr. Diamond," she called, following closely, but not too.

He turned. Again, the cap came off and his cheek dimpled right *there*. Sadie imagined kissing it. She liked the cleft in his chin, the bushy eyebrows. She liked his shaving lotion: the scent of peppermint floated across the foyer, promising walks in the woods, a dip in the Atlantic. Ice shavings in a frosted glass.

Herschl shifted the paper bag to his other arm. The puddle of water at his feet was now a widening pool. "Diamond," she said, "that is the work you do, or your name?" Men liked women with a sense of humor. He smiled. She was right. Make them laugh, and they're yours.

"My work," he held the bag at arm's length. Little drips were now bigger drips, a gray-white mass poked through a hole in the bag. "My work is *like* diamonds, if you don't mind fakes."

"Well"—she brushed hair out of her eyes—"that is a very, very interesting"—rolling the word over her tongue, as her English teacher had demonstrated—"point of view." She hoped to work *certainly* or *actually* into the conversation.

"Sorry to walk away." He moved toward the stairs. "Dinner . . ." The blue-gray eyes were clouded; he must be a worrying type.

8

She'd help him fix that.

"We are practically neighbors," she called after him. Two long words. He had to see she was a woman of learning. His foot was on the first step. "Schuster," she added, shouting now. He hesitated, but didn't turn around. "With an *s-c-h*, my late husband's name." He was almost at the first landing, his shoulders swinging so gracefully, she wondered if he was a dancer. "We must talk sometime," she continued, still shouting. He was on his way to the second floor. "You can call me Sadie."

He disappeared around the next landing. Sadie stood at the bottom of the stairs, looking up into the dimness, her words echoing against the walls, the railing, the landing, and finally, at her feet.

"Spirits!" She felt them hovering. Crouching, she peered into every corner of the vestibule, until she heard Herschl's knock on the door of the Rosenberg's flat: hard, clear, demanding. Like a call to war.

     ꙮ   ꙮ   ꙮ

Who knew better than Sadie how slowly the spirits moved? Who knew better how unreliable they could be, even when they liked you, what pleasure they took in hurting? They were not, after all, Jewish spirits. They and she were not kindred. They could turn on her at any moment, for any reason. Even for no reason at all.

Worse, even if it pleased them to give her Herschl, who knew what they'd demand in exchange? She needed a human plan she could control, but not a plan suggested by Yivvy. Her daughter laughed at the idea of finding love with the help of cotton knots. She laughed at finding love, period. Sadie needed Mitzi Beuhler, the newest tenant in her building; third floor rear, the biggest flat, three bedrooms, the only one with windows facing the patch of backyard, welcoming the afternoon sun into a spacious parlor. The rent was fifteen dollars a week—three times that of the other flats.

Mitzi didn't care how much rent she paid. She was a widow from Chicago and, she said, her late husband had treated her well, especially after he died. "Understand?"

Sadie did. Mitzi's story was her own story, with one important difference: Mitzi didn't worry that her money might run out. Sadie envied that. But not as much as she envied the way Mitzi looked and smelled. She smelled of flowers, and something else, something exciting and faintly foreign, like cloves. And her hair! Sadie had never seen such hair, a brilliant shade of red, flecked with golden tints, brushed into a shining pompadour, like a bright crown, and pierced by a long tortoiseshell pin.

Then there was the beauty mark under her full crimson lips. God hadn't put it there. And the high, full breasts swelling beneath silk shirtwaists. Hers? Or—*store bought*? Maybe Mitzi had her own magic tricks, something to do with the packages wrapped in flowered paper she carried home in her string bag. Sadie, hearing her tenant's quick, light steps, would open the door of her flat a hairline crack, and squint into the gloom at the bright vision passing, inhaling a trail of perfume. Here was all the proof Sadie needed that the world had been created in two unequal parts.

Time wasn't on her side. Herschl wouldn't last long in the bachelor business. Sadie slipped a note under Mitzi's door: "Today, please, we must talk. Four o'clock?"

Four o'clock gave Sadie time to visit her daughter Yivvy's antique shop, a dim cave of abandoned treasures on Houston Street, in search of Yivvy's specialty: hard-to-get street information.

From the moment the girl had learned to talk, she'd had only one response to her mother's suggestions. No to dancing: a waste of time. No to the moving pictures: too many people eating and drinking and talking, the piano player pounded too loud. No to sitting in cafes along Lower Broadway on Sunday afternoons: "What! Paint my face and put on fancy clothes, pay fifty cents for stale strudel?"

"All the nice boys go there, it's a place to—"

"*Nice*? With their sweaty hands, always patting and pinching. No, thank you."

"Not to marry with. To talk, have a few laughs, a young girl—"

Yivvy said she didn't feel young; she felt in a hurry. Her final no was the one that caused Sadie the most pain, even more pain than her refusal to help out or to maybe even clapping when she marched with her votes-for-women friends, holding a proud "Votes

10

for Women" sign. This no was to taking night classes at a teachers' college: "What for? Business. *That's* the future of America. I wanna be rich."

"Who doesn't?"

⟡   ⟡   ⟡

When Sadie arrived at the antique shop, she found Yivvy behind the counter polishing a brass samovar. She looked up. "Oh, it's you," she said as she went on with her work. She was short, like her mother, but skinny, as though all the fat in her body had been rendered.

Sadie squinted at her daughter through the gloom. Same black cotton dress, same tight curls, like she bought them at the five-and-ten, and glued them onto her head. "You oughta fix up a little, do something with your hair, wear red."

"Gee, Ma, a minute ago I was glad to see you." Yivvy blew at the samovar and stood back to admire her work.

Sadie thrust her hand into a wooden bin, and brought out a pair of dice. "Ivory?"

"Bone."

"I'll take 'em. Who knows when I'll have a customer in love with a gambler?" She dropped the dice into her purse.

"Ten cents."

"Put 'em on my account."

Yivvy carried the samovar to a display of lenses, binoculars, paperweights, magnifying glasses.

Sadie followed. "Ah." She pounced on a glass circle the size of a silver dollar, the color of night. It caught and held the light of the overhead gas lamps. It whispered her name. "How much?" She blew her breath over it, wiped it on her skirt. It winked at her.

"It's nothing; just cheap glass. Without the whach-a-ma-call-it"— Yivvy measured the height and width of a telescope against the empty air—"it's junk."

"Then junk you'll give for nothing." Sadie held the glass up to one eye.

"Ma, I want to thank you."

Sadie turned, the lens still covering her eye. "For what?"

"The way you move stuff out of here, it makes me feel like business is good."

Sadie slipped the lens into her purse and, clapping her hands, wiped them on her skirt. "You could use a little soap and water."

"Next time bring that, instead of advice."

"I came about something important—*two* somethings, actually—one short, one long." Sadie eyed the gas burner behind the counter. "A cup of tea while we talk? I brought my own sugar." She rummaged in her purse. They sipped tea, they talked. Yivvy asked questions. Sadie described Mitzi, shaping the air with her hands. Then she described Herschl, his horse, and wagon.

Yivvy took notes. She had friends: salesmen, street musicians, shopkeepers, politicians. "I call them my eyes and ears."

"Call them your belly button, get me the information. For her: where's she getting all her money? Something don't smell kosher. For him: how long was the marriage, was it happy, any children? Is he—God forbid, religious—where is he from, when did he come over?"

"Why?"

"Also, how old?"

"You workin' for City Hall, or somethin'—*what*?"

Better not to talk romance. Yivvy loved her father. Later could come a soft way to say she was lonely for someone to hold hands with, to listen. "Find first, then ask why."

"This got anything to do with those pushy women you meet at the library, and all their talk about how women are cheated if they don't get to vote? You know, Ma, the suffering jets."

"With a '*g*,' not no '*j*.' It makes me crazy when you on purpose pull apart the name, like it's something not important, like voting ain't something women should be doing from the beginning of this country. George Washington"—Yivvy's eyes were taking on their let-me-out-of-here look—"was not so smart like everyone says, or he would have written it down in the rules."

Yivvy shrugged. "I leave that kinda thing to fancy ladies who went to college. They got the time and money to *putz* around."

"*Money*, all the time money! It don't cost to read books, to *think*. It don't cost to change a law here, a law there, make over what

George Washington didn't remember when he was putting together America."

❧   ❧   ❧

Sadie knocked on Mitzi's door at 4:01 p.m. She didn't recognize the flat. Mitzi had furnished it like a scene from a fairy tale: gold brocade curtains, plaster statues of men and women draped in layers of filmy-white tulle. The gas lamps were hooded with crimson, tulip-shaped glass, the mirror above the mantle framed in a circle of gilt angels busy hugging one another. And, in the corner—milky, luminous, shining like a sky full of moonlight—a piano. On Orchard Street, a white piano, and she—*she* who missed *nothing*—missed seeing the men carry it in.

Mitzi, looking to Sadie like a walking bouquet in peach chiffon, waved Sadie toward a sofa.

"Nice material." Sadie ran her hand over the plush fabric.

Mitzi sat on a pale, yellow love seat, cradling a thin silver case in one hand. "Okay, hon, what can I do you for?"

"I never saw such a place, all these *things*." The cupids on the mantel winked at her. "Your mother's furniture?"

Mitzi laughed. "Somethin' like that."

Sadie waved at the piano. "You know to play? I hear music coming from here. I thought, a phonograph. I never dreamed a real piano."

"You didn't come knocking at my door to talk furniture." Mitzi tapped a latch, the cover of the silver case flew up. "Cigarette?"

Sadie hesitated. Maybe she should try, once. All the ladies who smoked in the moving pictures looked so, so—*American*. She shook her head.

Mitzi tapped the cigarette on the case, lit it with a tiny ruby-red lighter, and looked at Sadie with a half smile that wasn't smile enough for Sadie.

"I came for advice," she blurted out, and closed her eyes. When she opened them, Mitzi was all curves and draped chiffon, leaning against the cushions, smoking, looking more beautiful than Tootsie

McCoy in her last movie, when she ran through the woods in a silver crown and white feathers.

"About?"

"My best advice giver is the lady who writes in *The Daily Forward*, but this I can't go to her for." Mitzi's beauty mark shimmered. *That* was the secret, beauty marks. "Anyway . . ." Sadie continued—hoping her pronunciation made up for her accent—and talked about being alone in New York without a mother, without a husband, who had married her when she was just eighteen, and not because she'd picked him or he'd picked her, but because someone back in Poland did the picking.

"*So?*"

"So, now I want to marry with someone *I* picked out *myself,* and I need help getting prettied up." If Mitzi laughed, she'd raise her rent.

Mitzi crushed her cigarette. "Why do women always think, if I only had that guy over there"—she pointed to a male statue draped in black-and-red-striped cloth—"I'd be so goddamned blazes happy, I'd bust in half with joy?"

"You asking me, or asking yourself?"

"Women, females, ladies, girls. No matter what's the problem, they think the solution's a man."

Sadie knew that word, *solution.* She heard it from Lillian Pomerantz, the sweet-like-sugar schoolteacher who could gain a couple pounds, and maybe do something about all that curly black hair, not pin it down so tight, who talked better than anyone when she came to the library to say, "Shame on America, women can't vote." Women had to stand up and holler, march around, remind the men they were just as good.

Sadie stood up at one meeting and asked why that would work. Everyone marched around after the fire in the Triangle shirt factory, so many young girls killed, and then everyone forgot. Then Lillian Pomerantz said, in her soft, silky voice, pronouncing every word like she was born with a dictionary in her mouth, there was no easy solution, but they were making progress. Another high-class word.

Sadie wrote it down, *solution,* adding it to her night school word list, and practiced in front of her mirror, loving the way the *u*, the *t*, the *i-o-n* got worked into such a lovely *shooshing* sound. Now Mitzi looked at Sadie as though wondering why she'd allowed her into the flat. "You got a few bucks in your pocket, right?"

Sadie made a none-of-your-business face: *maybe yes, maybe no.* "Enjoy yourself, for Christ sake! What you wanna tie yourself up for?"

This was not the conversation Sadie had in mind. Talking to Gentiles was hard work. "There's enjoy, and there's *enjoy.*"

"You got someone particular in mind?"

Sadie told Mitzi about her horoscope, about Herschl. "He looks like a man who knows from"—should she use the Yiddish word for passion? Uh-uh. English. Mitzi should see her as a modern, one hundred percent New York woman—"passion."

"It's better if they love you. When you do most of the lovin', they make you pay."

"You—paid?"

"I could tell you stories, hon, but this ain't the time."

She had to stay, she had to fish out this woman's secrets, like how to talk with that careless shrug. Herschl would visit her often if she could do that, they'd practice talking American. They'd dance. "Interesting," Sadie said, the word strung out with only a hint of a Yiddish accent, "but, if you don't mind me saying so"—a pause, only a beat, but long enough to search her mind for another long word—"you don't look to me like a lady who suffered."

Mitzi laughed, an explosion that ended in a cough. "Tell me about you. What all do you do?"

"Well . . ." She couldn't talk about her marching ladies, and the vote, that wasn't Mitzi; she could smell it. Better to get on to the love knots, even if Mitzi didn't believe her, even if she'd say, like lots of people: *You crazy, lady? Get out!* "I make love knots." Sadie's hands crawled through her purse, pulling out a scrunched-up yellow-and-blue flowered knot. She shook it to restore its shape.

"So?"

"So, plenty." Eyes closed, Sadie swayed, chanted a mélange of Polish and Yiddish, squatting in a half twirl, urging the love knot along her throat and arms. "Touch, but only a fast pat, you shouldn't crush the spirits or frighten them." Mitzi tap-tapped the love knot with the tip of one crimson fingernail. Sadie snatched it away. "Enough! The spirits love pretty things, your nail polish excited them." She jabbed at the air. "Listen!"

"Hey, come on!"

"*Shah*, quiet. You don't hear a little humming?" Sadie whirled and pointed to the fireplace. "There!"

"The furnace, for Christ's sake!"

"In *June*?" Sadie slipped the love knot into her purse. "Like I tell my customers, first you believe, then you see."

Mitzi snuggled into the cushions. "Same as any other shell game, mumbo jumbo to fool the poor suckers. We all do it."

"You think I make up lies?"

"I gotta hand it to you, whatta way to turn a buck."

"Fifty cents, two for ninety-five." Sadie blushed. "I also do something else. I dance"—she shifted, staring now at the cupids—"pretty good. My late husband wouldn't, so I didn't do it too much, but play music, and I turn into a whole new person."

"What's so marvelous about dancing?"

"*What*? You touch, you don't feel so alone." How to say this? "It gives a chance to be anybody you want to be, to show off."

"Let me have a look at you." Mitzi gestured *up-up*. Sadie stood. Mitzi turned her in one direction, then the other. "Well, hon"— she sighed, scrutinizing Sadie's hair, face, shoulders, chest, hips, ankles—"it won't be easy, I'm not makin' any promises. A few fast turns with the rouge brush, some upgrading here." She fluttered her fingers toward Sadie's eyes. "A new corset."

She'd come to the right place. She could hug this woman, who didn't look like the hugging type. "You do me good," Sadie said, "I do you good. One hand washes up the other."

"Meaning?" Mitzi crossed the room to a red-lacquered break-front, and brought out a crystal decanter and two glasses.

"Who doesn't have a little dirt on her hands," Sadie said, "from time to time?"

Mitzi poured wine into each glass, holding one out to Sadie. "First thing I gotta help you with is that accent."

"I don't talk so good? I know a thousand fancy night school words—two thousand! Listen." She took a deep breath.

"Sumptuous, delightful, celebrity."

"It's not *what* ya say, it's *how* ya say it. Practice this every night in fronta your mirror." Mitzi cleared her throat. "Some sugar-filled delicacies satisfy practically all our appetites. Clear, strong *s*'s on the *some*, a soft hiss like *s-h* on the *sugar.*"

"You gotta be *meshuga* to talk like that."

"You want this ice guy to think you're a woman of the world? I'll write it down, ten days and you'll sound"—Mitzi made a circle of thumb and forefinger. "Then we'll go on to another mouthful." Sadie shrugged. "I like you. We got a lot in common, you 'n me."

Sadie wasn't sure how that was possible, but she loved the sound of it.

Chapter Two

Ten o'clock Monday morning, Sadie was at the corner of Orchard and Delancey. Even this early, the city was a frying pan full of sweet onions. Her pompadour, brushed to shiny obedience with Mitzi's hair oil, wouldn't keep its good looks for long in all this humidity. Perspiration beaded her upper lip, her throat, trickled into her cleavage. Her opening speech was ready.

At exactly 10:24 a.m., Herschl and his wagon rounded the corner. Sadie held up one hand, bringing the wagon to a stop. Dampness had curled his hair; ringlets fell across his forehead. The sight of his chest with his shirt unbuttoned made her shiver.

"Ah, Mrs. Schuster." The cap came off. His smile was polite, but wary.

He remembered her name. A good sign. She complimented his horse, the color of the ice, and said he was better for her health than the doctor. He looked puzzled. "In this heat, I mean." The spirits had so far done nothing to soften him up. She held up five fingers. "Fifty pounds ice, please. You deliver?"

"What else? I don't expect you to carry."

"Later," she said. Should she flare her nostrils? She hadn't asked Mitzi about that.

"You don't need now?" The hair on his arms was blonde, a surprise. She could see him on the dance floor in a starched white cotton shirt, pearl studs down the front, maybe a snappy bow tie in a flowered silk print. She'd wear red silk, something soft around the hips, pleats at the bottom.

"Deliver at six o' clock," she said, "stay for a bite of supper."

He sat down hard on the wagon seat. "I'll bring the ice, but I'm busy for supper." His eyes today were more gray than blue, Fivel's color, but Herschl's were more . . . open. Only now she saw the faintest flash of annoyance in them. Good. She liked a man with strong feelings.

A foxtrot, she decided, the dance for getting to know a man. It gave room to pull back on your shoulders, to turn away your head and look at him without looking at him, like you're paying attention to the music. Yes sir, he was a man to foxtrot around with, all right. She held up a dollar bill. *Now!* He took the money and counted her change, dropping each coin into her palm. When the final penny left his fingers, she cupped her hand, fast, but not fast enough. Her fingers grasped only air. This man was plenty smart. She felt her smile slip.

"You know, of course, where I live." She pointed across the street. "My own eight-flat building that has no mortgage."

Herschl turned his head and looked, then, turning back to Sadie, thanked her for her business, putting two fingers to the brim of his cap before clicking his tongue at his horse.

"Ah, one minute." Sadie knelt and retrieved a clod of mud from the wagon's footrest that must have fallen from his boot. Then, reaching behind him, she pulled a straw from under a tower of ice and patted the horse with a scrap of fabric she'd slipped out of her pocket.

"You need something?" His voice was polite, but cool. He'd loosen up once she got him dancing.

"Oh, no." *Why not?* She flared her nostrils.

The gesture was lost on him. "I can go now?" Without waiting, he flicked the reins, guiding the wagon away from the curb.

"Oh, Mr. Diamond . . ." The wagon was gliding away. "*Never-*

theless . . ." She sang out. It was a free country, she could use all the night school words she knew if she wanted to. She could walk down Orchard Street dressed in a purple silk corset underneath a chiffon robe, if she wanted to. Twenty-two years living with Fivel, two years, four months without, she was entitled to collect on her horoscope.

Herschl balanced himself on the moving wagon, half standing, half sitting, looking back at her. Annoyed, waiting. "Even if you're busy for supper tonight, come anyway."

The wagon was almost at the corner. Herschl opened his mouth, then closed it, and shook his head, or was he flicking off a fly? Then the wagon turned the corner, and he was gone.

"Some sugar-filled delicacies," Sadie shouted into the empty air, as she crossed the street. A little boy sailing a clothespin in the water spurting down the gutter looked up at her, blinking. Sadie stopped and, leaning down, hollered in his ear, *"Some,* with a clear *s, sugar,* with a soft hiss." The boy burst into tears, and Sadie hurried down the sidewalk. "Spirits, get ready, I need you."

ᒍᵒ   ᒍᵒ   ᒍᵒ

"Fivel?" From the ceiling, silence. "You don't know me in my new face?" Sadie, puckering her lips, examined herself in the hand mirror. She fluttered her lashes and pinched her cheeks, feeling full of hope for the first time since falling into widowhood. "It's me, Sadie, a new package outside, but inside, the same merchandise."

After a trip to Klein's Emporium, she'd gone back to Mitzi's flat with a string bag full of cosmetics and a hairbrush. That woman knew her business, suggesting a pompadour, then curling the stray ends around her ears and along her neck, and *this*—patting her cheek—a black beauty mark. Who ever thought Sadie Schuster would turn out looking so good, after looking so bad for so long?

She set out the clod of mud from Herschl's boot, the snippet of straw, the bit of *schmattah* with sweat from his horse, arranging the objects in a circle, then a triangle, balancing the straw on top of the dirt, then sticking it into the dirt, then powdering the dirt into a small pile, laying the straw on it crosswise.

Uh-uh. She didn't feel any *zoompah*. Tonight, the spirits were indifferent. Wrapping the dirt in a wisp of white cotton batten, then coating the straw with a dab of olive oil, she covered it lightly with the *schmattah*, careful not to bruise anything.

She had here a nice variety of snippets from Herschl's life, only a beginning; not enough for an absolutely, sure-to-succeed love knot. The spirits admired an overflowing of *chochkas* that suggested for-sure knowledge of the loved one: his ins, his outs, his secrets. She needed a button, a whisker, a toothpick, a touch of his sweat.

Humming, Sadie carried her tidbits into the bedroom. Tonight she felt that the other treasures were as good as gotten. At six o' clock, she changed into her new flowered voile dress, and set the table with platters of cold pickled fish, sliced tomatoes, beet *borscht*, sour cream in a cut-glass bowl, and sliced pickles, snapping her fingers and two-stepping between table and icebox. He *would* stay for supper, of course.

Herschl was prompt.

Sadie opened the door to an overheated man in a short-sleeved shirt, a red-and-white bandana knotted at his throat, balancing an enormous cake of ice on a square of black leather slung across one shoulder. He held metal ice tongs, and looked determined. "Hello, Mr. Diamond." She tried to sound calm, in control, but breathy. She'd been correct, all right: he sure had muscles.

"Where is it?" His eyes were friendly, but she wouldn't call him relaxed.

"*It?*" She couldn't decide if he'd noticed her new face.

He half lurched, half shuffled into the flat, forcing her to move backwards. "Your icebox, Mrs. Schuster, *please!*" He didn't wait for an answer, but circled the room, until, seeing the kitchen, made one powerful motion of arms and tongs, lowering the cake of ice. Carrying it into the kitchen, he thrust it into the wooden icebox.

"That took some strength, believe me!" Sadie, in the kitchen doorway, hoped he heard how impressed she was. "Thanks God you came; I'd have hated to see everything spoil."

His eyes were friendly, even lively, but so far they showed no sign that he considered her beautiful. He untied the bandana and, leaning against the wall, wiped his face and neck. "June, and it feels like August," she said, fanning herself with her hand. He looked around the flat. She should have covered Fivel's picture. "A good thing for you I suppose, the more heat, the more business." Show him she had a good head for money.

"Mrs. Schuster"—now his hand was on the doorknob—"fifty or so pounds; fifty cents." Such nice eyes, honest. You could believe anything a man with eyes like that told you.

"What a coincidence." There were not many ladies who could pronounce such a long word, and one with so many *c*'s going the wrong way. "I am just now sitting down to supper"—a peddler's cry floated through the open window as she continued—"*alone.*" The word hung between them, coming to rest, finally, at his feet. Herschl took his hand off the doorknob, regarding her with weary eyes. He looked suddenly exhausted. She'd be happy to massage his shoulders, or maybe his feet. Men who stand up all day loved having their feet rubbed, then creamed. Tickled, even. Or, so she'd read in *The Daily Forward*. Fivel, unfortunately, hadn't been a foot person.

Herschl wiped his hands with the bandana. Was she imagining, or was he looking at her more closely now, taking in the hair, makeup, the new dress? He seemed to hesitate, then shook his head. "Thank you, anyway."

"Nothing to thank, only a little cold soup, some homemade pickled fish, relish I seasoned myself, and for dessert—"

"I already ate," he protested.

"Just an everyday supper, I eat like this all the time."

He looked at the table, sighed, and wiped his neck again, thrusting the bandana down the front of his shirt.

"So, you ate a little. What can it hurt? Sit and rest, take a sip, cool yourself." What a waste if he should leave. She wouldn't look this good again soon. Maybe never.

His hand was on the doorknob again, but he didn't open the door. He was looking past her, maybe at Fivel. "Mrs. Schuster—"

"Call me Sadie."

"—you are a very, I mean, you know a lot of words, and you use them"—now he looked at her—"all the time."

Sadie smoothed her dress and summoned a look somewhere

between modesty and gratitude. "Everybody says so." Was that a yes she saw in his eyes? She felt him weakening. Maybe the spirits had taken pity.

"Me." He shrugged. Good shoulders for shrugging. "I don't like words so much." Frowning, he seemed to ponder what he'd said. "I mean, I *like* words, but not when I have to speak them out."

"Well"—she stepped to the table and poured beet soup from the pitcher into two bowls—"talk does not cool us like cold *borscht*." She felt his eyes on her bare arms as she refolded the napkins and straightened the tablecloth. "Please," she said, and gestured to one of the chairs. "Sit." In one swift motion, she pulled the chair out and pressed gently on his shoulders when he came forward, lowering him into it.

"I am a man who always knows what he wants to do," he said, shifting uneasily. "Usually."

"You're strong, definitely strong. Anyone can see that." She sliced the bread, remembering to look up at him between slices. "I admire strong in a man; I always have."

He looked skeptical, "Mrs. Schuster—"

"Sadie," she said, as she sat down opposite him.

He seemed suddenly shy, almost embarrassed.

She leaned across the table and patted his hand. "Speak up, Herschl; you can talk to me about anything. I'm a good listener."

He cleared his throat and leaned back, then pressed forward again. "I think a lot—"

"A sign of a good mind."

"—but words don't come easy, like they do to you." He frowned at his soup spoon.

"Then we'll talk less and eat more."

"I read," he said, and looked surprised, as though wondering: *Why am I telling you this!*

"*No!*" Sadie put her spoon down. "I read also, from the time I was a little girl in Poland. Anything I put my hands on, I put in my head. Tell me, what kind books do you read?"

"Poems," he said, softly, "in Yiddish."

"The best kind," she said, happy he hadn't said books about murders or animals. She waited for him to say more, but he looked down at his plate. "Well . . ." she said. From Herschl, more silence.

She dipped her spoon into her *borscht.* "Enjoy in good health."

"For me," he said, "that's not always possible." He sipped, paused, sipped again.

Sadie leaned across the table. "You were saying?"

"Blood pressure." He pointed to his head.

"*Aaaah.*" She made a clucking sound, hoping he recognized it as sympathy. "My late husband"—she gestured to Fivel's photograph. A good thing, not covering him. His picture was proof someone had loved her once. Fivel never said it was love, but she never said love to him either—"he suffered from blood pressure, but I kept him alive. The doctor couldn't believe—"

"A lucky man. Mostly, one is sick and one is healthy. With us— my late wife and me—it was both." He hesitated before adding, "She suffered a weak nature. Nerves."

Sadie put her hand out, hoping to cover his hand where it lay on the table, but something—a rattling at the window, a noise from the hallway—caught his attention. He pulled back. She shopped around in her mind for a safer subject, thinking, maybe votes for women, but decided that was too dangerous. Who knew if he was a yes or a no on that subject. "Children?"

"To my sorrow, no. Gittel had women's troubles also." He rubbed his abdomen. "I hoped, at the beginning we both wanted"—he opened one hand: *nothing.*

Before she could stop herself, Sadie blurted out, "I myself have a lovely daughter."

"That's nice." He avoided her eyes.

She felt him slipping away. *What now?* "Herschl"—she started again, drawing out the *sch.* He had a dab of sour cream on his lower lip; it looked delicious—"do you dance?"

"Dance? Yes, but before, not anymore."

"Not since—"

"You should have seen us, Gittel and me." His eyes brimmed with feeling. "Oh, did we dance! We never got tired. Sometimes we even . . ." He blinked, looking past her, then shook his head. "*Heh!* Over, gone, another life."

"No, don't! I mean, please—wait." She hurried into the bedroom, returning with a phonograph.

"Ahh, a music machine." He looked impressed.

"My daughter pawns things. What nobody picks up, she gives me for pennies."

Setting the phonograph down, she rummaged inside the china cupboard and held up a cylinder. "A foxtrot." Snapping it into place, she cranked the machine. High, thin, scratchy music—a piano, a clarinet, a violin, a saxophone—filled the room.

Sadie pushed the table to one side, put her hand out and pulled him to his feet, taking him into her powerful arms, guiding him across the patch of floor. They moved awkwardly. He pulled away, and she pulled him back. The music was lively, an anything-is-possible tune. It made Sadie feel twenty years old, twenty-five, tops. Herschl felt good to her. A dip, twirl, dip, and he seemed to relax. He moved easily, just enough of a leader, enough of a follower.

"You are born to dance, like me," she said. His next move—a smooth turn, a slight pressure on her arm to guide her this way, then that—told her everything she wanted to know. He smelled of cigars and leather; thanks God not of his horse. She smelled, she hoped, of perfume, not onions.

"I'm stale," he said, finally, "out of practice." His breath ruffled her hair. She hadn't been this happy since, since . . . she couldn't remember when. The music wound down and he pulled away suddenly, wiping his damp face with the polka-dotted bandana. He started work very early, his horse must be fed by four in the morning, time to go. "So, good night, Mrs. Schuster."

Then Sadie saw it, a loose button on his shirt. "Hah." Moving quickly, she plucked it off with a snap of her fingers. "Take off your shirt." Before he could answer, she hurried into the bedroom for her sewing basket. When she came back, he was bare from the waist up, looking just as she had imagined. No, better. She sewed quickly, switching one of the buttons from her sewing box with one of his. When she held his shirt out to him, he thanked her and shook her hand, but she couldn't get anything going with his eyes. "You enjoyed, I hope," she said, still holding his hand.

He wagged his head. His face told her nothing.

One thing about this man: he didn't lie. Sadie forced a smile. "Good, then you'll come for supper again." Not a yes or a no crossed his face, as if there was a law against showing his feelings. She walked to the street door with him. "Good night, Herschl," she called after him, "nice to dance with you." He waved without turning.

Back in her flat, Sadie lowered the gas jets, set out the clod of dirt, the straw, the button, the fabric that held his perspiration, placing each object in the center of a scrap of chintz she'd saved from a love knot put together just that week for a skinny young dressmaker with crossed eyes. After tying the four ends of the fabric into a plump round knot, she held it aloft, chanting, "Me, me, *me*!"

The spirits were watching, she felt their feverish breath. Nestling the love knot on a lace doily, she produced the lens from the glasses from Yivvy's shop.

"I got here in my hand"—one arm stretched forward into dimness, the lens cupped in her palm, she rubbed the dark circle of glass with the fingers of her other hand—"I have here a genuine evil eye!" Her voice was barely audible above the hiss of the gas lamps. "This magic can out-spirit the spirits! It can do anything I tell it to do—*anything*!" Was she imagining that whoosh off the bridge of her nose? *Them*! No other movement anywhere. Even the floorboards fell mute.

"So, all right, I give you a special problem, a man who won't say yes if he can say no. That's why I need"—sniffing at the dusty air—"magic!" Hard to say, they maybe left by now, angry, such a *cockamamie* problem: a practically brand-new widower who dances, but won't; who reads poetry books, but counts out his spoken words.

Circling the room, Sadie thrust the lens into every corner, twisting and turning it until, exhausted, she fell to the floor, where she lay listening. *Ha—finally*! This silence was different; full, not empty, waves of feeling floating past her, a weight feathering her earlobes. The spirits were awed by the powers of the lens! "You know who he is and how he is, now get to work. You're *for* me"— she pulled herself to her feet—"or *against*!" The flames in the gas lamps sputtered. "So," Sadie said, "a good sign."

The next morning Yivvy arrived early, talking as she came through the door. "The news about Mitzi Beuhler is . . ." Sniffing, she opened the oven. "Strudel?"

"Talk already. You got news?"

"Some could say there's news, some could say . . ." Shrugging, she sat down at the table and cracked her knuckles. Mitzi, she reported, was from Chicago, maybe a widow, maybe not, and good at running businesses. "*Businesses!*" she repeated.

Nothing registered on Sadie's face. Then, suddenly, the word hit. "No!" How was it possible—in *her* building?

"Why not in your building? Next door to the synagogue there's one, the *shammus* gets a dollar for every customer he sends over. So," she continued, removing the cake pan from the oven, "you gonna throw her out, or what?"

"Give me two minutes to chew up and swallow your news."

"Take all the time you want, but cut up the strudel while you're thinking."

"Get to Herschl Diamond." Sadie sliced. "Here"—she sighed, pushing the cake pan across the table—"help yourself."

"Okay, okay," Yivvy said, reaching for a slice, "but I wanna know what's goin' on. He's from Russia, Kiev."

"That's good. Not as good as Poland, but better than Rumania. Too peppery, those Rumanians, and also not so romantic like a Hungarian."

"Peddles ice, makes an okay living."

"That I know."

"A new widower, kinda—"

"That I also know. Gittel."

"She was a little *zahftik*"—Yivvy shaped two circles in empty air—"sorta like you. Not too much in the upstairs department"— she tapped her forehead—"not like you. Also good-natured, what you'd call sweet."

"He likes sweet, I'll be sweet. What else?"

"Somethin' about him likin' to read. He goes to the library over on Chambers like other people play pinochle, always buyin' secondhand books on Second Avenue." She refilled her plate.

"Perfect—eat up."

"So, what's this guy to you?"

"Nothing, yet, but"—Sadie eyed her daughter. Would it be too much for her to doll up a spec, get a couple of cute baby doll dresses, trade in that flat, old maid hair for a few curls?—"if I say I'm ready to, you know, do for me what I do for everyone else, what would you say?"

Yivvy chewed without answering. Then said, "You *know* what I'd say—what I *always* say when you wanna fix me up with some guy: who needs it?"

"Who said anything about needs? *Wants!* It wouldn't kill you to fix yourself up and go out—"

"Stop with me." She had that fire in her eye that Sadie recognized: here we go again, stay out of my business. "You already hadda good enough husband. Pa was a real sweetheart."

Sadie hooted, an explosion of air. "What if I told you your pa was *some* sweetheart?" Yivvy's mouth went slack, her eyes sorrowful. "What I mean . . ." Sadie chewed on a crumb. "Who's to say what's good enough? One lady's good enough is another lady's not-so-wonderful."

"You mean, you and Pa? I always thought . . . you know."

Sadie patted her daughter's hand. "Sure, I know . . ." Why paint Yivvy's rosy picture into a bitter black? Fivel had been a so-so husband, but a nice enough father. Leave it be. "It was okay, your papa and me. For twenty-plus years we were just what you said: good enough."

꩜   ꩜   ꩜

Mondays were the best days for love knots. Those who had endured a lonely weekend or had wandered into the Sunday afternoon crush of Moishe Pipik's, only to find themselves solitary figures surrounded by tables for two, often awoke the next day willing to gamble fifty cents on Sadie's magic. Also, Sadie's library ladies met in the evenings on Mondays, leaving her plenty of time to shop around for the odds and ends she needed for new customers.

By eleven o'clock on the Monday following Herschl's visit to her flat, Sadie had a twenty-five-cent deposit from five new customers; almost six, but Nussy Weinburg, at her door before seven, had shouted into the foyer: "Hello, Sadie Schuster, I'm here, don't open up. Not yet. First prove to me you're a real magic person. Tell me through the door what color is the shirt I'm wearing."

Nussy drove a fancy delivery truck for Bernstein's Department Store. "Brown," she guessed.

"Wrong," Nussy crowed. "Like I said yesterday to the guys at Max's Hot Dogs on Greene Street, you're no honest magician."

"Is that so? Well, like I am going to say today at Izzy's Delicatessen on Houston Street, you're not by me good husband material."

By noon, when she set out to pick up snick-snacks from the peddlers' carts and neighborhood shops, Sadie had covered eight note cards. Under *To Find*, she wrote: *red silk thread, ivory toothpick, a smidgen of shoemaker's glue, a snip of a label from two-cents seltzer bottle, one chicken feather, a shred of tobacco, a stamp.*

Under *To Do*: *Cut up three flowered schmattahs, two red-and-white oil cloths, one pink voile.* And, on the final note card she wrote, *Remember: for Hannah Finkel use special, fancy, long words.* Her sweetheart was a gentleman, very rich, in buttons and linings, two gold teeth, a genuine diamond ring on his little finger.

She began on Delancey Street, excusing her way among the pushcarts piled high with fruits and vegetables, wandering among towers of men's accessories—stacks of underwear, suspenders, belts, garters, socks, ties—all of it with Tybbe Kaplan, a no-longer-young, but not-yet-old milliner, in mind. Earlier that week Tybbe had bought a love knot for Fischele Grunskind, who delivered beer and whiskey to her brother's tavern on Market Avenue. Fischele fought amateur boxing matches on weekends, and had a red handlebar mustache shaped into two waxed upward points.

She needed to find leather laces, perfect for Tybbe's love knot, like the ones sporty fellas used for gym shoes, or a patch from a sleeveless undershirt, good for showing off muscles. If she couldn't find one of these, she'd have to sneak into the locker room at Silver's Gym on Canal, bribe the attendant, get him to open Fischele's locker for a fast look around.

At the corner, a man in the gutter was blowing on a harmonica, holding a leash with a hairy little animal on the end, a tin cup tied onto its back. Sadie stopped to drop a dime into the cup, and backed away when the animal sniffed, then stepped on her toes, looking that minute like he thought her shoes would make a good toilet. Somebody's elbow nicked her arm, and she turned in time to avoid a heavy woman clutching a baby. Glancing over her shoulder, she saw Yivvy arguing with a peddler, saw her with a *schpritz* of surprise, so far from the pawnshop. Same black cotton dress, same sorry hairdo, same no-makeup face. Same sad, sour expression.

"I'm glad you're here," she said, coming up behind her daughter, squeezing her shoulder.

Yivvy wheeled around. "Why glad? Hello, Ma."

"We can shop, find some new clothes for you. My treat."

"No 'hello,' no 'go to hell'? Right into your 'you-look-terrible speech'?"

"Who said terrible?" Sadie brushed lint from Yivvy's collar. "Not me, I didn't say terrible."

"Lady"—the peddler, a youngish man with a flat, pock-marked face and enormous ears, took a pull on his cigarette—"like I said, thirty cents apiece. They cost me twenty, but for you I'll make an exception." He held up a porcelain cat and dog with brightly painted faces and rhinestone eyes. "Take 'em both, I'll give two for fifty cents, wrap it up, whaddya say?" He ground his cigarette under his heel.

Sadie pressed forward, squinting at the porcelain animals. "*Feh,* junk!"

The peddler pulled his hand behind his back. "Who asked you?"

"Who waits to be asked?" To Yivvy, Sadie said, "Let's go."

"Take it easy, Ma, I got important business goin' on here." To the peddler, she said, "Two for forty, final offer."

"You gotta gun in your purse, lady, you robbin' me this way?"

"Save the sob story for the yokels. Yes or no," Yivvy said. The peddler hesitated. She took a half step toward Sadie, who had begun edging away into the crowd.

"*Yes!*" the peddler shouted, reaching for her arm. "I'm a fool, God only knows how I'll pay my rent."

"*Rent?* What rent?" Sadie stepped back to the cart. Peering upward, talking into empty air, she said, "Yoo-hoo, up there, you hear this, 'rent,' he says." Looking at the peddler: "You got a front door with a bell, a glass window, a fancy toilet? You're a regular *holdupnik*, anyone ever mention?"

Yivvy counted coins into the peddler's hand. "Don't thank me," he said, "and don't"—flicking his chin at Sadie—"bring *her* back."

"Give me your card, I'll send all my friends," Sadie called out, guiding Yivvy toward the corner. "I saw some nice things your size," she said. "You wouldn't believe how cheap, next block, let's go."

Yivvy stopped, so Sadie stopped. "Some other time, okay, Ma? I gotta go back to the shop, a guy's bringing some good goods he wantsta sell me, a whole warehouse of stuff he happened to fall into I can have for next to nothin'."

Sadie shrugged. "Sure, some other time. Maybe also we'll do a little something about"—she patted her daughter's hair.

Yivvy backed away. "Hey"—eyeing Sadie's bangs—"whadda we got here? And here"—touching the velvet beauty mark. A burst of amused understanding flashed across her face. "This got anything to do with that peddler guy you asked about?"

Sadie shrugged.

"It's okay. I can stand the truth, I'm a grown-up."

"Nothing to tell."

"Have it your way, only I gotta know, how's it goin' with, with"— Yivvy snapped her fingers—"that *nafke* business, Mitzi Meuller. No . . ." She frowned. "Booter. No, Beuhler! From Chicago!"

"*Shah*"—Sadie's eyes darted around the crowd—"hush up, not everyone has to know my business."

"So, you tell her you're onto her, you gonna throw her out, or what?"

"Not yet."

"Hey"—Yivvy put one finger under her mother's chin, forcing Sadie to look at her—"what gives? Somethin' smells not-kosher, such an aye-aye-aye honest lady, always tellin' me to be careful, don't mix up with the law and all."

"I'll tell her, but first I got some"—Sadie coughed into her fisted hand—"problems to work out."

"Such as?"

"Such as you'll be the first to know."

Yivvy said fine with her, only remember, the guys in the precinct captain's office smelled that kinda thing a mile away. She'd havta do some kind of payoff, or maybe Mitzi was doin' it already, if she wanted her building to pass code inspections, get garbage picked up. She knew how it worked around the East Side.

Sadie said sure, sure, she knew also, and appreciated the advice. Then, sensing that Yivvy was eager to leave, said, "Tonight, give me a yes, go with me to my ladies meeting at the library. We need lots of people to pass out papers."

"*Maaaa.* I keep saying: who cares if I can vote? Will it help me sell more stuff?"

Sadie ducked her head, "I just thought—"

"Well, don't think so much."

"That's like asking the dead to sit up."

As her daughter turned to leave, Sadie pulled up a weak smile and a hug, then watched her walk her rapid-fire walk down the street before vanishing around the corner.

Ha! Leftover pieces of Fivel spilled out all over her. No appetite for kissing, no time for sipping tea, for slipping off her shoes and wiggling her toes, for just enjoying. She'd say wanting Herschl was foolishness after all those married years. Sadie felt the futility of trying to explain. It was *because* of all those married years, because she never got to choose her own life, to say, *I want this, but not that.*

How to tell her daughter that with Herschl she'd dance, they'd talk about books and later, maybe, she'd sit with him at the moving pictures? She'd start up all over again. Yivvy couldn't understand *again.* She didn't want to start up in the first place.

Chapter Three

Herschl had disappeared.

Every morning just before nine thirty, Sadie—corseted, rouged, hair curled—posted herself at the corner of Ludlow and Greene, an eager sentry in a freshly laundered cotton shirtwaist and skirt.

Ten. Ten thirty. No Herschl. Throat parched, bunions on fire, she sought the solace of cold lemon tea and a chair pulled up to a bowl of ice chips set in front of her small fan. He would come back. She had the spirits, she had Mitzi. He'd come riding by, seated like a king on the seat of his wagon, with ice tongs and muscles and salt and pepper curls. His sweet smile, that polka-dotted bandana around his neck. An adorable Russian gypsy. Wait.

Sadie hated waiting. She'd found three books of Yiddish poetry at the public library, and knew what she'd say: "I just read a lovely poem written by the poet Shlinsky," or, "Do you by any chance know of Yevov?" And then add, not winking until she was sure he'd appreciate a wink, "Yevov brings up to my mind Alschler, two gorgeous"—a good word, *gorgeous*, when speaking about poets, as well as for practicing clean *s*'s—"poets; different, but nevertheless"—rolling all four syllables of *nevertheless* over her

tongue, taking care to sound breathy—"the same. Do you agree?"
In her mind, Herschl always did.

⌁ ⌁ ⌁

On Saturday Sadie, sitting on the front steps to catch up with any
cooling breeze blowing past, was reading a story in *The Daily
Forward* about a lady in Chicago who chained herself, with a
real iron chain, to a fence around City Hall, threatening never to
eat until she could vote. She'd been carried away to the hospital,
where they did something called forced feeding, a tube down her
throat. Against the law, it had to be. This wasn't Russia, Romania,
Hungary. Sadie knew what was, and what *wasn't*, okay to do to
honest people who wanted their Declaration of Independence
say-so.

She'd ask Mrs. Pomerantz, she knew everything, at their next
meeting. She had, that week, asked Sadie about her being in
charge of the next march, Delancey Street to Washington Square;
far enough to make a lot of noise, even sing patriotic songs, if the
crowd on the sidewalks didn't throw rotten fruit like they did the
last time.

She was scissoring the article out of the newspaper when a taxi
stopped in front of her building, and Mitzi, in red silk, carrying
two string bags filled with packages, got out. Ha! The very woman
who should know about finding missing men.

Mitzi pressed forward toward the driver, saying something that
made him laugh, then dropped coins into his hand and, turning to
the curb, raised her hem to step over the tins and crumpled papers
littering the gutter.

All this getting in, getting out, twisting and hopping up, without
a single bumping of that thumb-in-your-eye white straw hat she
was wearing. She sure knew how to move her moving parts. The
two women greeted one another like old friends. Sadie decided:
her advice first, then we'll talk about her business that she'll have
to cut it out.

Sadie mentioned having a lost-and-found problem, could she
drop up for another visit? Mitzi said, "Sure, three o'clock okay?"

The flat was lit up, sunshine spilling through white lace curtains, and smelled like a garden, not an easy thing to smell like on Orchard Street. On all the tables, the mantel, the floor, a convention of glass vases—short, tall, skinny, fat—and inside each one, a wild *mishmash* of daisies—pink, yellow, white—like someone was passing them out on the street, and Mitzi came along and said, "Whoopee, I'll take 'em all," and the daisies right away perked up, happy to be going home with this gorgeous person.

Sadie sat down on the velvet sofa, but couldn't settle back, twisting around to look at the door, at the hall to the bedrooms. If Yivvy was right, where were the customers? She'd seen men who could be customers in the downstairs hall, smoking cigars, twirling gold key chains, derby hats at a nervy angle, expensive woolen suits, spats, sometimes stopping to read an address scrawled across a slip of paper, then looking up when she peeked out, asking, taking off their hats, real gentlemen, "Oh, excuse me missus, which way to flat number six?"

And the girls, where were they? She'd never seen anyone in the hall or the flat who fit Yivvy's description of them: "A lot of skin, purple satin corsets, black feathers, sequins, lace stockings, enough perfume to knock you out for a week."

Sadie heard Mitzi coming down the hall, humming, snapping her fingers, sunlight blazing against her coppery hair. She'd changed from red silk to pale-green organdy, a ruffled robe that made her look like a walking bouquet.

Sadie said thanks to Mitzi's offer of cold seltzer, trying to decide, while they waited for Lila to bring their drinks, should she begin with: "I wouldn't allow no more hanky-panky going on here, I run a respectable family building?" Mitzi could say: "Who, me?" Or: "Remember me? I pay twice the rent you got for this dump before."

"So, hon," Mitzi asked, "what or who'd you lose?"

"Herschl Diamond," Sadie said, happy to talk out the easy part before getting to the Mitzi business. She told her about their supper, the poetry, the dancing. "But ever since, *pfffft*! Gone. If I can find him, I'll show him something he'll love." Sadie blushed. "Maybe."

"What's that?"

"My night school education."

"No kiddin'!" Mitzi laughed, the low, throaty laugh Sadie practiced, but couldn't get right. "Yeah, night school, books, they're fine, some men love it. Just the same, I gotta tip. Wanna hear?"

Sadie didn't like the you're-a-dumb-greenhorn look on Mitzi's face. She'd seen it before. In the eyes of sales clerks at the cosmetics counter in Klein's Emporium when they said, "Step right up, ladies, try this lotion, this lip cream, this eye pencil, guaranteed to make you young and beautiful," and Sadie said, "Lady, explain, please, how it works."

That look was also in the eyes of the cashier at the movie house on Eighth Street when she pushed her nickel through the grillwork cage and asked, "Tell me, lady, is this a good picture? At the end does the girl get the boy?" Right now, she'd say it, if this tip hurt her feelings, she'd tell Mitzi, you can take your business with the men coming in and going out, and move it out of my building.

"Flesh," Mitzi said, flicking ashes into her cupped palm.

"That's your tip, *flesh*?" Maybe she should learn how to smoke, after all. It made a woman look mysterious.

"*That's* what men want, that kinda education. Push flesh."

There! Practically a confession! "Speaking about—"

"'Course, you gotta find him first. Who the hell knows what hole he dropped into?" Mitzi turned thoughtful. Even now her face was prettier than that blonde movie star who last week threw herself in front of a train when her lover died of a real bad case of measles. "What does he do besides selling ice?"

"He reads."

"Reads?" Mitzi's eyes said: *huh*?

"Like I told you about the poetry, remember? Me too, we're like twins that way." Thinking, if she laughs, I'll right away cut off her hot water.

Mitzi patted Sadie's hand. "Well, tootsie, your work is cut out for you." Her look now was stuffed with sympathy. "Go looking for him in all the bookstores. Fight fire with fire, but watch out for the smoke." Mitzi smiled and shook her shoulders without moving the rest of her body, shook them in such an adorable way. Sadie was sure that if she could only learn to move that way, Herschl would be plenty friendly. She couldn't throw her out of her building now, even if one of those girls came out of a bedroom that minute without her purple satin corset.

Sadie bumped into the good goods Yivvy said she was expecting when she visited the pawnshop the next morning: cardboard cartons and canvas sacks strewn over the front of the shop, merchandise spilling onto the display cases and over the floor. She'd come to say, "I want a list of the best secondhand bookstores," a short, sweet story, not a word about Herschl. She'd look wise, calm, pretend she was taking a class at the Jewish Alliance. Calm was important with Yivvy.

Yivvy beckoned from the back of the store, where she was unpacking a large wooden crate. Sadie moved toward her, stopping suddenly when she spied an intriguing hodgepodge of hammered brass plates and trays. She scooped up several large round plates and an oval tray engraved with elaborate scrolling, along with a beaded crystal candle holder, reaching into the carton once more to find, at the bottom, several stacks of folded sheets and towels in pale shades of yellow, green, blue, pink. She squinted at her daughter through the gloom. "Who'd you say you got this from?"

"I didn't say."

Holding up a carved glass bowl rimmed with a twisted gold leaf pattern, Sadie looked around. "It must have cost you plenty. You won't sell this many fancy things in—I don't know how much time." Yivvy carried a silver dish to the back of the shop and began rubbing it with a cloth. Sadie followed her. "Let me help."

"I don't need help. What I need is some quiet so I can get these things counted."

Sadie studied her daughter for a moment. "What's so touchy? There's something about this junk."

"*Junk!*" Yivvy rubbed the dish harder.

"Oh, excuse me. There's something about this *merchandise* that's a secret, you're so touchy, like a sore boil."

"What kind of secret!" Yivvy wheeled around. "Always accusing!"

Sadie raised her hands in mock surrender, backing away. "I just stopped in to ask a simple question."

"So ask already." Yivvy turned to the back of the store.

The secondhand bookstores, which ones were best? She was thinking maybe of taking a class on Yiddish poets at the Jewish Alliance. She was almost shouting. Yivvy's ears weren't always so good, or maybe her head was too stuffed with all her new *chochkeys*. Her daughter came back, balancing an armload of platters and trays. "There." Pointing to paper and pencil on the desk. Sadie wrote down six names and addresses, noticing her daughter's worried look; the crinkled-up eyes, the too-thin lips, like being even a pinch happy was against the law. Sadie felt a ping of reluctant affection. "You look to me tired."

"I'll be okay." Then, brushing the hair from her eyes: "Ma . . . I'm sorry."

"Yeah, sorry," Sadie said. "You're like your papa. First you bite my head off, now you're sorry." She moved toward the door.

"Oh, I forgot," Yivvy called after her. "Izzy Wiznitzer, from the station on Canal, the desk sergeant. He came by to tell me, Mitzi, your Mitzi—"

"Yeah, my Mitzi—"

"Gimme a minute, I wanna get it right. Izzy said some guy who useta work in Chicago, but got sent here, knew Mitzi from when she ran a house on North . . . North"—she flicked her hand. "Son of a gun, I can't think, I don't know Chicago."

"*Think!*"

"Halsted, that's the street. North Halsted, where the saloons and vaudeville places are."

"I want the facts, she gives me a geography lesson."

"Hold on. The long 'n short of it is, Mitzi never had a husband, she's an old-time pro from way back. Her dough came from owning a business, same kinda business she got here, only in Chicago the cops started shakin' her down, so she packed up 'n took her show on the road."

Sadie sank against a large cardboard carton. "No husband?"

Yivvy shook her head.

"He's not dead?"

"Izzy says now that the boys here know where she's operatin', they'll be 'round to pay their respects. He wanted me to tell you."

"When?"

"Sooner, if not later."

Sadie opened the door. "Thanks, I'm happy for your news. Like my *bubbeh* was happy to hear the Czar was living in good health."

ↄ𝒥ᵒ   ↄ𝒥ᵒ   ↄ𝒥ᵒ

Three times that week she met her ladies in the library. Everyone agreed, Sadie would be the number one organizer of their next march, in July, good weather, from Houston Street down Broadway to Washington Square in Greenwich Village, ending in speeches and music, a volunteer ladies' orchestra, free ice cream and soda pop for anyone who came to hear speeches, and stayed to clap. Children were welcome, but no dogs.

Shayna Teitelbaum, a youngish redhead from Minsk, pretty enough, but not as pretty as she thought she was, with curves to spare, and smart besides, who ran an office for three dentists on Third Avenue, would be Sadie's second-in-charge.

ↄ𝒥ᵒ   ↄ𝒥ᵒ   ↄ𝒥ᵒ

In the late afternoons, giving Herschl time to finish his rounds, go home, change clothes and come out again, she went in and out of the secondhand bookstores on Yivvy's list. No luck. The owner of the Books by the Pound bookshop, a short, squat man with red suspenders and *gimme gimme* eyes, sold her four pounds of used poetry books and said, if she couldn't find this other guy, come back, ask for him. He loved reading out loud in the dark to ladies.

Late on Thursday afternoon, when the sun was losing its fire, the city beginning to cool, Sadie put on her white linen shirt-waist with the pearl buttons, white pleated sharkskin skirt and white kid boots. White made a lady look sincere. If she knew her men, Herschl was a good customer for sincere. She pinned a red grosgrain bow at the back of her hair, *right there*, where it nestled into her bun, standing back to admire.

How many years since she'd thrown away her *shaytel*, threw it down the toilet, Fivel watching, predicting she'd never make it into heaven—twenty, twenty-five?—and she'd never grown tired of admiring her hair, of running her fingers through the heavy, dark curls, of feeling the silky wisps where they curled against her ears and neck.

Maybe today she'd laugh like Mitzi, a high, tinkling sound, all silvery and delicate. She faced the mirror over her washbasin, inhaled, exhaled, held her breath, but nothing silvery came out. Well, anyway, she had her love knot, pale-pink satin, like a baby's bottom, blue velvet string to tie, round, plump, filled with his button, straw from his horse, a clump of mud from his boot, a speck of sweat. She cradled it, kissed it, held it to her cheek before settling it at the bottom of her purse and leaving the flat.

She'd try East Broadway, a fifteen-minute walk if she moved fast, which she wouldn't do. Too hot. She strolled, staying away from the dogs looking to pee, of which there were plenty, stepping around three little boys playing games with dripping ice cones, stopping to tap her foot and shake her shoulders in front of the pint-sized man in a derby blowing on what she thought, but wasn't sure, was called a clarinet, *Oh, you beautiful doll*, or was it *Oy, you beautiful doll*?

It felt good to be out, to mix up with a crowd. Since Fivel's passing, she'd been alone too much, even if she counted talking to him every day the same as having company. If it weren't for the half-pound of worry she carried on one shoulder about Mitzi's business, and the pound she carried on the other shoulder about Yivvy's new merchandise, and when was she going to find time to visit Milly Kaplan—sentenced to two weeks in jail for stopping traffic on Broadway, pushing headfirst between the cars and the bicycles and the trolleys, with her signs about how it was a shame on America to not let women vote—she could almost feel happy.

On Canal Street she paused, tapping her face with her handkerchief. Maybe crowds weren't such a good idea, so many pushing people, especially in this heat. Then: did she imagine, someone hollered out, "Hey, lover!" A raspy voice, a man's, definitely. "Hey lover!" again. Wheeling around to the nearest shop, Sadie looked into the eyes of a brilliant green parrot, its face ablaze with red, purple, yellow feathers, perched in a wire cage swinging in the doorway. The gold letters on the shop window read: "Frieda's Pet Shop. If it has four feet or two wings or one tail, we got it. Cheap."

The parrot lowered its head, studying Sadie. "Lover, lover, lover, hiya tootsie, come 'n get it!" A miracle! A bird that talked like a man and looked like a rainbow. *Tante* Zippke always said, "Parrots, good luck in the house, even better than a policeman for keeping burglars out." But feathers made Fivel sneeze, and too much talking made him nervous.

Sadie cocked her head; the bird did the same. "Come on, baby," it squawked. She'd never met a parrot with so much personality. Not yet five o'clock. Herschl wouldn't get to the bookstores until at least five. What was a few minutes' delay if she could buy a little good luck? She carried bird and cage into the store. The bald man reading a newspaper behind the counter looked up. "Ahhh, lady, you got some brains, this is a perfect bird for you."

Sadie regarded him with wary eyes. Too much enthusiasm could add to the price. "Who said anything about *perfect*? Interesting"—she ducked her head, chucking the parrot under its beak—"maybe."

"Whaddya talkin' about, I can smell a parrot-lover a mile away."

The parrot, clinging to the bottom of the cage, watched Sadie with sad, knowing eyes. "Love of my life," it squawked.

"See," the man crowed, "he's already stuck on you. Parrots are very loyal, affectionate animals, they're not like people."

Sadie sniffed. "Who taught it so many words?" She was finding a place for the bird in her parlor, not too close to Fivel's photograph, close to the phonograph.

"It came from one of the houses on Cable Street. You know what I mean, *houses*?"

"Skip, please, the *bubeh meises*, no stories, I'm running without time."

His face crumpled. "All right, I see you're all business. The lady what owns the house said, *smart!*" He rolled his eyes. "My grandchildren should only talk this good."

"What's his name?" Sadie offered her finger, the parrot pecked at it.

"*Nashoma*. Holy Spirit."

"*Spirit*! I can't believe—"

The parrot made a whistling sound, then said, "Hey, beautiful!"

The man patted the parrot's head. "Believe. A real high-class house, only the best customers."

The parrot looked at Sadie with pleading eyes. This could be a sign from the spirits: *Sadie, Herschl is positively about to be yours.* She couldn't ignore, the spirits hated to be ignored. Her future life depended. "How much?"

"So cheap," he said, "you'll say I'm lying." He held up eight fingers.

"Eight dollars, I can buy a living room sofa, a train ticket to Chicago." The parrot ducked its beak under its wing and scratched. "See!" She pointed. "Fleas."

The man snatched the cage from the counter and turned toward the window.

"Luvva my life," the parrot squawked, twisting on its stand to look back at Sadie, who stepped forward, pulling on the cage, sending the bird swinging on its perch. "Four," she said.

"Seven."

"All right, I'm a generous person. I'll take it off your hands." Sadie eyed the parrot, who was eyeing her. "Five."

"Six, and it's yours," the man said, pushing the bird and its cage at Sadie. "With it comes enough food for two weeks, and a custom-to-fit cage cover, it should go to sleep when you do." He reached into the window for a yellow cloth and a cardboard box.

"Kiss me, you fool," the parrot squawked.

Loving *Nashoma* was easier than carrying him. Five thirty, and the sun refused to go away. She could use a bowl of ice cubes, a soft chair, a fan. Iced tea, a little lemon. Sadie set the covered cage down on the sidewalk, eyeing the crush of people pushing past in both directions, and tapped her handkerchief across her forehead, down her cleavage, under her arms.

Five, even six blocks to the next bookstore. She'd be a sport. A quarter to the next boy flashing by with an empty wagon. Someone in heaven read her mind, maybe Fivel was following, sending good luck, even if he hated parrots. A short, chubby boy—glasses, beanie hat, about ten, eleven—turned a corner from a side street, pulling a battered blue wagon, rusted, empty.

"Sonny, stop!" Sadie called out, waving him over, "You want to get rich?"

The boy looked at Sadie, then at the cage. "Who you got in there?"

"Not who. *What*." The boy sniffled, running his sleeve across his nose. Sadie rushed on: "I say rich because I will pay you big money, a full twenty-five cents you should put this cage in your wagon and ride it"—she pointed down the street—"two, three blocks, nothing, a minute."

The boy shrugged. "I charge by the block."

"*What*?" Sadie held the cage out to him. "Take, feel, it's a nothing. Five minutes, we're there."

Sadie heard, "Hold the phone, hold the phone, tootsie," from the cage.

"Is it alive?" The boy lifted a corner of the cage cover.

"Don't touch, please"—she tapped his hand—"he's delicate."

"Fifty cents for pulling, ten cents extra for something that talks."

"You got a union what tells you what money to charge?"

"Take it or leave it, lady." Pulling the wagon, the boy turned away, just as Sadie's feet sent up a complaint.

"Wait a minute, sonny"—putting the cage in the wagon—"tell your mother I see for you a big business future."

Following boy and wagon, Sadie figured. Already this evening cost her more than she made selling twelve, thirteen love knots. Something good *had* to come up.

It did—but not immediately. Not until she'd been in the Slightly Used Bookstore long enough to find two volumes of Yiddish poetry. Sadie settled the parrot's cage on a nearby counter, patting the books' worn leather covers, sniffing them, smelling Luvel, the books she'd borrowed from the traveling bookseller. "I'll take—" she said to the shop owner and, looking up, saw Herschl enter the store.

"Hold for me," she said, thrusting the books at the owner, and moved—not as slowly as she wished to, but not as fast as she could have—toward the front of the store. And there he was, head down, paging through a book, looking like a regular sport in a blue-and-white-striped shirt open at the neck, sleeves rolled to his elbows, showing those wonderful muscles. Dark-blue wash pants, red suspenders, a soft cap crowning his curls.

"Why, do I see Mr. Diamond?"

Herschl looked up. "Ahhh—" Was that a happy *ahhh* or an annoyed *ahhh*? He pulled his cap off. "Mrs. Schuster." He looked, but not directly into her eyes. A pity. Her new eyelash pomade, Mitzi's suggestion, did marvelous things.

"What a coincidence," she said, *sussing* the *s* sounds. "I come here all the time." She gestured around the store. "You, of course, know how books can make you happy."

He showed no sign of knowing.

"You said at supper that night at my place"—lingering over *my place*—"Yiddish poetry." He was about to say something when, from behind them, a crash, then a whooshing sound and a harsh voice: "Hey, baby, how about some fun, lover?"

Sadie turned around and saw the opened, empty cage lying on the floor amidst a pile of books, the parrot swooping across the ceiling, dropping down here and there to perch atop a bin, taking off again, scattering books, signs, paper bags. "*Gevalt!*" she shouted.

"Someone you know?" Herschl asked.

"Lady, lady, get him, it's ruining my store!" The owner ran from behind the cash register waving a cardboard box in one hand, a broom in the other.

"Excuse me, I'll be right back!" Sadie squeezed past Herschl and between two bins, noticing, as she glanced back, that he was smiling; interested, almost amused. "*Nashoma, Nashoma!*" Clucking her tongue, she clapped. "Come back, little spirit."

"Pretty baby, pretty baby, come 'n get it," the parrot squawked, whooshing low, then rising to settle on a ceiling fan.

"*There!*" Herschl hollered, pointing up and behind her.

Sadie rushed in that direction, flapping her arms, singing, "Here, here, here," to the ceiling, upsetting books stacked on the floor as she turned one way, then another. The parrot, hovering perilously close to a gas jet, looked down at Sadie with what she could swear was friendship. The smell of charred feathers floated across the store. "Hey, sweet cake," the parrot screeched, flying to the opposite side of the shop, "hot potato, hot—"

"Look out, it's throwing down!" Herschl ducked as the bird's claws scraped along a sign, shredding it, sending pieces of cardboard sailing down onto a white-haired gentleman in a gray derby and high starched collar.

The owner shook his fist at the parrot, threatening to turn it into a pillowcase if it didn't come down this minute.

"No—*there!*" Herschl called to Sadie, hurrying to help the white-haired gentleman wade through the sea of books, as a young man ran into the street hollering, "Police, fire, a wild bird!" Several people came into the shop, demanding to know what was happening. Someone in the street blew a whistle.

Then, a small freckled boy of seven or eight, tears streaming down his face, fists pushing against his mother, cried, "Leave me alone! I didn't let the birdie out on purpose, 'n besides"—stopping to hiccup—"mustn't put birdies in cages, they could suffercate."

The parrot, perched atop the highest shelf in the store, cackled, "Hiya, sweet cake, pucker up!"

The little boy's mother, a redhead with an orange feather boa around her neck, fixed Sadie with a fierce look. An enormous feather floated atop her blue straw hat. "That your bird?"

Sadie, now holding the broom, preparing to climb atop a shaky stepstool, paused to look at mother and child. "That your little boy? He should be teached to keep his hands off other people's belongings." She noticed Herschl brushing the man's jacket, smiling and looking—was it possible?—like nothing so terrible had happened.

The mother pulled her little boy closer. "Such a dumb thing, stuffing a bird under a cover, my Herbert's right." Herbert brushed his sleeve across his nose.

"You got a friend who's a parrot what told you where parrots like to be put?" Sadie asked.

The woman glared at the shop owner. "Ya hear what she just said ta me?"

"I'm ruined," the owner shrieked, clapping his hands at the parrot, now walking tightrope across a ledge. He shook his fist at Sadie. "You'll pay!"

"Don't you threaten her!" Herschl came up behind the owner with an armful of books, "It shouldn't have happened the way it did, but nobody got killed."

She could kiss him right here, that sweetheart, to defend her in front of all these people. She teetered atop the stool, trying to catch Herschl's eye to signal her gratitude, but he was in conversation with the store owner. Slowly, careful to avoid the broom handle, she backed her way down the stool.

"Wait, you'll fall!" And Herschl was there, holding his hand out. *His hand.* She'd dreamed of holding it, of his holding hers, just tightly enough, long enough, to make her feel that in some tender, silent way, he'd claimed her. The woman marched out of the shop, pulling her little boy along, leaving the door swinging open behind her. With a frantic beating of wings, the parrot was through the open door and over First Avenue.

Sadie, unwilling to drop Herschl's hand, watched the bird disappear, two thoughts colliding—*Six dollars,* and *Never have I been so happy.*

"Look, just look!" The storeowner, slumped in a chair, waved at the debris of books strewn across the store.

"Give us twenty minutes," Herschl said and, stooping, began gathering books, dusting them off, then stacking them on bins.

"Fifteen," Sadie said, doing the same.

ᒍᎭ   ᒍᎭ   ᒍᎭ

Thirty minutes later, the store returned to its normal order, Sadie brushed her clothes, checked the bottom of her purse to make certain her love knot was still in place, and moved toward the street, where Herschl was waiting, looking in the direction of the East River. An idea buzzed into her ear.

"Oh, lady," the owner called after her, "next time take your business somewhere else."

Sadie turned around. "I don't charge you nothing for the birdcage, tip-top new, a present." She joined Herschl at the corner. A cool breeze ruffled her hair. "Such a beautiful night," she said to the back of his head. *If he walked away now!* Her best white clothes, her new perfume, and what about all that let-me-help-you business inside?

"Tell me, Mrs. Schuster—" He turned.

"Sadie."

"—do you always take your parrot with you into bookstores?"

Was that a twinkle in his eyes? She couldn't tell; the light was terrible. Maybe he had a sense of humor, even if that night at dinner he acted what she'd call *ungeblozen.*

Straightening her shoulders—Mitzi said straightening narrowed her hips, making her look slimmer—she said, "If you have a minute, we can walk down to the river, find some breaths of cool air, buy an ice cone, talk, I'll answer your question." He hesitated; then, without a yes or a no, he put his hand on her elbow, the slightest, easiest touch, and guided her down the quiet, darkened, almost-deserted street towards the East River.

Nice, walking with a man. It made her feel so . . . safe. Sadie glanced at Herschl from time to time, but he seemed lost in his own thoughts. She cleared her throat, as though about to speak, but hesitated to break the intimate silence, like they were close friends who shared so much, they didn't have to always say it out loud. Wonderful luck, the walk along the river was empty. She knew just the bench she wanted, near a streetlamp, but not too near, and pointed it out.

Seated, Herschl pulled a small book out of his pocket. *"Dreams of the Fathers*, Komaroff," he said. "You know it?"

"No." She took the book and leafed through it. "Tell me, how do you know so many poems?"

He talked about his parents; his father, a teacher in the *gimnazye*, reading to him at home. The light from the gas lamp was tangled in his hair. Sadie had never noticed how beautiful curly hair could look on a man. "Then we came here, and nobody wanted to hire a Russian-Jewish schoolteacher who didn't talk English good, so"—ducking his head—"he peddled ice, and I went with to help."

More words than Fivel had talked to her in six months. And such words, like a sweet, sad "Bintele Brief," a story out of *The Daily Forward.* You didn't go around talking like this to just any stranger. If she knew him better, she'd press forward and pat his shoulder. So hard to keep her hands folded in her lap, a toucher like her.

He shifted toward her slightly, sitting even closer now. She wanted to tell him about how she'd felt once she'd stepped into New York, that her life was stretched as wide as that river down there, with night school English and newspapers, the moving pictures, so many new ways to dream. And about Fivel, the way he was picked out for her, a good person, but no talking between them—never. She felt happier this minute than she felt after dancing a whole evening at the Irving Street Saturday Night Social Club.

He fussed with the book, opening, then closing it, finally putting it back in his pocket, and said, "Mrs. Schuster"—at the same time she said—"Well, Herschl." They laughed, then neither one spoke, and she decided: *now*! "Your wife," she said, "she was also from Kiev?" Did she feel him stiffen, pull back?

"We lived in the same *shtetl*, we were babies together, Gittel and me." He said her name like he was reading a poem. "I'm sorry"— she strained to hear him—"I can't talk about her without—"

"How long is it?"

"Four months."

"Four months," she repeated.

"And three days."

Sadie waited. She'd never seen anyone look so wounded without having a bleeding something or other. If she could make him feel this sad, she'd be the happiest woman in the world.

"Speaking of selling ice." He stood up. But they weren't speaking of selling ice, they were speaking about Gittel! "I wake up early."

Sadie stood up. He must have seen the disappointment on her face, and went on: "I enjoyed talking to you. You're a very, very nice person."

Well! A very-very. Something, at least. Her heart settled into her chest, a cement block. "I'm sorry," she said, not knowing why, exactly, but sorry was such a big part of what she was feeling.

"What?"

"We were married twenty-six years, a lifetime. For me, this"— he gestured toward the lamppost, the sidewalk—"is too soon."

Call me Rosh Hashanah, Halloween, call me Thanksgiving,

Hanukah, New Year's, I'll wait. But he was taking her hand, squeezing it, saying, without saying, *Enough talking.*

They walked along the river to First Avenue, then along Bryant Street to Ludlow, with more silence than talk, unless she counted his "Watch out!" and "Such crazy drivers!" whenever a runaway pushcart rumbled into their path.

Somewhere between Bryant and Ludlow, Sadie cupped her love knot in her palm and rubbed it against Herschl's shirt sleeve—once, twice—pretending she was shooing away flies. At the corner of Ludlow and Greene, he shook her hand, stiff and polite, like a friend who had good manners. But she didn't need another friend: she needed someone to love; someone to read to; someone to talk to; someone to let her put her icy feet against his warm back on cold nights. Someone to love her . . . like Fivel never could.

From her palm, a faint pulsing sensation. Her love knot oozed a flowery scent. She was about to toss it into her pocket, when a dark shape and a rough beating of wings caught her attention. Stepping back, Sadie looked up and saw—"*Oy!*"—*Nashoma*, perched atop the gas lamp across the street, head cocked at a crazy angle: *Come catch me!* For sure, her eyes were playing tricks. Herschl's face, even half-shadowed, didn't show any sign he heard or saw nothing and was, in fact, a perfect picture of calm.

"Goodnight," he murmured.

She opened her mouth to ask if he saw what she saw, but, without even a squeeze on her fingers, he was stepping away from her, tipping his cap, leaving her on the corner to watch him vanish down the dark street, admiring his healthy stride, the proud set of his broad shoulders—*gone!*

Chapter Four

Sleep was impossible. Sadie pulled her Herchl love knot from under her pillow, listening, waiting. No sign of Fivel. Maybe he was this minute laughing at her, thinking, *take that*, Sadie Schuster. Shame, shame, for running after passion.

"Spirits," she crooned. The air was too thin, too cool. She felt none of the heat, none of the spidery weight against her skin. The only sound was water dripping from the corner of the icebox. Maybe the spirits were busy. Summer—they had lots to do: weddings, babies being born, taking care of all the find-me-a-new-job wishes, the move-me-away-to-another-city wishes. It would be nice sometimes to have spirits not mixed up with any other business, only full-time making people fall in love.

That noise *there*! At the window. Sadie peered into the gloom toward the band of light seeping into the room from under the window shades. Again, a faint whooshing.

"Come, my lovelies"—she raised her arms, palms up—"Sadie needs you." One, then another window shade snapped into a wild spin, round and round on their rollers, circling at whirlwind speed, slowing to a final *plip-plip-plip*. "So"—shivering, she sat back against her pillows, pulled the quilt up to her chin—"you're in a hurry." Puckering her lips, she blew softly three times. From across the room, a faint echo. "I'll be quick. Herschl Diamond, the one who's in here"—she thrust the love knot into the air—"the one we talked about, remember?"

The room was dense with their listening. "Things were going good tonight"—no need for too many details—"then I, I—talked too much. But what I maybe did, you can undo, if you want."

Quiet without end, until dim light became a blur of wings, a dark speck beating its way toward her and—*aahhh*, on the fingertip of her left hand, the softest tap-tap. "I don't think I'm asking too much when I ask you, give him to me. It's my turn to pick out for myself." She hesitated. Maybe Fivel *was* hovering. She glanced at the clock on the bedside table. One o'clock. He never stayed up this late.

A deep pull of breath. This was no time to hold back. "Last time, remember, when I got a husband, I didn't do none of the picking out for myself." She felt the sensation of air parting, and then—*yes!* A weight on her eyelash, a poof, or was it her lashes sticking together from her new pomade? The sensation again, then a tickle at the tip of her nose. They were sending a message: *We'll help.* She sank into her pillows, caressing her chin, throat, shoulders, back and forth, back and forth, with the love knot.

ᒍᐤ   ᒍᐤ   ᒍᐤ

That week Sadie tried to pull the subject of the police into a conversation with Mitzi, beginning with how safe the neighborhood was, so many patrolmen day and night, but, *My, my, it must cost the city plenty*; hoping to jump from there into: *I wonder, how much do policemens get paid?* and, from there into: *I bet there's all kinds ways to finagle extra dollars here and there, those who don't mind bending the law, I mean.*

But Mitzi was impatient, turning talkative, saying things like, *Jeezus, the price of flowers, she loved having 'em in the flat, but a few lousy daisies and two dried-up roses set her back half a buck.*

To which Sadie asked: *Was Chicago a cheaper place to live than New York?* Hoping to arrive at the front end by coming around from the back, she added: *Was it true what she heard about Chicago policemens, they were not so friendly like the New York police, in fact, even a little—should she say, pushy?* Maybe that would open the door to some honest talking. Maybe, once-warned, Mitzi would ask for help in handling the police, or offer to close up her business, to move—*something!*

"The Chicago Police pushy?" Mitzi said. "That depends. Who'd you hear that from?" Who'd have thought that warning Mitzi, without accusing, would be such a slippery problem? Sadie had only Yivvy's word. Yivvy had only the say-so of the people she called her eyes-and-ears-on-the-street. Until Mitzi confessed, this was some tricky business, as tricky as finding Herschl.

Sadie had to admit, but not out loud, that her concern for Mitzi was half affection, half greed. These past weeks she'd grown fond of her, of that brave, stylish swagger Sadie found so touching. And, in the greed department, Mitzi paid a hefty rent. Not every day did you find that kind of money thrown at you on Orchard Street. . . .

ﻊﻤ﹏ﻴ   ﻊﻤ﹏ﻴ   ﻊﻤ﹏ﻴ

Thinking about greed led Sadie to Yivvy, how jumpy she'd been when Sadie asked about the new shipment of goods. This wasn't Yivvy's usual tight-lipped, none-of-your-business *mishagas*. Something important was upsetting her. Part of Sadie said: *Butt out, she's a grown-up person.* The other part brought her to the shop later that week, where she found her daughter at her desk, frowning into a ledger book.

"Just sit, darling," Sadie called across the shop, "don't rearrange yourself, I'll make myself at home."

Yivvy glanced up, "That's what I'm afraid of."

Most of the newly arrived merchandise was still on display. The best way to fish for information would be to bait her hook with flattery. "My, my, so many gorgeous pieces"—Sadie fondled a string of tawny amber beads—"who could not buy?" She continued to wander among the display cases, examining carved ivory figurines, moving next to a display of engraved brass boxes inlaid with jade, then a nest of painted wooden dolls, each one fitting into the other, *oohing* and *aahing* her delight.

Yivvy watched, smiling a smile that was two-parts sour; one-part amused. "Save the drama for when I gotta store fulla customers."

"Happy to. When will that be?"

"Who knows? Tomorrow, next week, maybe never." She jammed her hands into her pockets. "Maybe this stuff's too high-class for my customers."

"Send back."

"Back? Back *where*?"

Sadie shrugged. "Where it came from, the man from where you got it."

"You gotta be kiddin'."

"Yankel the fish man sends back all the time, whatever don't sell."

"Well, good for Yankel, but this stuff ain't *gefilte* fish."

"Too bad. *Gefilte* fish you can eat."

Yivvy focused on a column of figures, adding the numbers under her breath. Sadie watched for a minute, then did an *mmmm* clearing of her throat. Yivvy made no sign she'd heard, and Sadie repeated the sound, louder, until Yivvy looked up, annoyed.

"You couldn't?" Sadie tried to sound offhand. Nothing to worry, a simple question. "Send back, I mean."

"Not possible." Yivvy studied her hands. "I made a big mistake, I'll havta live with it."

A weight, like indigestion, settled into Sadie's chest. "You know," she said, straining to keep her voice light, "you never told where you bought these from."

"You're right, Ma, I never told"—Yivvy stretched and yawned, her old self again—"and I'm gonna keep it that way, if it's okay with you."

⌒﹆   ⌒﹆   ⌒﹆

A week later, three days before the deadline on her agreement with Mitzi to pursue Herschl *her* way, he hadn't knocked at her door or appeared on Orchard Street, or been seen in the secondhand bookstores. Sadie dreamed he was sick and alone, unable to get in touch with her. Using the telephone in the candy store on the corner, speaking slowly, in her best night school English, she called the only East Side hospital with Yiddish-speaking doctors on the staff.

Describing Herschl to the woman on the phone, Sadie asked if anyone fitting that description had been carried into the hospital injured by a horse or a trolley or motorcar. "He's too healthy to be there with a terrible sickness," she explained. "Maybe a little high blood pressure that don't look serious." The only Diamond in the hospital had just given birth to twins.

She went to his flat on Avenue C, waiting at the corner for sight of him or his horse. None. Finally, she knocked at his landlady's flat and asked, any empty places to rent, any sudden vacancies brought on by accidents or illness? Again, nothing. No sudden vacancies, either, at the stable on Cooper Street, where Herschl boarded his horse.

So. Nothing terrible had happened to him—something terrible had happened to her. He was on-purpose avoiding her, pretending their supper, the bookstore reunion, their sit-down along the East River, had never happened. She'd dug herself a hole with her tongue. Now she'd have to figure how to bump her way out.

The library ladies sent a card. Tuesday night, a questions-and-answers get-together. The speaker was a famous lady from Washington who happened to be in New York that week—what luck!—and had a bundle of information about how to push yourself onto the pages of the newspapers in a ladylike fashion, you shouldn't be seen as dangerous, or like your head was out of order, to explain about getting the vote for women, how important it was, and now was the time.

Two more ladies, Libby and Tillie, who Sadie knew from the early days when she rolled cigars in a damp room with no windows, one toilet for forty workers, a boss with slippery hands when he got you alone, were also speaking. Even back then, they were ambitious, graduating from eighth grade, a small miracle for poor Jews, especially girls, moving from rolling cigars to working in a newsstand in Times Square, finally buying the business.

And now, they were real-life heroines, just out of jail—sour soup and stale bread, a lumpy blanket on a concrete floor—for tying themselves to the fence around Gramercy Park, holding up signs: "Women Are Citizens, Too." But never mind, the announcement read, we are going to win. Losing is not in our vocabulary. Five syllables. Sadie had written the word in her night school notebook.

Sadie loved that thumb-in-the-eye confidence the suffragette ladies had. She'd had it, from God knows where, back in Luvel, telling Fivel, "Let's go, let's go, you'll love America," not sure he would, sure she would. She'd felt the pull to go, the *need*, in her *kishkey*, close to the way she felt now about wanting to vote, one hundred percent American, through and through, never mind she wore a skirt.

Sometimes she thought, what would Fivel think about ladies and voting? Not a peep from him in a week. Maybe he'd found Gittel Diamond. He could use a good friend, someone to help him think about all the ways she, Sadie, was going in the opposite direction from what he believed in. There had to be days, Sadie blushed to admit, when Fivel wasn't sorry not to be at home on Orchard Street.

The library was near the East River, seven, eight blocks, a good day for walking. Lots of people in the street, lots of noise and horse shit, peddlers and carts lined up like herrings, everyone hollering something: "Ladies' stockings, combs, two for a nickel, ladies' intimate wear for sale." Two men the size of wrestlers, but not so hot-headed, derby hats, bow ties, spats, carrying chairs on their backs, stools on their chests, hollering, "Shoeshine, one thin dime, step up, sit down, walk away clean."

She pushed her way between carts, fingering a lace scarf here, a silk blouse there, buying an ice cream cone, dropping five pennies into the box held out by one of the young girls singing on the corner; red satin skirts, sassy red hats, dancing to lively accordion music, "Some of these days / You'll miss your honey. . . ."

Sadie took a seat in the third row from the speaker—not too close, not too far. In minutes, the women began arriving. Some, the younger ones, wore high-heeled boots, lipstick and rouge, snappy piled-high hair do's, peeked into the room, then took seats in the back. Several, moving with the strong whiff of knowing where they were going, stepped up to the front row, took out notebooks, unwrapped sandwiches, crossed their legs, revealing their silky American ankles.

Sadie glanced around the room, thinking that a few ladies looked like possible love knot customers, especially that plump lady across the aisle, hair two shades of blond, too much rouge, no wedding ring. She rifled through her purse. No, she forgot to bring her business sheets. Maybe for the best. She was here to ask questions: How could she help with getting the vote, but not go to jail? No need to go into confessions in public, but she had a problem. Herschl. Would he think she was poetic if she mixed into politics? Could she do illegal things—yes, *illegal*, she couldn't call a mule a horse—and still be sweet, feminine? Was it important what he thought, if she knew what *she* thought? Her head hurt, and the evening hadn't even started.

Suddenly—surprise, surprise, with the room almost filled, and the unwrapped sandwiches sending out pickle and mustard and salami smells, some sipping seltzer from glass jars—there was her night school teacher, Lillian Pomerantz, on the stage, all pale-blue silk and soft voice, dainty pearl earrings, hair combed into a smooth pompadour, calling the meeting to order.

The important lady from Washington missed her train. Not too terrible, Lillian Pomerantz assured, smiling her schoolteacher smile, sending out waves of calm strong enough to quiet the room and bring to the stage Lilly and Tilly, looking healthy after their time in jail.

Lilly, the shorter, rounder of the two women, talked with a lisp, but Sadie caught her meaning: they needed new members, especially if they were typists, envelope stuffers, or knew about talking on the telephone. Also—and now her voice was louder—

they needed office supplies, rent was due on their tiny office, the light bill. Any new ideas on how to raise money?

Feet were shuffled, paper bags rattled, a few whispers, but no one stood up, until Sadie did. Mrs. Pomerantz beamed at her student. "Ah, Sadie Schuster, always good to see you."

Pressing her sweaty hands against her cotton skirt, she hoped the *thomp-thomp* of her heart was invisible. Mrs. Pomerantz was still smiling. Finally: "Hello, Mrs. Pomerantz." Sadie waved a weak wave.

Mrs. Pomerantz nodded. More foot shuffling. From someone, a sneeze, followed by a "*Gezuntheit.*" Sadie closed her eyes and saw Fivel, Herschl, Yivvy, all mixed up together, whispering, "*Shah, shah . . .*" What was she doing here, hanging out her own personal private laundry for everyone to hear? Opening her eyes—filled with guilt over not doing enough with the voting ladies, even with the march to plan for, pushed by her terror of talking too much private talk here, in front of strangers—she pulled in a gulp of air, and plunged ahead. "My own personal gift to helping the fight for votes, I will pay this month's lighting bill."

Chapter Five

Push flesh.

S adie translated Mitzi's advice into: *dance*. It made perfect sense. Who danced as graceful? Very few women who lived on the Lower East Side and, of those few, who else also owned income property that had a new, completely paid-up furnace and was fully rented?

Also, the timing for dancing was perfect. The once-a-year dance contest at the Henry Street Saturday Night Social Club was in August. Almost two months. She'd enter and invite Herschl to watch. Once he saw her on the dance floor—wasn't he an old-time hoo-ha dancer himself?—his love of dipping, of bending his body, flesh pressed to flesh, would spring back to life, like new tulips popping through cracks in the sidewalk. He'd realize, no matter how much he'd loved Gittel—it was sweet, all that loyalty, *but*—he was still alive, and life goes on.

Only one problem. Yivvy said it two days later, when Sadie, eager to get to Klein's Emporium to find red dancing boots, something in snakeskin with curved, tricky heels, was hurrying to deliver a love knot to Manny Kupperman in his wholesale linens store.

Glancing up the street, she saw her daughter on the corner in serious conversation with—no! That man talking with her, it couldn't be—a policemens! Seeing Sadie approach, the officer—younger looking than he appeared to be from a distance, and plenty good-looking, with that blonde hair and that moustache—took a card from his pocket and, handing it to Yivvy, tipped his hat and hurried off, swinging his club.

"Troubles?" Sadie stared after the retreating figure.

Yivvy buried the card in her purse, and murmured, "Fine, fine, fine," or, "Nine, nine, nine." Sadie wasn't sure. "So, Ma, imagine, whatcha doin' in this part of town?" Yivvy smiled a tight, unhappy smile: *See, no problem, nothing to get excited about.* "You get down here often?"

"I need special permission to come to Broome Street?" She studied her daughter closely. "All of a sudden you got business with a policemens?"

"What kinda business? We met by accident, I know him"—blinking—"not a lot, I don't know him a lot"—talking faster now—"only a little, from up there, my neighborhood, near the store. He wanted to know, how's business? A nice guy, but a little, you know"—Yivvy spun one finger next to her head—"kind of a *yenta*, always pokin' in everybody's pot. Nothin' better to do, you know how police are."

"No, I don't know nothing about policemens' personal questions." She looked up the street again, then back at Yivvy. "So, how is it?"

"What?"

"Business."

"Oh, *that!*" Yivvy studied her shoes. "Okay, it's okay, good, no complaints."

"The new stuff is selling?"

"Not exactly."

"It's *not* selling?"

Yivvy rotated one hand, "So-so."

"What's his name?" Sadie poked a finger toward the corner.

"*His*? Oh, Quinn, yeah, Thomas Quinn, Junior. It's on his card, he gave me his card"—she held up her purse—"in case I ever need somethin', I can ask for him at the station. You know how all policemen look alike, you need a name to find anyone."

"I was noticing that Quinn policemens looks like the Kelly policemens that walks around my street, and *he* could be the twin brother from that other policemens, Sullivan, that stands on the corner by Delancey. Like you say, you can't tell one from the—"

Yivvy looked like she was about to leave.

"Wait." Sadie grabbed her daughter's arm. "What's new, since you asked, is dancing." She explained: The Henry Street Saturday Night Social Club's contest was less than two months away and, since she loved to dance, not mentioning the Hirschl part, she'd always wanted to enter. Why not now?

"Sure, why not? The only problem, the right partner. You'll dance good, but with who?"

"Not with *who*! 'Dance with *whom*.' My night school teacher said so."

"Well, *excuuuuze* me!"

"One letter, one, at the end of a word, leave it out, the world hears how green you are. Put it in, the world hears your educated American mouth."

"You know what, Ma?" Yivvy's nose twitched with annoyance. "You oughta forget about dancin' 'n find yourself a talkin' contest."

◡୬ ◡୬ ◡୬

The Henry Street Saturday Night Social Club was more than a club. It was a sweet ending to the bitter workweek. Two large rooms off Houston Street, above the Real Romanian Bakery, rented out on weeknights for lectures, union meetings, pinochle tournaments, and cousin clubs' meetings. Saturday evenings were strictly for dancing, fifty cents admission, no IOU's or poker chips accepted. The customers with steady jobs said, Why not, what's money for? Cheaper than Moishe Pipik's Cafe on Broadway, where all you did was eat and drink, but never touched. Others said: *Robbery!* Fifty cents, too much to pay for moving around a dance floor hoping, if you were a man, for a fast feel; hoping, if you were a woman, to meet someone who'd buy you a glass of seltzer, walk you home, someone who'd ask to see you again and, God willing, if this was your lucky night, might turn out to like marriage.

Everyone who was single came. In the first room, Lippke Axelrod, the bartender, stood behind a wooden table dispensing whiskey and beer to dancers over twenty-one, seltzer and grape juice to everyone else. Lippke was a smiler, a watcher, a kind man, unusual in someone who made his living spilling whiskey. While he spilled, he noticed: who were the *kibitzers*, which bragger, acting like a *macher*, was really a *schlemiel*? No one fooled him.

"Look out for the one with the greasy head," he'd warn female customers. "He has busy hands when the lights go out." Or: "Don't leave with Hymie, the Hungarian. A bad memory. Show him a pretty face, he forgets he's married."

In the second room, the band, Moishe's Melody Makers—two fiddles, an accordion, a set of drums, a piano, a clarinet—sat on a raised platform. In front of the piano a large white cardboard sign read: "Applause Is the Only Tip We Accept."

The women sat on wooden chairs against the walls, waiting to be picked, pretending not to care if they weren't. The men circled the room, making eye contact with this woman, avoiding the next.

Most of the women who came to the Henry Street Saturday Night Social Club were younger than Sadie, but none was a better dancer. When the music began, she felt it as surely as she felt the wooden chair and the silk taffeta of her shirtwaist. It entered her, lifting her from her seat, carrying her onto the dance floor, her face a bright moon burning with excitement. Even if, occasionally, she had no partner, dancing was dancing. She waltzed, box stepped, cakewalked, dipping and swaying, in and out among other couples and across the waxed wooden floor, as though she had not feet, but wings. As though she were twenty and slim, rather than forty-one and soft.

Most Saturday evenings she had enough partners. Often, too many. Men like Yankel the carpenter, Nate the barber, and Izzie the fishmonger, younger men conscious of their rough good looks and strong, muscular bodies. Not men to talk with, not a reader among them, but they worked hard at dancing, pumping their legs, sweating inside stiff starched collars and cheap woolen suits to keep up with her, because she looked good when she danced and she made them look good.

On the first Saturday night after her decision to enter the Club's

Chapter Five

dance contest, Sadie arrived early, expectant, hopeful she'd find not only a partner, but also a couple of love knot customers, and a place to tack up the news about her march. She'd brought a hundred red, white, and blue announcements in her purse. Good dancing; good business; good advertising. Perfect.

Tonight, Sadie counted six men lounging against the bar. One, with the build of a wrestler, wearing a straw hat, striped suit, and yellow suede spats, waved at her. Sadie nodded, the barest dip of her head. Always nice to be nice, but too much enthusiasm too early in the evening could be dangerous. Why get nailed down with one partner?

She looked good—a pity Herschl wasn't here to see her—thanks to Klein's Emporium, Mitzi's makeup tricks, and the not-so-reliable electric lightbulbs strung around the hall.

Her new marquisette earrings whooshed a satisfying sound against the lace collar of her silk taffeta shirtwaist. Her corset was also new, bought the day her mirror told her she'd lost three pounds, maybe more. Mitzi, helping her get dressed, had pulled hard at the corset strings until Sadie had hollered, "Enough!"

"You're sure ample, hon, but interesting."

Sadie asked what *ample* meant, and Mitzi made a circle of thumb and forefinger. She couldn't breathe, then she couldn't sit. Men didn't men wear bone torture chambers under their clothes, they'd never put up with it. Take them or leave them, that's what you got. Worse, her new shoes, shiny and red, with curving heels, made her feet—her best feature, everyone said so—look smaller, but hurt even more than the corset.

She was still standing in the entry, thinking that the path leading to Herschl Diamond was through the first room, into the second, that nothing good comes from doing nothing, when the band struck up a waltz. She wiggled, hoping to loosen the hold her corset had on her right thigh, rotating one red leather shoe, then the other. Resisting the impulse to plunge ahead, she walked slowly, head up, stomach in, toward the bar and Lippke.

"So, Sadie"—he smiled, his gold tooth winking. He needed a new dentist, she decided, maybe the one on Dean Street upstairs of the barber who sold Fivel those beautiful teeth the summer before he died—"how's the marriage business? How many weddings this month?"

65

"Some good beginnings starting up, no endings yet. Ask me next week." She slid two coins across the bar. "Who is here tonight?"

"A few regulars." Lippke half filled a small shot glass. "Summer, things get quiet."

Sadie glanced into the next room, where the women were taking seats along the wall. "I see Nussy Fishkin's back from Atlantic City. Probably lost his job, and also his what's-her-name?" Sadie crossed her eyes. "The healthy-looking redhead with all the money, and the funny look to the eyes."

Lippke nodded.

"And Jake Zeisler, still a shifty look on his skinny face." Not like Herschl. God-only-knew where he was tonight. Home, maybe, reading poetry, those sweet, serious eyes.

Lippke sucked a wooden toothpick in silence.

Sadie turned to him. "So? You got something to say, say it." She emptied the shot glass.

"Tonight I got a good one, a new fella, Ike something from Riga." Lippe pointed to the other room. "Off the boat one month, a good dancer, a smart talker."

Sadie, following Lippke's pointing finger, saw a young man, taller than the others—taller than Herschl—wearing a checkered suit and a pleased look. His hair was like black patent leather, probably pomade. Sadie watched him smooth his pompadour, straighten his tie.

"He looks to me like a pint of trouble, that one." Thirty, thirty-two, a *pisher*. She pushed her empty glass across the counter. "Sometimes a little smart turns into too smart."

"I'm talking dancing, you're talking is he a *mensch*," Lippke said. "What's one thing got to do with the other?"

"I'll let you know," she said, moving toward the music, then remembering, took the announcements of the womens' march out of her purse and handed them to Lippke. "Please pin up." She took a seat next to Malke Dlugatch, a thin blonde with watery eyes. Sadie's corset strings pinched, but Mitzi said, one, two dances, she'd forget she had it on.

Malke put a damp hand on Sadie's arm. "I'm coming to see you," she said, eyeing a tall, skinny young man with a giant-sized moustache across the room. Sadie rubbed her handkerchief over the toe of her shoe, and gave him a quick once-over. "Make an appointment, I'm very busy this month." The young man ran a comb through his pale hair. "Only, make it soon, you don't have time to waste. His kind, all the girls want."

The band moved into a lively two-step. Sadie watched Ike approach, pause in front of the plump lady two seats away. He certainly knew how to wear a suit, a regular walking clothes hanger. Probably not much to talk with, but good to look at.

Moving closer, he nodded to Malke. Herschl marched across Sadie's mind, in work shirt and suspenders, the polka-dotted bandana, his cotton cap, his book. She'd hug him this minute, sweat and all, if she could get her hands on him.

Ike was watching her from the corner of his eye. She knew the look, a come hither, mixed in with a little I'm making up my mind, like he owned the world and you should pay him rent. He took his toothpick out of his mouth, wiped it on his sleeve, slipping it into his pocket, and stopped in front of her, half bowed, and held his hand out. Sadie took it and followed him onto the dance floor. "Permit me," he said in Yiddish, "to tell you I was once the dance king of Riga." Sadie held herself very straight. The corset relaxed its pinch. "Latvia," he added.

"Good to know," she said, and sniffed. He smelled of *schmaltz* herring and hair oil; not as good as Herschl's leather and cigar smoke.

Ike led like he was born to lead; she followed easily. She'd talk to him in Yiddish. At her age, her weight, dancing and talking mixed together was not easy, especially with someone like this man, who probably gave two meanings to every word.

"Teach me to talk American," he said, "and I will teach you to dance."

Sadie stopped dancing. "Excuse me, if you will be so kind as to notice, I am doing that." They resumed dancing. "Dancing, I mean."

"Of course." He said he'd watched her the week before, he knew she was good. He, however, was better. He'd also heard her speak, and knew from Lippke that she'd studied English in night school. "Do we have a bargain?"

"Your name, please?" Why tell him Lippke had reported news of

his name, city, brains, dancing talent? He was already too puffed
up with his own importance.

"Tabatnik," he said, and executed an elaborate bow that involved
swinging one arm in a wide arc. "Ike Tabatnik, just two weeks off
the *S.S. North Atlantic Princess.*"

They continued dancing. This was not a man to have a calm
conversation. From him she'd never hear, "I'm not too good with
words." She closed her eyes. Herschl's sweet smile beamed at her.
Ike twirled, she dipped. His hand touched the middle of her back.
He was nudging her without looking like he was nudging, a man
who liked to be in charge. A real let-me-take-over type. All right,
Ike Tabatnik, we will see who's the pusher and who gets pushed.

"Your job is?" she asked.

"A fresh meat butcher." He led her through two dips and a whirl.
So, not a clothing model after all.

The band struck up a cakewalk. Ike hesitated. Sadie put her
hand out. "An American dance, permit me." Now she led, he
followed. They made an unusual-looking pair; a short, slightly
wide, intense woman propelling a taller, younger man across the
floor, gesturing: *this way, this way; count, one-and-two-and-three.*

He felt good, not in the same way Herschl had felt good that
night in her flat. Herschl was a man, this one was a boy. It was
another kind of good, more about the dancing than the thinking.
His shoulders and arms were strong, but not too. His hands were
a nice kind of easy moving. This one, yes sir, this one just might
be the one to help her win the dance contest.

She smiled. Herschl was asking: "Who's that good-looking
young man you danced with?" She'd murmur Ike's name, then add:
"Just a boy I met at the club, no one important." Then, Herschl
would say, in his strong, quiet, poetic voice, "Enough! From now
on, Sadie, you will dance only with me."

The cakewalk ended. Ike dipped, bending Sadie backwards in
an extravagant arc, his face close to hers. A sharp, pungent scent
floated past her nose, making her eyes water. An onion eater, bad
for dancing. "Ah," she breathed, "onions!" He said nothing. Mister
Chutzpah, all right. She patted her face with her handkerchief, her
mind racing. Good dance partners with nice muscles and shining
pompadours were not hanging from every tree on the East Side.

The judges liked nice-looking, it counted high, right up there with nice-moving. Maybe she could interest him in a love knot.

The music began. He folded his arms across his chest. This man, like all men, made nothing easy. "I agree," she said, "A good time to rest," and, inviting him to sit with her over a glass of seltzer, moved into the next room without waiting for his reply, found an empty table, set her purse in the center, then went to the bar to buy two glasses of cold seltzer.

Lippke's eyebrows were question marks. Sadie shrugged. "So far, the dancer part wins over the *mensch* part." She glanced around the room. "My announcements?"

"Why pin? I give two, three, to everyone who buys a drink. If they take ten papers, ten percent discount."

No time now to talk about voting. She gave Lippke a wink and a smile, and got back to Ike, who was waiting at the table. "Friends?" she asked, sitting down. He wore a tight smile. Probably an only child, or his mama's only boy, fed the plumpest piece of chicken, the juiciest bit of brisket, before anyone else got a swallow of cold water. She raised her glass. "So, tell me about you."

He was, he said, a man who made the most of every chance. His job was cutting up meat in a wholesale market on Fulton Street, but he planned to have his own shop soon, a man couldn't be expected to work for strangers. Not in America.

Even sitting down, he seemed to swagger, and whoever made his teeth did a good job, or was it possible they were his own?

"Your wife?" she asked, eager to get the love knot question settled.

"Wife?"

Maybe he didn't understand her Yiddish, she didn't speak it often, her words were rusted up. "You know." She shaped a female figure in the air.

He nodded, but said nothing.

"Wife," she repeated, and rocked an imaginary baby in her arms.

His story was familiar. His wife, their two children, waited in Latvia for him to send tickets. He took a sepia-colored photograph from his pocket, and slid it across the table. Sadie saw a sad, but pretty, young woman in a marriage wig, a little girl perched atop a stool, and a younger boy clutching his mother's skirt, both children smiling as though sharing a secret.

Married. Bad for the love knot business. He'd never ask, so she'd fill him in about herself, he should know good luck was on his side. He'd met an American with a soft spot for greenhorns. She told him about Fivel, about Yivvy, about the eight-flat she owned on Orchard Street.

"You are living at the present moment—where?" Sadie asked.

He was a boarder, he said, in someone's flat, a cousin of a man he met coming over, and gave an address close to hers.

Aaahhh . . . an idea took shape. If he lived in her building, they could practice evenings; dancing, nothing more, *no funny business*, she'd make that plain from the beginning. "I have in my building a nice flat," she began. His nod seemed serious enough, no lights blinking in the eyes. "Much better than being a boarder, your own kitchen.

"Your husband left you rich?"

Rich! The word smarted, salt on a cut finger. "He left me too soon, but"—he was beginning to look bored—"I'll look over your pushy question if you'll look over my pushy answer, and down the hall a clean water closet. Cheap."

"I need a place free, not cheap, the wages I get."

Not so easy, arranging these things. She'd begin all over, talk up the dance contest. "How about going in?" she asked. The first prize was ten dollars, good money, even split fifty-fifty. No, please don't thank her, everyone knows how generous she is.

He asked her had she thought about how she'd spend her prize money.

She described the fox scarf with both eyes missing in the window of Klein's Emporium. Or, the purple lace gloves in a shop on Rivington Street, chocolate cream tortes from the Viennese Bakery. Also, she saw a frosted glass perfume vial with the tiniest chip in the stopper, in her daughter's pawnshop. Last, and she held up one foot, showing off her new red shoes, white leather boots with gold leaf hearts embroidered on the cuffs. Anything was possible with five dollars. "And you?"

"Spats," he said, "pale-grey suede spats."

"Not for the steamship tickets?" He looked like he didn't understand. "For your wife, the two little babies."

"Oh, mmm"—he cleared his throat—"of course." He looked away.

This man could use loyalty lessons from Herschl. She began to mention how much he must miss his family, but the music started up, a polka, and he jumped to his feet and led her onto the dance floor and into a lively two-step.

Was she imagining it, or was his hand on her waist more insistent? He broke into a whirl, a fancy shuffle, ending in a graceful clicking of his heels. Two couples stopped dancing to watch, applauding. Ike half bowed, his face bright with pleasure. He was good, all right, but she had a few dancing tricks of her own. He slid backwards, she glided forward, the perfect response. He looked impressed.

"Of course, we'll win," she said. "Absolutely."

He'd begun a fancy arms-high-in-the-air maneuver, but stopped abruptly. "Repeat, please, that word, I like it."

"That word is your new word," Sadie said, "a present from me, no charge. *Absolutely*, in four American parts. Write it down."

Ike Tabatnik—the first words in her head when she woke up the next morning—was going to help her win Herschl. The dance king of Riga, Latvia, if she could believe him. Greenhorns step one foot into America, and brag about who they were in their old lives, not all of it true. She summoned his face: the sleek black hair; dark, snappy eyes; flashing smile. A made-to-order partner for winning, and enough of a looker so that, when they won and Herschl claimed her—when she claimed *him*—seeing Ike would be an extra squeeze on his heart.

Later, hearing Mitzi's heels tip-tap in the foyer, Sadie opened her door to see her tenant, looking like a bouquet of lilacs in lavender chiffon. Stepping out to admire, Sadie said, "You smell as good as you look," and patted the row of tiny pleats circling Mitzi's hips.

"Nothing's too good for church."

"*Church?*"

"I meet some interestin' people there. Surprised?"

"From you, nothing surprises. Tell me, do you talk to the priest, you know"—her throat was dry like a sand dune—"any secrets? I heard it can help. You tell to the priest your sin, and that minute you're innocent." She swiped one palm across the other. "Good-bye secrets."

Mitzi smiled. "Wrong church, hon, that's Catholic. I'm the other kind, Methodist. We sing." She started moving toward the street door.

Now! "You got a minute, I got questions?" Mitzi made no sign she'd heard. "About Chicago, your home city."

Mitzi turned. "What about Chicago?"

"That policemens in Chicago who took money from you, that's what's about."

Mitzi glanced at the door, then at Sadie. "You got something to say, say it."

"He's not in Chicago, he's here"—Sadie pointed to the floor—"and he says he's gonna do the same thing in New York. It's not only him who says so, the whole police department where he works says so." She felt the wall behind her, and sank against it.

Mitzi studied her, saying nothing. Then: "Well, *well.*"

"That's all you got to say?"

Mitzi shrugged. "Who you been talkin' to?"

Sadie ducked her head.

"Okay, just tell me this—when?"

"They didn't say for sure."

"Thanks for the warning; I'll handle it."

"How?"

"I said, I'll take care of it!"

"Only"—Sadie pointed to the ceiling—"your business, you didn't say what you do up there."

"You didn't ask."

"I ask now."

"Don't get too pushy, I gotta lease." Smoothing her gloves, turning toward the door: "Well, toodle-oo, I have to get to my prayers."

72

She needed Mrs. Pomerantz, with her smart mind and her lawyer husband. She needed the spirits. Mostly, she needed a glass of ice water, which she drained in a single gulp. Then, holding the frigid glass to her cheeks, too agitated to stop to lower the window shades, Sadie whispered her chants, then said them aloud to the mirror over her washbasin, before pulling a chair into the center of the room—*Look like you're not afraid*!—climbing onto it and, rotating slowly, hands clenched, singing out chants to all four corners of the room.

Almost at once, a shaft of sunlight seeping into the room became a blur of wings, a speck of brilliance beating and humming its way across the room, pausing for a moment before arranging itself into two pulsing particles on the tip of the nail of her forefinger on her right hand.

The dots of light flared, like Fourth of July sparklers, then dimmed until they were extinguished, swallowed by the surrounding dust motes. One vanished. The other radiance, a pinpoint beyond the tip of her nose, seemed to be lingering, suspended, pulsating midair. Sadie shivered and scarcely breathed, watching as it once again floated onto her fingertip, seeming to melt into the nail until, barely glowing, it became a part of her.

Chapter Six

S adie started strolling through neighborhoods on the other side of Rutgers Park, in her purse, her Herschl love knot, Komaroff's new book of poems, *Coming to America*, and handouts advertising the upcoming march, pausing at pushcarts to pinch a plump tomato and smell a fragrant apple, to examine a secondhand, but good-as-new, china cup, and snap a pair of elastic suspenders. A beautiful summer day, everything peaceful. Who knew what nice surprises could turn up?

Late in the morning on the fourth day Herschl turned up.

She heard a lusty voice pinging its way across the humidity, calling out something about his ice and your icebox, two things made for each other, and there he was, rolling toward her, looking so good she could kill him, in his polka-dotted bandana and rolled-up sleeves and cotton cap. She stepped to the curb, and waited. Thanks God she had worn her purple-and-white-striped cotton skirt and pale-lavender shirtwaist, and had taken that extra minute to tuck a shiny shell comb behind her pompadour.

This wet heat—dabbing at her face, her arms—if a love knot customer her age came to her this hot and bothered, she'd say: "Wait, don't buy, not yet, go see your doctor, get a checkout."

Herschl saw her and pulled at the reins, edging the wagon toward the curb. "Mrs. Schuster . . ." His voice was surprised, but serene. His face let nothing slip out, a mountain of calm with a strong peppering of dignity thrown in. He looked down at her with an expression Sadie decided to call *friendly*.

"What a lovely surprise," she said. No answer from him, but a flicker of a smile lit up those sweet blue-and-gray eyes. "I am just inspecting a building I hear might be up for sale"—Sadie waved a hand vaguely, hoping he'd think: *My, my, a lady of property*, but that he wouldn't ask: *where*? Should she show him the womens' marching news?

"You wouldn't be shopping for a new parrot?"

Wonderful! He had a sense of humor. What a relief. Sadie peered up at him. "Once is enough; maybe too much." Glancing at her wristwatch, she said, "Can you believe, time for lunch already?"

He squinted in the direction of the sun. "Twelve o'clock. It so happens, I have a sandwich, a jar of lemonade, cold, of course." He smiled. She allowed a soft giggle to escape. "If you enjoy Swiss cheese on *challah*, we can sit there," he said, looking down the street and pointing toward the park.

"Perfect!" The word slipped out before she could catch it. She shouldn't be so enthusiastic, play hard to get, say a simple yes without shooting off fireworks. Herschl was guiding his horse toward the park, and she followed.

They sat under a tree close to the street, so he could feed his horse. "Sorry not to offer you as good as you fed me in your house," he said. Dividing the sandwich in half, he filled two metal cups with lemonade.

So! He remembered their supper. He probably also remembered how she'd talked too much when they sat along the East River, asking too many questions, like the question she was about to ask: *Do you make your own lunch?* but swallowed, along with the lemonade. Raising her cup, she said, "To new friends." He hesitated, then tipped his glass toward her and sipped.

"I usually read while I eat," he said, pulling a book out of his paper bag.

"What a coincidence . . ." Sadie let the word hang in the

air between them, her clear, strong *c*'s spoken like *s*'s, before plunging her hand into her purse, and pulling out Komaroff's book. "*Coming to America*," she said, holding it up.

"*No*—how?" He took the book from her, and paged through it. "Where? I wanted this but can't find it."

"I was lucky. I looked, and there it was." She hoped she didn't sound boastful. Boastful was not a selling point with this man.

"I can't believe . . ." He continued to leaf through the book, pausing to read a few lines to himself. "Listen!" Looking up at her, then down at the book: "Now that I turn from home," he read.

Sadie stopped eating. The sun glinting through the leaves, falling across his hair as he bent over the book, struck a shade of dark silver in the salt-and-pepper curls. Such a gorgeous picture it made, she felt like crying.

"My heart finds its new home," he continued. His reading voice was deeper than his talking voice, also quieter, like someone reading from a holy book, someone praying.

Better than praying.

He stopped, looking up at something behind her, something at the far end of the park, his eyes shiny. Sadie thought, *Don't talk, don't*; struggling against squirming, but the grass tickled, were those ants crawling? Or—too much to hope for!—the spirits, their lovely little wings quivering, sending a message: *Sadie, yes, yes, yes*! She glanced at her finger and the tip seemed, even in the harsh sunlight, to wink up at her.

Herschl sniffed and, pulling out his handkerchief, wiped his nose. "Well"—now he was looking at her, smiling, but not a happy smile—"excuse me, please, Komaroff does this to me." He wiped his nose again.

"Please," she said, "nothing to excuse. We're lucky to find people who feel like we do"—she swallowed, working to keep her voice steady—"in books, or outside."

His eyebrows expressed surprise. "Mrs. Schuster—"
"Sadie."
"—I like that, what you just said, like a poem."

"Why, thank you." If she died this minute, she'd die happy. "It's nothing, really, I always . . ." She gulped the rest of her lemonade and peered into her empty glass. "Do you have more ice?"

"Oh!" He looked at his watch, jumped up and began gathering his things. "I have the finish of my route to do before five o'clock." They stood for a minute, her hand in his. Then his cap, which he had just put on, came off. "So, good-bye, Mrs. Schuster."

Her mind raced. He couldn't feed her half his lunch, read to her from a book of poems, and just walk away, *pfffft*. Suddenly, almost without meaning to, she found herself scratching her ear and heard *Supper*, barely a whisper. "Maybe sometime we could have a little supper," she said, "at my place. It is after all my turn"—he frowned—"after you fed me lunch," she added.

Herschl fussed with his cap.

"Nothing special, a little cold smoked fish, beet *borscht*. You loved my *borscht*."

"I am still . . ." He looked stricken.

She knew, not wanting to know.

"Not even six months since Gittel died. I like talking with you, but"—he shrugged—"I'm not ready." He wagged his fingers in a limp farewell wave, and would have been on his wagon and gone, but she saw the book lying on the grass where it had fallen, and ran after him, calling and waving, insisting that he take it, no, no, she wanted him to have it. He nodded, smiling, but not a full-force smile.

"Wait!" She took two marching notices out of her purse and slipped them between pages of the book. "A little something, also to read." She couldn't think of any American words to tell him, *This is me also, I have my important ideas, take it or leave it*, knowing she needed him to take it, knowing—and not wanting to know—he would maybe leave it.

ᒍꝰ   ᒍꝰ   ᒍꝰ

She cut through the alleys to avoid meeting anyone, simmering with a feeling of—of being *cheated*. This time she'd said the right thing, she hadn't said too much, he said what she said sounded like poetry, and where was she? She felt a small sliver of happiness that she'd slipped in the marching news, which he *had* to see was about more than a march.

A small gray dog yapped its way between her legs, forcing her to sidestep and embrace a garbage can, which overturned, spilling a waterfall of tins, jars, celery leaves, watermelon rinds, and oranges over her shoes. "Typical!" she hollered into the humid, rancid air. "That's all I got, garbage!"

Sweating, Sadie stood outside the door to her flat, one hand on the banister, glaring upward. How could she run to Mitzi for advice when they weren't even talking? Plus, any minute a man with an axe and a whistle could knock down the front door and ten or twenty men in blue uniforms could fly up into Mitzi's flat, hollering, "Hands up, this is a raid, and you, Sadie Schuster, you criminal landlady, you're going to jail!" Sadie smiled in spite. In jail, she could count on being with some of her friends.

Mitzi, in a pale-green chiffon robe, answered Sadie's knock. "I found him." Sadie marched past her. Her this-minute-crisis couldn't wait. Time later for wiping up the leftover pieces from their last discussion.

Mitzi followed Sadie into the parlor. Her coppery hair was brushed to a brilliance, fastened in place by a spiral of trailing green satin ribbons. Sadie eyed her, wiping at her face with a soiled *babushka*. "All this heat, and you look like the angel on top of the cake in the window at the Viennese Bakery. God must not be Jewish." She sat down on the red velvet sofa.

Mitzi settled opposite her. "I ain't seen you since our last shoot-out."

"You're mad at me?" Sadie asked impatiently. Mitzi made herself busy with a red velvet pillow. "Because, if you are, that makes us two evens."

"Why would I break into a sweat getting mad at you? We're two single ladies floating in a sea fulla snapping men."

"Good, so I can tell you my today's hard luck." She did, finishing with, "My terrible *mazel*, I picked out a man in love with a dead woman."

"Well, I say the hell with him: good-bye and good riddance."

"Easy for you to say, with your face, that hair, like the burning bush."

"You think I'm telling you to go hungry and I'm sitting down to a banquet?"

Sadie's head ached, her feet ached. Maybe she should stay home more, a woman her age, concentrate on making love knots, go back to reading books, see more moving pictures. March with voting signs, never mind Fivel hollering down on her, *Sadie, shame, shame!* and, for sure, never mind what Herschl could think on that topic.

"Make him jealous," Mitzi said.

"Jealous? Did you hear me? He's still married." Sadie shook her head. "In a way of speaking."

"I know what he said, but all guys are the same, the only difference between 'em is the siza their wallets. They're like kids," Mitzi went on, "don't want a piecea candy 'til someone else has his mitts on it."

"It wouldn't work."

"Look, you want this Ike to dance with so you could win the contest"—she ticked her points off on her fingers as she spoke—" 'n impress this ice guy."

"So I was wrong."

"Let me finish! He thinks you're an okay lady, more than okay. He *says* he's not interested, but soon as he thinks he's lost ya, wham, bang."

"And what's going on inside the brain of Mr. Ike, he should be happy to *schlep* around with a woman old enough to be his, his . . ."

Mitzi twirled the ribbons. "What's it worth to you to make it worth it to him?"

Sadie stood up. "My head hurts all the way down to my toes. Could be that passion feels better when the weather's not so hot."

Maybe Mitzi made sense. Maybe not. Sadie wrote a letter in her best Yiddish: *Dear Mr. Tabatnik: A basement flat in my building is, surprise, surprise, empty. Free to you if you take down the trash, sweep the stairs, clean out the furnace. Nothing too much.* Some days after supper, they could play her phonograph, brush up on their dancing for the contest. She added, *The empty flat is yours, with or without the dancing. I wait to hear, and wish you only good things.*

Should she sign it, *Yours, Sadie Schuster?* Or, *Yours, Mrs. Schuster?* She decided upon *Sadie Schuster, Landlady.*

The letter was partly true. The basement flat *was* empty, had been for six months, since Mrs. Lustein died, leaving her furniture, curtains, a few dishes and pots. Sadie, when her bunions didn't burn, and her sciatica didn't squeeze, did all the janitor duties. A strong pair of muscles to help her out would be nice.

But there was the other part of the letter, the part she'd left out, the "make-sure-Herschl-sees-us" part. Sadie reread it. This could be trouble. Ike was a hustler, the I'll-take-anything-I-can-get type. She knew his kind, just off the boat, chewing up America and spitting it out. She had to be careful he shouldn't think she meant something she didn't, a woman alone.

P.S. Please don't get the wrong idea, this is a strictly-for-business arrangement, like a mother—she erased *mother* and wrote *sister—would do for a brother.*

ᒎᔆ   ᒎᔆ   ᒎᔆ

Sadie walked six steaming blocks to a red brick building on Division Street, fourth floor rear, where Ike was a boarder in the flat of a woman Sadie knew from her visits to the pushcarts on Orchard Street. She knocked at the door, smiled at his landlady, gave her a new twenty-five-cent piece, and the note, and told her to be sure and give it to Ike when he came home for supper.

The landlady pocketed the coin and the note and eyed Sadie. Sadie recognized the look. Suspicious, layered over curiosity. "I'm his teacher," Sadie said.

"Yeah, whaddya teach him?"

But Sadie was gone.

She read the advertisement in *The Daily Forward*: BeBe Delight and Harold Farrell—together! Two gorgeous people, with straight teeth and straight noses and perfect-sounding English, her creamy shoulders and the beautiful way his pants fit, starring in the just-out movie, *Love of My Life*, beginning that afternoon at the Eighth Avenue Movie Palace. Exactly the right medicine for soothing her in-an-uproar nerves.

Going to the moving pictures in the middle of a weekday? The same as serving beef brisket and cheese blintzes together. Going to the movies instead of stuffing up envelopes for the next suffrage ladies meeting? A sin, but not a big one, she could stuff the next day. Fivel was gone and Yivvy, also gone, in a way, now that she'd moved into two rooms behind the pawnshop. *Do it.* Maybe Ike's answer would be waiting when she got back. Maybe Herschl would feel an attack of loneliness and show up at her door hungry.

One o'clock. She stopped under the marquee to admire a life-sized cardboard cutout of the stars. That BeBe Delight, some body. Something mysterious about the way Gentile women didn't put on fat.

Sadie elbowed her way through the crowded lobby toward a man selling chocolates, soda water, peanuts. "A two-cents bag of popcorn," she said, as someone's heel jabbed her ankle.

Wheeling around, she bumped into a blur of blonde hair, red suspenders, navy-blue shirt, broad shoulders. Now her ankle throbbed, the heavy air was a damp blanket wrapping her skin, and the smell! *Feh!* Garlic, pickled fish, *schmaltz.*

"*Klutz, klutz, klutz!*" she shouted, hopping now, groping to grasp the wounded foot, lowering herself finally as gracefully as she could onto the dusty flowered carpet, everyone staring down at her, especially the red-haired woman in the pink feather boa chewing gum, looking guilty.

"Ma!"

Sadie heard Yivvy before she saw her and, when she managed to see her, she understood why her daughter looked embarrassed, on top of frightened. She was with the young man wearing the red suspenders, and he had not only golden hair, but also a golden moustache, and was, from up close, anyway, at least six feet tall.

"I got here a broken foot," Sadie said, pointing. Yivvy yanked Sadie to her feet, helped her hobble across the lobby and into the chair an usher had rushed from the manager's office.

Seated, sweating, Sadie's curiosity swallowed her pain. "Who is . . .?" she asked, tilting her chin toward Yivvy's companion.

The young man bobbed his head. Sadie, mopping her face with her handkerchief, tried to remember where she'd seen so many freckles on one face. "This is Thomas," Yivvy said, "Quinn."

The young man clapped a cap onto his head, snatched it off again and, leaning forward, thrust out an eager hand.

"Junior," Yivvy finished.

Canal Street. She'd seen those blue eyes, like two lumps of the sky, on Canal Street, wearing a uniform. "The policemens from the other day?" She ignored the young man's hand.

"Thomas Quinn, Junior, patrolman," he said, and grasped Sadie's hand until he'd squeezed it into a handshake. "Very pleased to make your acquaintance."

Sadie pulled her hand away; then, seeing Yivvy's stricken face, added, "The pleasing is mutual, I'm sure." She patted his hand. Thomas cleared his throat and coughed. Yivvy sniffed and avoided looking at her mother. "Well," Sadie said.

"Well," Thomas repeated.

"How're you feelin'?" Yivvy asked.

Sadie wiggled her foot. "I'll live." Bracing herself on the arm of her chair, she stood up. "So far, so good." She scrutinized Thomas. *That* color yellow she'd seen on wheat, on butterflies; but on hair, never. "So, you like BeBe Delight?"

"Who?"

"You told me you never go to the moving pictures," she said, turning to Yivvy.

"We happened to be passing by."

"Twenty-five cents, no, thirty cents"—Sadie blinked—"you paid, because you got tired of walking?"

Yivvy said, "No," and Thomas said, "Yes," and then they both said, "Oh," and Yivvy looked at her wristwatch and said she had to get back to the shop.

"Who's watching?"

"No one."

"So, go."

"I am." And they were gone, Thomas looking back at her as they hurried through the lobby door, his face crinkled into an expression somewhere between regret and embarrassed delight.

Sadie hobbled home to soak her foot and think. She didn't need new glasses to see that here was a problem, but whether Yivvy brought it on herself, or it was brought on to her, was a question. She needed the facts but, from her daughter—with a mouth locked like a tomb—she'd get as much help as she'd get honey out of a stone. The well to dip into was named Quinn, with a Junior on the end.

⁂   ⁂   ⁂

Sadie had never visited a police station. Along with her mother's milk, she had drunk in a fear of the uniform, believing what everyone in her Polish town believed: no one wearing a uniform was a friend to the Jews. Never mind that there were Jewish firemen and policemen in New York. Sadie knew what she knew. She would go to her grave without putting one foot into a building built for policemens. Until now.

The right makeup, a beauty mark or two, curl up the hair. Show Mister Blue-Eyes Quinn that Yivvy has for a mother not a greenhorn, but a woman who knows her way around. Tell about owning her own building, maybe, even about the love knots, but no talk about suffragettes, who only fought with the police, banging up some of them with their wooden signs.

Mornings were the best time to carry out important business. If Thomas Quinn was out patrolling, she'd leave a message. If she found him, she'd say, coffee, tea? Let's sit and *schmooze*, only she wouldn't use that word, even though *schmooze* said what she wanted to say better than any American word.

The next morning, she arranged a face somewhere between I'm-going-dancing and I'm-going-shopping; stingy with eye shadow, generous with the lipstick, leaving out the beauty mark at the corner of her mouth. She dressed in black and white, adding her red straw handbag for a color punch-up.

She arrived at the police station in a taxi—who could walk after that foot stabbing—at eighteen minutes past ten, moving fast enough to look like she had no time to waste, but slow enough to look confident. Start out with: "Please, is patrolman Thomas Quinn at home?" She'd rehearsed, pronouncing every word, wrapping her mouth around the *q-u* in Quinn, puckering her lips, so she wouldn't flatten it out to *Keane* or, worse, *Cohen*.

She didn't ask for Thomas Quinn. He was writing at the desk when Sadie stepped up to it, recognizing her at once, looking surprised but happy to see her. So happy, in fact, that he reached over the desk to pump her hand *Hello*, blue eyes shining. She felt a strange squeeze on her heart, a ping of something too complicated to have a name. This young man would be easy to like. Sadie hadn't come here to like him.

"I'm Sadie Schuster," she said, "Missus."

"Of course, Ma'am." His voice was deep and musical, sounding like he was singing some of his words. "Yivvy's mother." He pressed farther forward, until he was staring over his desk at Sadie's shoes. "How's your foot?"

"Better, thanks." Now they were both looking at her feet. "I came to talk." She looked directly into that smile; so open, so honest, it pulled at her mouth, making her want to smile back, but she didn't come here to smile.

"Happy to, Ma'am," he said. That word again—it jolted her. No one had ever called her that, it sounded so young, so not Jewish. "If you can wait a few minutes, I'm due for a break. That is, if you don't mind going down the street to a little coffee shop I patronize, nice and clean, the kind a lady'd like."

Sadie read the sign above the window, "Pasteris the Greek." It was, as Thomas said, clean, and almost empty. She took a table near the front, studying the menu, until he came whistling down the street, waving at her through the plate glass, waving at the sour-looking waitress behind the counter, then at the skinny man with the handlebar moustache and big ears reading the newspaper behind the cash register.

"You're some kind of politician," Sadie said, when he was seated opposite her, "you go around waving to everybody?"

Thomas leaned back, looking around the cafe as though being there was a wonderful idea. "Not everybody, but almost. These are kinda my people in a way." He looked around the room. "Being I'm out on the streets so much. One big, happy family, in a manner of speaking."

"I believe it," Sadie said. She wasn't sure she trusted so much smiling. He had to be hiding something. Leaning forward: "I got important things to discuss."

He didn't look alarmed, or even curious. Signaling to the waitress, he called out, "Two coffees, please, heavy on the cream." Then, turning back to Sadie, elbows propped on the table, chin cupped in his palms: "You were sayin', Ma'am?"

"Yivvy and me," Sadie said, "we're close. A mother worries."

Thomas said, sure, he had a mother, she worried all the time. "She says it's because she's Irish."

"*No!* I thought it's because I'm Jewish." Thomas laughed. So— he was a laugher, *and* a waver. "You know, of course, I'm Jewish. Yivvy, too."

Thomas said he knew about Yivvy, so it was no surprise to him that she was. "Anyway, that's nice."

Nice? No one ever said being Jewish was nice. It was hard, *hard*, didn't he know that? The waitress set down two cups of coffee, slopping liquid into the saucers.

"I mean, Ma'am"—he sipped and gestured vaguely—"there's all kinds of people in a town like this one."

"Ha—just what I want to discuss! Jewish is not all kindsa people, it's . . . it's"—Sadie struggled for the right word. Yivvy wasn't like him and he wasn't like her—"Jewish is different, that's all."

"Well, the way I see it, you're whoever"—he pointed to her—"and I'm whatever." He tapped his chest. "And we're humans, so that makes us alike, doesn't it?" Sadie opened her mouth, but he went on. "That's the way I got it figured out. So far it's been workin' real good for me."

"Why beat behind bushes? Do you and my daughter go to the moving pictures a lot?"

"I don't go to anything a lot, Ma'am, I'm too busy studying for a promotion. Exam's comin' up next month."

He looked so proud, Sadie almost blurted out, *Congratulations.* "Excuse my question, let me start from the beginning. Since she was little, Yivvy never liked boys." He looked interested, but not surprised. "I mean, she maybe *liked* them, but—how to say this right?—nothing for romance." He nodded. "Not to hurt you, but only to talk the truth, you're a busy man, and me, too." Now he looked amused. "I said something funny?"

"At first, she said the same thing to me, and I told her I'm no boy, I'm a police officer." He sat up straighter and patted his tie. "Did she tell you I got my high school diploma, might go to night school, study law?"

"*No!*"

"Yes."

For sure, no ordinary policemens. Awe washed over Sadie's face. She couldn't stop herself, she smiled into Thomas' smile; except—so, one more lawyer, what difference in her life? She put her smile away and fiddled with her handbag, trying to look uninterested.

"Anyway, Ma'am, what I'm tryin' to say is, I don't plan to waste her time, or mine, just get to know her better, and vice versa. And, besides"—he was suddenly solemn—"Yivvy and I didn't just bump into one another at the movies."

A headache knocked on the inside of her head, "What *did* you do?"

Thomas frowned. "Maybe you better ask her, Ma'am"—he shuffled his feet—"I don't wanta talk too much outta turn."

"Sure you do!"

Thomas glanced at his watch, put his cap on. "I hope to see you again sometime soon. I like you, Mrs. Schuster, Ma'am." He picked up the check. "But I think it's a good idea if you talk to Yivvy 'bout this." Irritation, a hot, hard lump, hit Sadie's chest.

"Except, I got this to say"—he stood up—"your daughter is a fine person."

"Who said she isn't?" But he was walking toward the cash register, where he slid coins across the counter. "*Who!*" she hollered after him. Turning, just before stepping into the street, he tipped his cap and smiled.

An Irish Ike Tabatnik, this Quinn, full of *chutzpah*, hidden under that one-big-happy-family smile. Where did he get off with *your daughter's a fine person*! She didn't need his approving stamp to know how fine Yivvy was, never mind all their fighting.

☙ ☙ ☙

Yivvy's shop was four blocks south and one block east. Sadie banged the shop door open, then closed, rushing to the rear, where she found her daughter dusting lampshades. "Ha, you're here," she said, sinking into a chair.

"Where would I be on a Monday morning?"

"I'll be quick. Thomas Quinn Junior."

"You *saw* him?" Yivvy's eyes flashed a warning signal. "Where? When?"

"We sipped coffee, now, this morning."

"You're kidding me."

"Yivvy"—Sadie's voice was a miracle of calm—"he's Irish." Where was Fivel when she needed him? Dying was one way of avoiding these terrible times.

"So?" Yivvy carried a lamp into the next room. Sadie followed. "I hope you behaved like a lady."

"I behaved like a mother."

Yivvy set the lamp down on a polished wooden table, stepping back to admire. "Looks good here."

"I'm talking life and death, she's talking lamps." Sadie's eyes on the ceiling: "Fivel, wake up, are you listening?" Looking at Yivvy: "My foot needs a chair." Yivvy pointed, Sadie sat in the chair behind Yivvy's desk. "Okay, begin, tell me why you think Irish and Jewish mix good."

Yivvy began with how she'd seen Thomas Quinn here and there, he was the cop on the beat, they'd stop and talk, exchange street gossip. Nothing personal. Even when he began stopping in the store, they were friends, that's all. "Oh, sometimes we'd take a walk, go for a cup of coffee, nothing special."

Until last month. Some guys she'd never seen before showed up offering to sell her a load of merchandise, imports, mostly; figurines and bowls and jewelry, fancy *chochkas* people with money go for. Sadie's footache moved higher, hovering somewhere around her belly button.

They named a price she couldn't turn down, her chance to make a few bucks, enough to buy the shop, turn it into a high-class place, be in business for herself. Wasn't that America, a chance to get rich? How could she say no?

"But you smelled something not kosher?"

"I smelled and I didn't smell. It's easy, lookin' back." When she paid, the guys spilled the beans: "The stuff was off a ship that just came from China through that canal, 'n worth ten times what I paid, twenty times, but hot."

"*Hot?*"

"Stolen."

Sadie saw her daughter on Riker's Island wearing a baggy striped dress, talking to her from behind steel bars. Now her ear itched. She ignored it. What good was a magic spirit against the whole New York City Prison Department?

Yivvy went on: The two guys told her to forget she met them, just as Thomas Quinn showed up, following tips about a gang selling stolen imported goods. "He asked a lot of questions."

"He knew what you done?"

"Not right away but, when he saw soma the stuff layin' around waitin' to be unpacked, he got suspicious, wanted to know where I got it, how much I paid. He's a smart cop, I gotta say that."

"He put six and six together?"

"Yeah, only—"

"It gets more worse?"

"Depends. By that time we was"—Yivvy shrugged—"seein' a lot more of one another. The moving pictures, concerts in the park, you know."

This, Fivel couldn't fix. "What happened to your 'I-don't-want-to-waste-my-time-with-men'?"

Yivvy shrugged. "Tommy—"

"*Tommy*? No more Thomas?"

"—didn't seem like sucha wasta time, I suppose. Listen, you don't know what a friend he's been, not one word did he spill about any of this."

"You mean he's breaking the law over *you* breaking the law?"

"Why do you always put things . . ." Yivvy tented her fingers and looked past Sadie, as though listening to something Sadie couldn't hear. "Yeah, I guess you could say that, only he says with a little luck he'll find these guys 'n I can give 'em back the whole messa things, everything I didn't sell, let 'em keep the money. They'll be happy, 'n I'll be clean, 'n—"

"Yivvy, he's *Irish*."

Yivvy sat up straight. "So?"

"Catholic, too?"

"I guess."

"You *guess*! About these things, we don't guess. We *know* who is and who isn't. We gotta know, like the mouse knows where is the cat." The ache had risen; the squeeze was on Sadie's heart now. "For *this*"—she fisted and unfisted her hands—"your papa and I walked out of Poland, vomited our way across an ocean, no family, no money, no English to talk, nothing! *That* part is worse than monkey business in the store with *goniffs*."

"You're afraid, Ma."

"Hurray. For once in my life you can see how I feel."

"That don't mean you're right. Open up your mind, times are changing."

"Some things, these kinds of things, don't change, never. Irish is Irish and Jewish is Jewish, and never mind what you call *the times*. People can run around getting divorced, ladies throwing away their corsets for silk something or other. The whole world can sink in the ocean, but I know what I know."

Yivvy moved toward the door. "You'll get to know him, you won't be afraid."

"That will be the day when I turn into a skinny, blonde fan dancer."

Chapter Seven

The next morning, Sadie woke up early, eager to catch up with Fivel before he turned too busy.

Lowering her foot into a pan filled with cold water, she sang out, "Fivel? We got to talk, things couldn't be worse." The room hummed with silence. A bad time of year to yoo-hoo to heaven. Summer. Everyone up there busy relaxing, no one paying attention to business. But this couldn't wait until Fivel got tired of floating around in the sunshine *schmoozing* with anyone who talked like a rabbi, picking up tips on how to treat his lumbago, stopping at a friend's place for a sip of *schnapps*, a few *Talmudic* stories.

Heaven didn't have no clocks, and down here time was running. Yivvy could meanwhile do something foolish, even—God forbid!—marry with the policemens. Sadie raised her foot out of the water and wiggled her toes. That would be some earthquake for the Schuster family, a relative who's a police person who's Irish and Catholic. Plus having someone in the family go to jail.

Seven o'clock already. She should move faster before the day escaped her. A pounding at the door, someone shouting: "Mrs. Schuster!" Fivel, it couldn't be. He never came into their house through the door since he died, and why would he call her Mrs. Schuster? The pounding came again, the "Mrs. Schuster" again. "Open," Sadie struggled to concentrate. Ike Tabatnik! Pulling her robe over her nightgown, she opened the door a crack.

"I'm here," Ike said.

"I can see." Sadie opened the door wider, pulling her robe closer, raking her fingers through her hair, wishing she'd had time for makeup, her corset, earrings, a spray of perfume.

He carried two suitcases. Three cardboard boxes were stacked on the floor. His shirt collar was open, a jacket slung over one shoulder. He wasn't wearing spats but, still, he looked *fahrputzt*, dressed up, not like a butcher on his way to cut up meat. It must be his hair; so much of it. She preferred Herschl's salt-and-pepper curls. Even Thomas' blonde silk was more honest.

"I accept your offer," Ike said in Yiddish.

"*Now?*"

"You said she died and the flat is empty."

"Are you always so fast?"

He closed his eyes for a brief moment. He had all the right movements memorized. "I make time to do what I want to do. Like they say, life is short, so we must work hard to make hay."

"*They* say! Nobody in Latvia says that!"

"Latvia for me is over." He did a joyous shuffle that was, even to Sadie's fierce glance, fully graceful. "Take it easy," he said, in English.

Take it easy! Was she hearing good? This man was not to be believed.

"You like my new American words? I learn from the girls."

"Welcome to America."

He flicked his finger against the brim of his derby, sending up a snappy ta-ta sound that bounced off the walls of the vestibule. "I take down my things, then I go to my work." And he was gone.

"Girls? *Girls*! You're married," she shouted into the empty air. Thanks God she didn't fix up her face or comb her hair for *that*. A dance king turned into a *chutzpah* king, wrapped in tight pants. But she hadn't been out in the open with him, so maybe they'd made a tricky bargain. She hated him. She needed him. They'd dance, be friendly, go maybe walking and, if she was lucky, they'd bump against Herschl who, Mitzi promised, would be feeling lonely, and ready to pop his eyeballs out at the sight of her with such a looker.

Cooler, calmer, she decided, invite him to supper, buy a new cylinder for the phonograph, something lively, a peppy two-step, a couple of foxtrots.

She dressed, and did a few quick things to her face and hair, enough to carry her to the shopping streets, then a quick look-in on Yivvy, a friendly what's new, not one word about Thomas. Left alone, the romance might dry up and blow away. But first, she'd put finishing touches on a pair of love knots she'd deliver on the way. The two sisters who'd ordered them told Sadie that, unless they found husbands by Labor Day, they'd return to Budapest.

One sister already had a beau, a trolley car driver with a baritone voice, who preferred evenings with a quartet to staying home with a wife. Sadie told the second sister that her possible husband, the owner of a pickle shop on Avenue B, was for sure a special good catch. His mother had just died, leaving him, an only child, dishes and pots and recipes, and no one to use them.

Sadie set out bits and pieces for each knot, arranging them in two piles on the kitchen table: a shredded bus ticket, a broken uniform button, a belt buckle, and earwax for the bus driver; a smidge of pickle brine, dirty threads plucked from an apron, a tattered eraser, and moustache clippings for the pickle store owner. Placing the fragments *just so*, each pile in the center of its own cotton snippet, she knotted the fabric around them, creating two soft, round poufs, each one small enough to fit in her palm.

Lowering the shades and igniting the gas jets, she passed her hands in front of her eyes, beating at the air with frenzied fingers, pointing at the knots, until they sent up low, husky, humming sounds.

Good! The spirits were paying attention today. Sadie chanted, a mixture of English and Yiddish, plus a smidge of Irish from her days in the cigar factory. Today, she needed for-sure falling-in-love magic.

The knots continued to vibrate, the spirits' signal: *We're ready.* Sadie blew on them, jiggling them until, eyes half-closed, she felt certain—yes, yes!—they were full of liveliness.

"Spirits . . ." Something pinged against her ear. Keep it soft, whispery. Another ping, the other side, and a *whoosh*, a sweet breath across the back of her neck. "These men, these women"— Sadie cradled a knot in each palm—"bring them love." Encircling her now, a spiral of light, a fluttering of something invisible, but felt. As good as done.

She left her flat, the love knots wrapped in red tissue paper, tied with gold ribbons. She also carried two string shopping bags containing a silk shirtwaist to be returned to Klein's Emporium, and a loaf of strudel and two *challahs* she'd baked for Yivvy. Opening the street door, she bumped into a tall, uniformed young man holding a bouquet of peonies, blazing pink. "Mr. Quinn!"

"Mrs. Schuster!" He pulled off his cap, smiling his sunny, isn't-life-grand smile that told Sadie what she didn't want to know: why Yivvy liked him so much. "I almost missed you."

"You did miss me," she said, stepping around him. "I got things to do and I'm late already." Did Yivvy send him? *Be nice to my mother, an old lady, easy to push over.*

"Well, then"—he shuffled his feet. Today, the eyes looked closer to navy than royal blue—"here." He thrust the peonies at her.

She stepped back as though to ward him off, dropping one of her packages. "I couldn't—absolutely not!"

"You've got to!"

Sadie grasped the flowers and, when Thomas stooped to retrieve her package, she couldn't resist: she inhaled and buried her face in their fragrance. "Flowers," she murmured into the enormous blossoms, "I love flowers." Thomas went on smiling, looking pleased with himself. *Now look what you done, you made him think you like him!* "I got no time," she said.

He tucked the dropped package among the others. "You just go on where you were goin', I'll take these inside for you Ma'am." A shred of peony landed in his hair, a bright star floating on a golden sea.

"Here"—she pushed the bouquet at his chest, jiggling it until he clutched it—"and don't never again try to soften me up, Mister Policeman Quinn, because I'm not your everyday house lady who doesn't know about what's what."

She began backing away, ignoring the hurt look on his face, ignoring the petals dropping onto the stoop. "Not me, no sir!" She hurried down the steps and walked quickly toward the corner, stopping to look back just before turning. "Anyway," she hollered, "why ain't you at work catching robbers? What do we pay you for?"

ᒎᕪᕞ   ᒎᕪᕞ   ᒎᕪᕞ

By the time she got to Grand Street to deliver the love knots, she found herself missing Fivel—except, now that she thought on it, he wasn't such a *hotsy-totsy* reliable person, not getting in touch about Yivvy. Men picked and choosed. They'd worry about *this*, they'd not worry about *that*, so sue 'em.

She placed the love knots against the door of the sisters' flat on Clinton Street, along with a note: *Dear Luba, Dear Sophie: Sell your tickets home, buy white dresses. Love, Sadie Schuster.*

Moving in and out of food stalls on Ludlow, then Essex Street, gathering the makings of a banquet, soothed her, as though eating could cure heart pains. She bought two chickens, garlicky sausages larded with fat, pickled herrings dripping with wine vinegar, and olives and spices, fished out of wooden barrels by plunging her arm into the brine.

At the pushcarts she pinched tomatoes, pressed fragrant parsley to her face and sniffed, and picked radishes, carrots, celery. She ran golden beads of barley through her fingers, like silken grains of sand, adding dried mushrooms, split peas, and wine-red kidney beans. One thing with Jews, she thought while squeezing a cabbage, eating and drinking was a kind of a blessing. Food was love. *Come, sit, enjoy.* Hadn't Abraham spread a table for the angels?

ᒎᕪᕞ   ᒎᕪᕞ   ᒎᕪᕞ

A fast circling around the cramped shop of papers, pens, and notebooks, on Delancey Street, and she saw what she needed: square white paper, thin—meaning not expensive—then a set of blue and red marking-up pens, a ruler, to write out more news about the march. When she told the lady owner, skinny like a beanpole, squinting eyes covered over with thick glasses, about the march, she shushed Sadie, closing the door to the back room.

"Take," she whispered, sliding two small boxes of red and blue paste-on stars across the counter. "My present, to doll up the announcements."

A man's voice called, "Dora, come help pull down boxes."

"My husband," she whispered, "he doesn't like your kind of ladies."

"Dora . . ."

Sadie gave the owner a quarter and a dime, the owner gave her a bag. "Tell your husband for me, he can take us or he can leave us. We'll do this: we'll get the vote."

"From your mouth to God's ear," the owner called after Sadie as she left the store.

⁓⁓⁓ ⁓⁓⁓ ⁓⁓⁓

Only one shop sold phonograph cylinders. Sadie stopped there last, and asked for a cakewalk, a foxtrot, a two-step, the kind of music the piano player had played to accompany the movie she'd seen twice the week before: *Love Comes to the Big City*. About to leave, she hesitated. One more have-to-have, the tango music the pianist in the movie theater had played last summer for *Mexican Madness*. Never had she heard music that made her palms feel that sweaty, and her heart race like she was running up and down five flights of stairs collecting rent. Dangerous for her health, but good for everything else.

The clerk brought the cylinder. Sadie held it in both hands, turning it carefully, running her finger around the edges. A magic wand, as mysterious as the spirits. All that music stuffed inside this shiny-black roll no bigger than her palm. Only in America did such magic seem like an ordinary, everyday thing. She closed her eyes and heard the music again, felt the excitement she'd felt the first time, sitting alone in the dark theater, so aroused she was more off her seat than on it, swaying, snapping her fingers, humming, until everyone nearby ordered her to please, for Pete's sake, *shush!*

She imagined Ike—shoulders, arms, hips, wound up tight—clasping her hand, the pair of them moving like they had only one skin, one set of feet. She bought the cylinder, and was back on the sidewalk, arms filled with packages, when she saw the mannequin in the window of a secondhand clothing store. Sadie pressed against the glass, breathing so hard, she fogged the window.

She had never seen anything so beautiful: a long shawl in vibrant reds, yellows, greens, blues, a pale, braided fringe around the edge. A silken waterfall, just like, splashed across the mannequin's ankles. A shawl for a young girl in a white dress waltzing across a ballroom floor in Warsaw; a shawl to wrap around herself when walking by the river with Herschl. Sadie rushed into the shop, dropping her parcels onto a chair, and pointed to the mannequin. "Yoo-hoo, anybody home? On the dummy, that shawl, how much?"

At the back, a gray-haired man wearing a skullcap sat on a stool, sewing. He looked over glasses that had slipped to the tip of his nose. Sadie couldn't wait. She reached into the window, gathering the shawl from the mannequin. A shiver ran down her back. The man continued to sew.

The shawl looked the way the music made her feel; warm to the touch, like it had stolen heat from somebody's flesh. It made her feel anything was possible. She had to have it to wear in the dance contest, to look at Herschl as he looked at her, wrapped in its elegance. She wrapped it around herself and stood in front of the full-length mirror. The sight of herself in such silken splendor was almost too much ecstasy to take in all at once.

"You like it, lady?" the man asked.

Sadie rotated her hand. "So-so."

Turning to a high partition behind him, he called out, "The silk shawl from the window, the one that looks like it comes from the Czarina, how much?"

"Ten dollars," a woman's voice answered. "Positively."

The man looked at Sadie. "Did she say eight dollars? I don't hear too good."

"Six, she said six dollars, I hear perfect." Sadie turned toward the window, tugging gently at the shawl until she had it gathered in her hands. She felt like a big-time moving picture star, maybe even like Lila DeLuva in *Summer Paradise*.

"Ben," the woman's voice called out, "go clean out your ears, maybe nine, not a penny less."

"My wife loves that particular shawl," the man said. He sighed and returned to his sewing. "Her mother's. Not another like it in New York."

Sadie draped the shawl across one shoulder like a banner, and walked a few steps, allowing the end to trail behind. She arranged it in folds around her waist and wiggled her hips. It had been put on this earth for her; she would not leave without it.

The man clucked his tongue in admiration. "A shawl like that, priceless. Eight dollars, but only for you." He put his finger to his lips and, lowering his voice, pointed over his shoulder. "She'll kill me."

"I'll take it." Sadie swept the fringe back and forth across the tips of her shoes. She'd maybe even let Yivvy borrow it sometime, introduce her to some of the good-looking hotshots at the Henry Street Club. A little grape juice and soda, a few jokes, and she'd forget about the policemens.

The man walked to the front of the shop. Sadie took a tight wad of dollar bills out of her purse. "Here, six dollars cash." She counted the bills into his hand.

The man raised sorrowful eyes to Sadie. "You want my wife should divorce me?"

Sadie pulled another dollar out. "Alright, seven."

"It's yours."

"Don't bother to wrap." Draping the shawl across her shoulders, she gathered her bundles and left the shop. She walked home almost as happy as she'd been the day Fivel said yes to America, almost as happy as at that moment when the midwife, holding the infant aloft, said, "A girl. Sadie, you have a daughter." Things were going to get good again, she could feel it. Shifting her bundles and walking even faster, despite the heat, Sadie announced aloud to the gritty, humid, empty street: "July, nineteen hundred and thirteen, Sadie Schuster in America, and happy."

That afternoon Sadie slipped a note under Ike's door: *Supper tonight?* No need to sign her name.

Six o'clock, seven o'clock, no answer. She went down the back stairs and waited outside his darkened flat, finally pressing her nose against the single window. Nothing.

The next morning, before six o'clock, she stationed herself outside Ike's door. At six twenty, dressed, whistling, he stepped out and onto Sadie's foot.

"You want me?" He looked calm. Sadie had hoped for guilt, but would have settled for embarrassment.

"My invitation."

He had it—where? Oh yes, right here. He produced the slip of paper from his shirt pocket, and smiled. Not a forgive-me smile, not a sorry-to-hurt-your-feelings smile, but an I-know-I'm-damned-good-looking smile, picked up—where else—from the young *machers* who hung out at the cafes along lower Broadway. He'd worked late, visited friends, came home and worked again to settle into his new flat.

She mentioned the stairs, the trash bin.

"Tonight, you have my word."

"*Your word*! That and five cents wouldn't buy me a trolley car ride to Coney Island. And after you finish up," she said, deciding, never mind this man's terrible manners and lack of gratitude, "a bite supper, nothing fancy. Then, a short time, some, not too much, dancing."

⟨⟩⟩⟩ ⟨⟩⟩⟩ ⟨⟩⟩⟩

Ike was late. This time she'd kill him, but first she'd throw his things all over Orchard Street. When he arrived, he thrust a swirl of green tissue paper at her.

Sadie unwrapped a pink carnation. "My, my, my, no one, not even my late husband"—she glanced at Fivel's photograph—"*especially* my late husband, gave me flowers."

"Good," he said.

"*Good?*"

"I mean, it's good you like flowers." She watched him inspecting everything, like he was doing a memory test. He was a *real looker*, like lots of the young fellas just off the boat, with snappy-looking hair and muscles and good teeth. She bet he went walking around the city pretending he was a real Yankee Doodle, just like the rest of them.

"Your place is nice." He circled the room, stopping at the china cupboard to study Fivel's photograph. "A fine-looking man, what'd he die from?"

"Pneumonia. Not even one week, then gone."

No word yet on her face and hair, no sign he knew how lucky he was. Generous ladies who owned buildings and danced good, and also liked greenhorns, were not on every corner in New York. She pointed to the table. "Sit." Swinging a chair around, he sat down. She ladled steaming beef barley soup into two bowls and sat down opposite him. "To your good health."

They spoke Yiddish, easier for him, he said, "But not for long, I'm learning American fast."

"I believe you."

He loved New York. This country was made for him, and he was made for it. He had big plans, really big, she couldn't imagine.

"Oh, yes, I can imagine, but go ahead, tell me anyway." Between the pickled beets and the tomato salad and the stuffed cabbage, he told her. Before six months had gone, he'd buy a wireless radio, a phonograph, two new, not secondhand, wool suits and a straw hat. He'd always wanted a straw hat. He stroked an imaginary brim. But who wore straw hats in Riga? There they knew nothing, had nothing. Thanks God he got out of there when he did.

He said yes to another helping of stuffed cabbage and added a matched bedroom suite in carved walnut, a sofa, and gray suede spats to his shopping list. Maybe a box camera also.

"And steamship tickets?" she asked. He looked puzzled. "Your family in Riga, the picture, the wife with the babies," she reminded him, as she served the roasted chicken and noodle pudding.

"Those, too."

Spooning honeyed carrots onto his plate she said, "You have

big ideas. Do you also have big money?"

"Soon," he reassured her. Sadie looked skeptical. "America is, is *op-por-tu-ni-ty*!" He concentrated, counting out all five syllables on his fingers. Did Sadie know the word, he asked, but didn't wait for her answer. "I only heard it the first time today." Pushing his empty plate away, he lit a cigar, blowing smoke rings at the ceiling.

"Time for dancing," Sadie said, and brought the phonograph from the bedroom.

"*Ah!* Just the thing I want to buy," he exclaimed, cranking it up. "How much?" The thump-thump tango beat filled the room. Ike's eyes widened in delighted surprise, his shoulders quivering, his hands opening and closing as he listened.

Yes, yes, he agreed, this music was, well, how to call it in American: *romantic*. He did a few fancy shuffles. They were going to win, no question about. He pushed the furniture to one side. "Let's begin." Sadie put her hand out, concentrating on moving, on pausing, on counting, turning when he turned, sliding forward when he slid backward, her eyes half-closed, until she wasn't concentrating, only dancing.

They danced for an hour, sweat rolling down their faces, half-moons growing in their armpits. Ten more minutes, and Ike begged for mercy, throwing himself onto the sofa, unbuttoning his shirt to his belt. Sadie released the top button of her shirtwaist, and pushed her head out the window.

They sipped lemonade, took turns wiping the back of each other's neck. "One more time," he said, as he pulled her to her feet. Thirty minutes later, Sadie said her feet ached up to her ears; they should stop now before she was crippled for life.

At the door Ike touched the fingers of one hand to his lips and then pressed them to Sadie's mouth. "Sadie, Sadie," he said, and shook his head.

She pulled away, murmuring something about: *no air in here.* What did he think he was doing, anyway? What was *she* doing? "So, good night, Mister—"

"Mister Dance King," he said, and laughed, "of Riga, in Latvia."

"Only this is New York, in New York," she said, trying for a calm she didn't feel.

"Tomorrow night," he said, "I'll be back."

Chapter Eight

S adie woke up the next morning with a feeling she couldn't name. It clung, just out of reach, a tickle at the back of her throat. Last night hadn't gone as she'd planned. Where was the sister doing a nice favor for a brother, like she wrote him in her letter? Ike-the-pusher pushed his way plenty far past that line, and she—*don't deny!*—didn't pull back while he pushed. She asked: Are you proud of yourself?

She wasn't.

Passion, she thought. How did passion get mixed into the Ike part of her life? It belonged in the Herschl part. Her reflection over the washbasin—you want the truth, go ask a mirror—was no comfort: pasty skin, bloodshot eyes, puffy around the edges. And *there.* Sadie pressed her finger into the ample curve of her cheek. New wrinkles. A reminder, not that she needed one, that, come Passover, she'd add up to forty-two.

She puckered her lips. How old was Theda Bara, and that skinny Felice something or other she saw last week in the new movie at the Orpheum? Thirty-five, thirty-six? Older than Ike. Which circled her back to last night. That was some aye-ya-ya thing he did when he said goodnight, kissing his finger, then pressing it to her lips. He didn't learn how to do *that* in Riga! The faint something she'd felt when she woke up wasn't faint anymore: guilt. As thick as chicken fat spread over *zizel* bread. She slipped a bathrobe over her nightgown, went into the kitchen, and set the water kettle on the stove. A married man, a man with two children with sad eyes waiting for tickets to come to America, and what about the wife with the frightened face and the ugly dress? And, spooning tea leaves into the teapot, a man how many years younger? Nine? She closed her eyes and admired Ike's shining black hair. Eight? His dark eyes snapped at her. Seven, for sure.

Which says *what*? The minute Ike's kissed-up finger touched her lips, she was cheating on Herschl. She could ask Mitzi, who knew everything about men, maybe too much. Mitzi would say, laughing her musical laugh, "I knew it all the time! Remember me, I said from the opening, this Ike Tabatnik. You enjoyed it, right?"

Mitzi had a terrible habit with which Sadie wished Jews could be afflicted: making everything seem simple. If it wasn't black, that's because it was white. Sadie poured boiling water over the tea leaves and pondered the puzzle of how she could enjoy what, by every rule she'd cherished, should not be enjoyable.

She poured tea into her cup and felt chest pains. That proved it. Who needed this kind of passion if you get sick from it? Didn't Fanny Jacobs from across Avenue B die the same year her husband passed, from a weak heart, right after she got married again to her sister's brother-in-law, who was five years younger, thirty-two, more or less Ike's age?

"Ma!" A knock at the door, the knob rattling. "Open up!"

"Yivvy?" Sadie pulled her robe closer and hurried to the door. A coincidence, all right. Here was a person with just the tongue for the truth. Pulling the door open, she began to say, *Why so early?* Seeing her daughter's stricken face, she said nothing, as Yivvy pushed past her and sank into a chair, elbows propped on the table, her head cupped in her hands.

"A little tea?" Sadie asked.

"No."

Sadie sat down and drummed her fingers on the table.

"Don't!"

Sadie sipped her tea and looked out the window. Hearing sniffles, without turning her head, she pushed her handkerchief into Yivvy's fisted hand.

"Yeah, tea," Yivvy said, dabbing at her face with the handkerchief. "Here." She tossed the balled-up handkerchief at Sadie. "I'm all right now, we gotta talk."

"So, talk." Sadie got up, poured tea into a cup and slid it across the table.

"I need a hundred bucks." Yivvy kept her eyes on Sadie.

"Who doesn't?"

"Don't make jokes, this is serious."

"A hundred dollars? Some joke."

"I wouldn't ask if I wasn't crazy-desperate scared."

Sadie swallowed. The tea was a lava stream. "Scared, why?"

Yivvy looked away, her voice a whisper. "I can't say, you don't want to know."

"The import guys what sold you all that stuff?"

Yivvy frowned at the wall behind Sadie. "Okay, okay, the detectives, the guys who were investigating the sale of stolen goods." She heard about it from Thomas, after he heard about it at his station house. They were coming to her shop, but she didn't have enough time to get rid of the stuff. Thirty minutes later, a team of detectives came into the shop with a list of shopkeepers who'd bought. Maybe the hijack gang was caught and traded information for special treatment.

"At first, they poked around, like they wanted to buy something, then they pulled stuff off the shelves, hollering, 'We gotcha!' "

"They *touched* you, they pinched—"

"Worse. They said they hated seeing such a young girl goin' to jail, they want to make things easier for me."

"A hundred dollars to catch a forgetting disease," Sadie said. Yivvy nodded. "You pay, and how do you know they won't come back for more, or some other policemens won't come, say the same thing?"

"I just gotta take their word."

Yivvy had five days to pull her money together, giving Sadie time to talk her plan over with Fivel, visit the bank, and a little leftover time to fit in dance rehearsals. This left no time for thinking about Ike and his finger kissing, or the upcoming march, with ten, twelve ladies waiting for her to tell them what the new announcements should say, where to pass them out, and where to find free folding chairs, popcorn and streamers.

One o'clock already. She stood at the window watching the children on Orchard Street running through a waterfall gushing from a fire hydrant into the gutter. "Fivel!" Her voice was raspy but, if he was around, he'd recognize.

Almost at once, lightning stabbed at the cloudless blue sky, followed by a drumroll of thunder. "Good, you're there. About time." Laughter floated up from the street. The children were chasing each other, splashing, a small army of small people acting happy. It made Orchard Street look happy.

"Fivel, our little girl needs a lot of money." Lightning again, so close, Sadie's heart pounded, like a bird was trapped in her chest. Slamming the window shut, she shook her fist at the sky. "Hey, listen, slow it down. We got babies playing here."

The rain began, a furious slanting that scattered the children. "There's no mortgage," she said to the ceiling. "I could ask the bank." The rain slackened. "I won't *nudgy* you over details. Just send a sign it's all right for me to do what I gotta do."

Two o'clock. The heat was exhausting. She opened the icebox door and sniffed: onions, milk going sour, strong two-day-old cheese. The ice block, its white-blue skin of crusted crystals, the ammonia smell of it, the surprise sting on her finger, conjured up Herschl. If she could get her hands on him this minute, she'd rake them through his black-and-white tweed curls, she'd kiss that adorable dimple in his chin until his eyes weren't anymore sad.

A graceful shuffle, a slide into a dip, and she knew what had to be done about Ike.

First, the phonograph. She got it from the bedroom. Then, the shawl. She trailed its fringe across her bare feet, pulled it over her head and draped it into a graceful hood, before arranging it under her chin in a fabric waterfall. Perfect!

This shawl could be her protection against hanky-panky, a custom-fit protector, reminding Ike about where she ended and he began. Maybe she should talk about Herschl when they stopped for cold tea. She wound up the phonograph to find some music that was less—less fiery. She listened for a few minutes, but the music was too loud, the drums, mostly, or was that knocking she heard?

"Who is?" she called out. Twenty minutes until three o'clock. Too early for Ike, Yivvy was in her shop, she didn't owe nobody money. *Who?*

Silence. Then, barely audible against the blaring music: "Mrs. Schuster, Sadie, it's me, Mr. Diamond. Herschl."

Sadie stopped the phonograph, threw the shawl onto the sofa, shoved the pile of newspapers under the sofa. She smoothed her hair, got a smile ready, and grabbed the doorknob, before she realized she was still barefoot, wearing a robe, and naked underneath. "Just a minute, don't go away!" she called out.

Scurrying into the bedroom, she pulled on corset, slip, stockings, shoes, and the first shirtwaist she could find—red cotton, a little tight—and a dark pleated skirt, ran a brush through her hair, reassembled her smile, and pulled the door open.

"I hope I don't bother you," he said, almost sheepishly. He was in work clothes: blue shirt and pants, blue-and-white polka-dotted bandana, his cap in one hand, a book in his other, his face shiny with sweat.

Delight as strong as a fist squeezed Sadie's heart. "Ah, Mr. Diamond"—she hoped all her buttons were buttoned—"come in." She waved him into the flat. "Please."

"I came from my ice route." Standing in the middle of the room, he cleared his throat, and asked for a glass of water. "A scorcher out there," he said, wiping his face and neck with his handkerchief.

"Aaahh, one water coming up, with ice." She opened the icebox door and, taking an ice pick from a drawer, began hacking at the ice block.

"Here, let me." Herschl took the pick and broke off a handful of ice chips. Water dripped from his hand.

Taking two glasses out of the cupboard she said, "Sit, please." She filled the glasses at the sink, thinking, is this a good visit or a bad visit?

"I brought this," he said, holding up the book of poetry she'd thrust at him when he left her in the park. "It's yours, you paid. I was passing your house, so I thought . . ." He shrugged and sat down.

Passing by! The nicest thing he could have said. He couldn't be passing by; his route was in the other direction. Sadie paged through the book. The precise, spidery-black Yiddish letters were both strange and familiar. She felt a rush of memory, like longing. "I hope you enjoyed." Should she ask about the marching notice she'd slipped into the book?

"I read it two times and was beginning again, when I thought, no, Sadie Schuster maybe wants to read her own book." He laughed, but his partly blue, partly gray eyes looked sad. "I have all his books, five." Herschl held up five fingers. "A book can be a good friend to lonely people." He studied his hands. "It takes me places without me having to go."

"What a nice thing to say, the way you said it, almost, well— almost like you're a poet." Give him back his own compliment. "I know all about being lonely," she said, glancing at Fivel's photograph.

Herschl studied Fivel's picture. "How long?"

"Long. Two years, four months"—she was trying to look solemn without looking depressed—"three weeks. Time, it's such a help."

"I wasn't like this before."

"Like *this*?"

"Before Gittel passed. I liked doing lots of things."

Sadie waited. He looked dreamy, as though he'd lost his train of thought. "You said," she prompted, "lots of things," trying not to jiggle her foot.

"I'm a strong man," he said, sitting up straighter.

"I can see that."

"A healthy man. I play horseshoes, I"—he grinned—"ride a bicycle."

Sadie sucked in her breath: "No! If there's anything I love, it's a bicycle." Why was she saying such a thing? She was afraid of bicycles. "A man who rides a bicycle is a real sport in my book!"

"I'm glad to hear you say so, lots of women don't like—"

"A lot of women don't understand—"

He interrupted: "Riding on my bicycle makes me feel like, like . . ." He shook his head. "The closest thing, I think, I feel on my bicycle like people say they feel when they fly. I don't talk about it, but I won a prize once, second place, the Russian *Landsleit* Fourth of July bicycle race across the Brooklyn Bridge."

"How wonderful!" Bobbing her head, smiling, she glanced at her watch. Three fifteen. Three hours until Ike and supper, plenty of time to keep Herschl talking, get to know him better, invite him to a moving picture, bring up the voting question, doesn't he think it's a good thing to do?

"They gave me a silver cup this high"—he shaped a tall, narrow object—"I have on my dresser with paper flowers stuck in, roses I picked up cheap."

"Roses," she repeated, "roses in your bicycle prize! I absolutely adore roses. It so happens"—she looked around the room—"I'm all out today. Always, I have a big bunch"—she pointed to her bedroom—"on my dresser. They make the room smell so good for sleeping."

Herschl listened with polite interest, but said nothing. The room filled with silence, the only sound, water dripping from the bottom of the icebox. She pretended to be rubbing her wrist, but stole another look at her watch. Three thirty. "Just look at me, such a terrible hostess, what must you think! Cold tea? I just baked my delicious almond cookies."

"No, please, I must be going, my horse waits in the street." But he continued to sit, to talk about the bicycle race, as Sadie, nodding and *mmming* from time to time, pulled glasses, a pitcher, plates, spoons and forks out of cabinets and drawers, set cookies on a plate, and poured iced tea into two glasses.

"Please," she said, moving to the table, "I need you to tell me more about Komaroff. I wouldn't dream of reading his book without hearing what you think."

He looked at the table as though surprised to find it covered with food and dishes. "I couldn't," he said, as Sadie pulled a chair out. "Well," he added as he sat down, "but only for a minute." Sipping, dropping sugar cubes into his tea, he looked at her and then into his glass. "I talked too much. Before. I don't know what happened, I never talk so much, and to a stranger."

Sadie felt a stab of pleasure. "Well, then, Herschl"—lingering over his name—"it must be, we're not anymore strangers." Three forty-five. "Which reminds me," she continued, "do you happen to have an enjoyment for the moving pictures?"

"The what?"

"There is one this week at the Bijou Theater on Avenue B, Douglas Morris and Vivian Fox. I saw them in *Polly's Folly* and laughed so hard I almost cried."

He looked suddenly sorrowful. "I'm still in mourning," he said, pushing his chair away from the table. "The moving pictures . . ." Standing, gesturing. "I'm sorry. I wouldn't, I couldn't."

Sadie jumped up so quickly, her hand upset the sugar bowl, spilling brown cubes over the tablecloth. "I didn't mean . . ." She straightened the bowl. "Of course, how foolish, how could I suggest!" He turned toward the door. "You're not going, you didn't touch the cookies." She felt a wild mix of fury and regret. What was the crime, talking about the movies, *only talking*! Forcing a half smile, she followed him.

"Thank you for the cold tea," he said, turning.

"Don't mention, what's a little cold tea?"

He murmured something that could have been: *Never mind*, or, *Take your time*, she wasn't sure. When the door was all but closed, he added, "Good-bye," and was gone.

"Go!" she hollered at the door. She hadn't gotten to the voting, the marching, he should know she had a high-class mind. "See if I care, see if I—" She flung herself onto the sofa, ready to work up to a howl, but suddenly sat up. Her fingernail. At this minute quivering, a sign from the spirits. Sadie, this man is a thinker, he'll come back to say, a movie, what a nice idea. Be patient.

Sadie was not a first-class patient person.

Chapter Nine

All that worrying that Ike would appear for more dancing, and more finger kissing—if not worse—and nothing. No Ike; no note. Not a surprise. Men say one thing, and do two other kinds of things. No excuses, no sorrys.

The next morning, she wrapped the book of poems by Komaroff in white tissue paper, burying it in the third drawer of the china cupboard, under her mother's embroidered tablecloths. She would, if she didn't have Yivvy's worries nibbling in her ear, write a note to Herschl, invite him to supper, a poetry reading at the Jewish Institute on Broome Street. A walk along the river. Tomorrow, maybe. Today was for Yivvy.

Still no word from Fivel. Even dead, with so much time on his hands, he loved silence, a shoulder shrug, a wiggle of the eyebrows. Anything but words. She'd have to save their daughter on her own. Mornings were the best times for performing important business, especially with a bank, which closed early so the bankers could spend the rest of the day counting their money.

She put together a going-to-business outfit: a dark-blue pleated skirt, white silk shirtwaist, sensible shoes, she shouldn't trip while walking into such fancy offices. The mirror told her she looked serious, but not boring; good for talking with banking people.

Getting the money was a simple business, because—surprise, surprise—she suddenly, when she needed it, knew how to talk with important men. The dark-blue part helped. Words came easier when you looked good. And, of course, an important fact: she had *collateral*—a word she had no trouble pronouncing, caressing all four syllables like sugar in a baby's mouth—and *that* told them who she was. Count in her rented-up building, plus no mortgage, and on-the-dot tax payments, and probably she could show up in her underwear, and get a loan. Although, the men in black suits, black ties, and starched shirts—the ones who asked questions— had never heard of smiling, and looked to her like they had no time for ladies with or without underwear.

Settled. When Sadie left the Union First National Bank, she'd arranged for a new mortgage on the Orchard Street building, and $200 in cash: $100 in tens for Yivvy and $100 for just-in-case money to be put into Sadie's savings account.

The possibilities of the just-in-case part helped sweeten the bitterness of the Yivvy part. At the final moment, she'd decided to deposit an egg in her nest. Who knows what might happen? A wedding? Hers? A honeymoon vacation? A few pieces of new furniture, should she have to pick up and relocate to a bigger flat?

She'd surprise Yivvy on her way home, drop into the store with the money and a hug. *Never mind thank-yous, darling, what's a mother for?*

᧞ ᧞ ᧞

The surprise was on her, in the shape of Thomas Quinn in Yivvy's shop, reading behind the counter. He jumped up, beaming like she was the very person he was hoping would come through that door. Yivvy was out on an errand, gone until twelve o'clock, when he had to get to work himself. That minute he was studying—holding a book up—for his examination. Then he said, "You're looking very special today, Ma'am, like a fashion lady you see in a department store window."

He had manners, this boy, she had to admit, even if he couldn't forget that *Ma'am*, or jumping up from his seat when he sees her, smiling that big, easy smile that announced: *We're friends, aren't we?* Even though they weren't.

His clothes were not exactly like a dandy, but more like a man with a serious job who enjoyed looking good when he didn't need his uniform. A striped shirt open at the collar, and dark pants, and the red suspenders she'd seen him in at the moving picture show. A sporty American look, all right, and not a bad build besides; nice and tall—too tall for Yivvy—but not too skinny, not too fat. Who would guess that underneath all that he was a policemens?

"Can I help you, Ma'am?" Then: "Oh, darn!" He punched his fist into his palm. "Sorry, I didn't mean Ma'am. Anyway, not exactly. If you'll excuse me . . ."

He looked at Sadie with such remorse, she wanted to pat his arm and tell him, *never mind.* But he couldn't trick her, this was what Yivvy warned. If she got to know him, she'd like him. "Help me?" she said, stiffening up her voice. "Uh-uh. Tell Yivvy I dropped by to help *her*. She'll know."

Sadie tried to look around the shop to see if the new merchandise was still there, but such poor lighting, she saw nothing. Half turning toward the door, she nodded, but he bounded out from behind the counter, around her, and over to the door, pulling it open. "Always a pleasure to see you." Again, that smile, like she was Santa Claus, and he just got a shiny new bicycle, ice skates, *and* a box of chocolates.

Sadie patted his hand as she stepped past him, "Likewise, I'm sure."

ॐ   ॐ   ॐ

Yivvy appeared in Sadie's flat an hour later, between Sadie's putting finishing touches on her beef barley soup, and trailing cinnamon along the length of a strudel loaf, her hands heavy with flour and bits and pieces of raisins, nuts, and cinnamon. Sadie tilted her chin toward the envelope on the china cupboard. Yivvy crossed the room and, without speaking, folded the envelope into her purse.

"Oh, you're one hundred percent welcome," Sadie said.

"Thanks." Yivvy started toward the door.

"A cup of tea, a glass of water, a toothpick?"

Yivvy shook her head.

"A piece strudel, a little conversation?"

Yivvy turned, lips pressed together, her nose pinched-looking. *That look, a Fivel look!* It gave Sadie a stomachache. "You got new help in the store?" She went on sprinkling cinnamon over the strudel.

"Don't think 'cause you got me this money you bought me."

"*Bought you!*" Sadie pressed her hand to her chest in mock surprise. "For a hundred dollars? Not even the down payment, that's how valuable you are." Yivvy made a sucking sound with her teeth. "To me, anyway," Sadie added.

"Well"—Yivvy shrugged—"maybe lemonade, you got some cold?" She sat down at the table.

Sadie got a pitcher of iced tea from the icebox, filled two glasses and gave one to Yivvy before sitting down opposite her.

The two women sipped without speaking. Then Yivvy said, "I'll give it all back."

Sadie waved her hand. "A present. I'll leave you that much less when I die." Yivvy cracked her knuckles. "When?" Sadie asked after a moment.

"They sent a guy who said Saturday."

"Should I come be with you?"

"Naaaa"—Yivvy drained her glass—"I'll be okay."

"It wouldn't hurt, an extra pair of eyes to watch you give them the money, so later they can't say you didn't do it, or some other *cockamamie* lie." Her fingernail felt heated up.

Yivvy went to the door.

"I'm talking," Sadie said to Yivvy's back.

Yivvy turned. "No witnesses, they gotta stay clean. In, out, get the money and run."

"I'll hide in the back and listen." Sadie held her glass against her cheek. "Times like these, a girl needs her mother." She glanced down, her nail looked puffy. It got that way when she got agitated.

She plunged it into the iced tea.

"Whatcha doin' that for?"

"You got my fingernail upset."

"Huh?"

"Nothing, stick to the subject."

"Okay, okay. If I hear what time, I'll let you know."

⌇⌇⌇ ⌇⌇⌇ ⌇⌇⌇

Suddenly, her life had enough tangles to send her to bed with a hot water bottle and aspirins, except, her other headache, Mr. Tabatnik, was coming for supper and more dancing, if he bothered to show up. Over her dead body would she let him knock at her door and find her in bed.

That night, and the next, Sadie and Ike ate supper and danced, the two-step, a foxtrot, a cakewalk. Not a finger got kissed. On the third night—still no word from Yivvy—he said he had to hand it to her; she looked so, so what they called in the magazines, *hotsy-totsy*, even in this weather.

This was not a conversation to push into. If she could keep them dancing and talking—only a few more practices until the contest—and, if Fivel didn't object too hard, and the spirits loved her and they won the dance contest, she'd have something good going with Herschl.

He was waiting, she was thinking. Don't, she told herself, make him angry. Like one night last week, he got all worked up and stomped around the flat, picking up and putting down, then opened the window and poured a pot of cold water onto children playing on the sidewalk.

They were making too much noise, he'd said, ruining his concentration. He'd warned them, and they went on screaming and clopping on the garbage cans. It was a hot night and the children had been delighted by the surprise shower, but Sadie was shocked by his fury, from a father of babies, especially!

Now he said, "What goes on here?"

"A nice thing is going on. We dance good together."

"I like dancing as much as the next person, but how much

dancing already?" He sat down on the sofa looking up at her with what she called his "ain't-I-beautiful" look, all wide-eyed and smiling, fanning himself with a folded newspaper. "A man is not made from stone."

She could have said, *You think a woman is,* but this was no time for clever. "Better you come back tomorrow night, or next week, when you can pay attention to your feet, and nothing else." She closed her eyes, only a fast minute, and Ike was patting his tie and putting on his jacket and standing at the door.

"I give you time to think on what you want to do," he said, and was out the door.

Sadie flung the door open and called, "Good night, Mr. Tabatnik, come back for dancing, and nothing else," slamming it shut, as Mrs. Mehuvich came onto the second-floor landing in her night gown and hollered, "When can decent people sleep around here?"

She leaned against the door, breathing hard. Who did he think he was? Well, she was Sadie Schuster: magic-maker, landlady, doing fine on her own. She could do fine alone for the rest of her life. Longer, if she had to. She'd better quick, catch him, tell him, forget the contest. Over. She opened the door, hearing footsteps coming down the stairs, and half closed it.

Only one person in the whole world walked like that. She heard Ike say something in heavily accented English, something sounding like "*Excuse* me!"

Suddenly he was a fountain of manners, a regular Mr. America in the excuse-me department. Then she heard Mitzi say, "Hey, mister, watch where you're goin'!" Sadie opened the door in time to see Ike tipping his derby to Mitzi, then handing her the umbrella he'd just retrieved from the floor.

"Well, who do we have here?" Mitzi stepped back to take a better look, smiling at Sadie, who was now in the hallway. "You are?"

Ike turned to Sadie. "Help me out with my words," he said in Yiddish.

Sadie studied the ceiling, saying nothing. Together, these two were like a lighted match thrown into a pail of kerosene.

"Sadie"—Mitzi kept her eyes on Ike—"don't tell me this

gentleman is our new maintenance supervisor?"

"All right," Sadie said, "I won't tell you." Mitzi's coppery hair, white feathered hat, white suit, gloves, and boots were a regular sunset on snow.

"I gotta tell you, mister, you *look* maintained," Mitzi said.

Puzzled, Ike looked at Sadie.

"She thinks you look good," Sadie said in Yiddish, "for a greenhorn."

"I'm Mitzi Beuhler." She extended her hand.

Ike flashed his know-it-all smile, and half bowed. "Ike Tabatnik, of Riga, Latvia. Very happy I knew you." Turning to Sadie, he said in Yiddish, "I said it good?"

"Since when do you talk American?" Sadie asked.

"I learn where I can," he said, in Yiddish.

"So," Sadie said, "I wanted you two should meet." Why didn't Mitzi's clothes ever wrinkle?

"She is our neighbor?" Ike asked Sadie in Yiddish.

"What did he say?" Mitzi asked.

"He is surprised there are not any younger people living in my building."

"Pretty fresh for someone who don't talk English," Mitzi said. "I like men with a fresh mouth."

"In what flat is she living?" Ike asked Sadie.

"He says he needs five dollars until payday," Sadie said to Mitzi.

"Huh?" Then: "Oh, I get it. I'd shoo away the other dames, too."

"Pleased to meet you," Ike said in English. Turning to Sadie he began, in Yiddish, "Tell her—"

"Tell him, ask her, where do you think this is, night school? I'm giving you a friendly warning like I'm a friend. This"—Sadie snapped her head at Mitzi—"is no Jewish lady. Be careful."

"You're not tellin' him anythin' mean about me, I hope," Mitzi said.

"Only that meat and milk don't mix on the same plate."

"Listen, kids," Mitzi said, "don't mind me, I'm just passin' through." She pulled the street door open.

"Don't forget your other important business," Sadie called.

"I never forget what I gotta remember," Mitzi said, and closed the door behind herself.

"So good night, second notice, Mr. Tabatnik," Sadie said, and went into her flat.

ᗡꝑ   ᗡꝑ   ᗡꝑ

Sadie sat straight up, blinking sleep out of her eyes, astonished. Never in her life did she sleep to ten o'clock!

"Mrs. Schuster?" A knocking on her door. "You at home, Ma'am?"

That policemens, Thomas Quinn, Junior. What was he doing, who did he think he was? She didn't invite him here! She struggled into her robe and, tiptoeing, pressed her ear against the door. Someone shuffled his feet, cleared his throat, then knocked again. "Who?" she called out.

"It's me, Thomas Quinn. Yivvy sent me."

She pulled the door open to Thomas Quinn's eager "Hello!"

Remembering to tie her robe tighter, Sadie beckoned the young man into the flat. He glanced around the room, clearing his throat, frowning at his cap, which he was twirling, before looking out the window, obviously unwilling to look at Sadie in her cotton robe. She did a come-here signal with her hands and, clutching her robe at the throat, sat down and urged him to never mind her clothes, *talk*!

"They're coming today at noon."

"I'll be there."

He murmured something that sounded like *sure*. Then, taking a hesitant step toward her, he stopped and shook his head, put his cap on, took it off and breathed a few noisy breaths, finally blurting out, "I'd be there, but I can't. You be careful." Sadie started to say that careful was her middle name, but he interrupted: "I'm crazy about that girl," then bit his lip before adding, "Ma'am."

Sadie surged out of her chair. "No, you're not, you only think you are!"

Thomas stepped back, startled. "I know you're not happy about this, and I'm sorry, honest."

"*Sorry*? Sorry is for breaking a glass, sorry is for stepping on somebody's foot." Sadie tried to catch her breath. Time. She needed time. She shouldn't say something she'd have to apologize for; he shouldn't say something she didn't want to hear. They needed tea, tea always helped. "Wait." She raised her hand. "We'll sit and sip."

Hurrying to the icebox, she pulled out milk and a butter dish, dropping them onto the kitchen table, flung cupboard doors open, grabbing plates, cups, knives, spoons, a loaf of bread, a bag of sugar cubes.

Thomas was still standing in the middle of the kitchen. "Tea?" she asked. Without waiting for his answer, she filled the kettle, put it on the stove and, now sitting at the table, pulled a chair out and motioned for him to sit down.

His eyes weren't blue; they were *blue*. No Schuster had eyes anywhere near that color. It was like they were from another world, which, she supposed, they were.

"I like you," she began. He brightened and seemed to press forward, seemed about to lean across the table and grasp her hands. "It isn't you." Thomas licked his lips. "It isn't anything . . ." Sadie frowned into the corner, then sat up straight, so she'd look like she meant business. "You, Mr. Quinn, Junior, are not Jewish."

Thomas blinked. "So?"

"So—*so*! You and Yivvy, out of the question, not possible *that's* what's so."

Her head was pounding. Everything all at once, her life was too much for her. Where was her fingernail spirit?

"Like I said just now, I'm sorry you feel that way, Ma'am, 'cause we say otherwise. We say it's possible." He looked surprisingly calm, sure of himself.

"We? Who is *we*? Yivvy isn't no *we* with you, not if I got a say-so." She rubbed her fingernail up and down against her pocket. That should wake it up.

"When two people love—"

"Don't talk love!" Sadie covered her ears. "I'm clapping my ears over!"

The tea kettle shrieked, shooting steam into the air. Sadie jumped up and poured hot water into two cups, sliding one in front of Thomas, who pushed his chair back and stood up. "I gotta get going." He looked at his watch. "I'm on duty at noon."

"We didn't finish our talk." Was that a faint twitch she felt in her finger?

119

Reaching out, and before Sadie could turn away, he grasped her hands in his. "I sure wish you could be happy for us."

Pulling away, Sadie inspected her finger. *Nothing*! He'd crushed it, pulling on her hand that way, all that policemens' strength.

Sadie, in her navy-blue outfit that had brought her good luck at the bank, stepped out of her flat to find a note wedged against the doorknob: "Dear Sadie," she read, "You can sleep easy, kiddo. I threw a few crumbs into the ocean, and now the big fish are gonna gobble up the little fish. And if that don't frost your bonbons, get this: For all your trouble, and because business is enjoying what I call a heat wave, I agree to a 10 percent raise in my rent, beginning at once. Love to you from the Eyetalians and me, Mitzi."

Well! It was time she made a profit from something. Maybe she'd charge sixty cents for the knots. Ten cents more for every love knot, times thirty or forty knots between now and Thanksgiving—she counted on her fingers—that could buy a used fur something or other.

She went back into her flat to put the note under her pillow, next to the Herschl love knot, and felt a ping of sadness. Sometimes, doing nothing is the worst thing you can do. Tonight, she'd write to Herschl, invite him for a cooling supper, a talk, maybe a reading from a new book of poems.

Life felt suddenly full of hope. Humming, she left her flat, ready to protect her daughter against the New York City Police Department.

Sadie hid behind the curtains separating Yivvy's shop from the rear, her hand clapped over her mouth. "Keep your hand there," Yivvy said, "Every time you feel like interrupting, don't. You're not here, can you remember that?"

"When did I ever forgot where I wasn't at?"

The front door opened, setting off a clamber of chimes, followed by heavy feet moving toward the back of the shop. Yivvy stiffened and looked at her watch, shushed Sadie and, whipping between the curtains and into the shop, sat down at her desk, head down, as though writing in her ledger book.

Sadie ripped a tiny tear in the curtain, just big enough for her to peek through.

She saw only Yivvy, then a man—no, two men—both wearing dark pants and shirts, top buttons open, sleeves rolled to their elbows, suspenders.

The one in front, the short square-looking one, had a lot of wild, dark hair and a heavy mustache. His stomach pushed out over his pants, and he kept mopping his face with a handkerchief. The man who came up behind him was bald, built like a tall child, narrow shoulders and chest, bent over, as though standing up straight was too much work.

Yivvy looked up at them and, sniffing, smiled a sour half smile. "Can I be of help?"

Before either man could answer, a man's voice called out from the front of the shop, "Hurry up, you guys." The skinny man jerked his arm in that direction and scowled.

"We're here to help *you*," the first man said to Yivvy.

Yivvy tapped her fingers on the ledger before closing it, stuffing it into a drawer. "Yeah," she said, standing up.

"Nice place you got here." The skinny man looked around.

"I like it." Reaching into a bottom drawer, Yivvy pulled out a pile of papers.

"Hey," the voice called, "whatcha doin'!"

"In a minute," the heavyset man hollered.

Sadie clutched the curtain and inhaled, breathing in a cloud of dust until, high up in the bridge of her nose, a steamroller of a sneeze threatened to explode. She grasped at her nose, pinching hard, holding on. That's when she felt a flick of fire brush her cheek, her fingernail practically burning up, quivering, changing color from a bruised-blue to black to a brilliant red.

"What!" Sadie breathed, as a siren shrieked from somewhere, from everywhere, from her nail!—enough wailing for two, three police wagons, bouncing off the ceilings, pouring out of the walls, surging through the floor boards. Sadie saw the two men freeze, heads whirling in all directions, then the heavy one grasped Yivvy's wrist.

"What kinda business?" he demanded, screaming to be heard over the siren.

Yivvy looked terrified and opened her mouth, but nothing came out.

Sudden silence, then: "Who's out there?" the skinny man hollered.

"Ain't nothin'," the voice hollered back. "What the hell's goin' on?"

"Scat, beat it!" Another voice now, louder, deeper, like someone making an announcement through a megaphone, or from the far end of a long tunnel. "You got ten seconds!"

"They're comin' in from the back," the skinny man hissed, pulling at his companion. "Let's git!" They ran toward the door, and may have reached it—Sadie couldn't see—before the siren started up again. All she could see was Yivvy, flattened against the desk, cheek twitching, hands pressed over her ears.

Sadie made tea, she patted Yivvy's head, shoulders, hands, she made more tea, and talked. She'd been brave, her daughter: how many young girls could talk to those hoodlums without bursting up in tears? She was for sure a hero, a double hero, staying calm, pretending everything was hunky-dory, not fainting or screaming when the sirens broke out.

She was about to add that Thomas would be proud, but why talk like they were one small, happy family? She was about to say, *It's a story you can tell your children.*

"Ma . . ." Yivvy was beginning to look less pulled apart, her chalk-white face showing a sign of pink. "The sirens. Who . . . where?"

Should she tell Yivvy about her fingernail spirit? No, too much to throw on her after such a terrible frightening. "Who knows? Sometimes good luck comes wrapped inside a surprise, and the best thing, the only thing, to do, is say, "Thank you for my *mazel*." Yivvy looked less unhappy. "And maybe your papa"—Sadie peered at the ceiling—"has important friends who can do anything they want by a snap on their fingers."

Herschl. *Him.* The person she wanted to tell about Yivvy, the store, the men, the siren. And also about the lesson to be learned on good luck and bad luck, and why you never knew which you would bump into. But this man was here one minute and gone the next four weeks. One night, in a fit of fury over his it's-too-soon philosophy, she reached under her pillow and pulled out her Herschl knot.

"Hey, Mister Too-Soon," she shouted into the empty air as she pulled the knot apart, "you see what Sadie Schuster can do? Throw you away, good-bye! You can beg me and you can beg me, I wouldn't go to the moving pictures with you, nothing, not even to see LuLu Murphy and her dog Schmendrik." She shredded the bits and pieces of straw, books, horsehair, flinging them everywhere. "Go, read your poems to your horse!"

Chapter Ten

Yivvy came to Sadie's flat the following afternoon. Using her key, she walked in without saying hello, sat down at the table opposite Sadie, who was finishing up a love knot for Sarah Channowitz, who wanted to marry Leibe Weinstein, her dentist, recently widowed, but only if Sadie's spirits could also make his mother move to Detroit to live with Leibe's sister. For this last part: an extra fifty cents.

Yivvy watched her mother trim red velvet into a perfect square before speaking. "Okay, Ma"—drumming her fingers on the table—"spill."

"Spill!" Sadie looked up. "This is the way you to talk to your mother?"

"What exactly went on last Saturday? And no stories, the straight stuff."

"After *spill* you'll tell me *bleed*, or—"

"You're stallin'."

"I'm asking for a little respect."

"I'll respect you better if I know who you're hanging around with. Some *cockamamie* magic, it coulda blown my place up, and you 'n me along with it. You crazy?"

Sadie shifted in her seat, cupping the velvet square, arranging a smidgen of toothpaste, a shred of paper mask, a tiny pliers in the center of the fabric.

"Okay." Yivvy stood up. "You won't talk, I won't talk." A rush of breath. "About what Thomas 'n me decided."

Sadie's head snapped up. "Sit down."

"I'm sitting." She sat down.

"I got my special assistance"—she loved saying that word, all those clean *s*'s—"for special emergencies." She twisted the love knot into a plump bundle.

"More of your mumbo jumbo from—"

"The gravedigger's wife." Stroking the love knot, Sadie said, "Laugh, be a know-it-all. You saw with your eyes. I mean, ears."

"You coulda scared me ta death."

"Did you see the look on that fat one's *punim*?" Sadie scrunched up her face. "I bet he wet his pants."

"The least you coulda' done is warned me."

"I couldn't know what would happen until it happened." Pressing forward. "Did you hear from, you know, *anyone*?"

"Nothin'." Yivvy made a circle of thumb and forefinger. "Zero."

"That's good?"

Thomas heard, she said, through a friend of a friend at the station. The three officers were so glad to get away before the paddy wagon—which they were sure was parked behind the store—could get 'em, they swore off risky business. "No more shakedowns."

"Too bad I didn't borrow my special assistance to Mitzi, she'd save herself a bundle."

"Whatever that means," Yivvy said. "Here." She took an envelope out of her purse and slid it across the table. "The hundred bucks you gave me."

Sadie slid it back. "Take it. Like I said, subtract from what I got to leave you."

Yivvy hesitated. "That's what I wanted ta tell. Thomas 'n me talked it over. I wanna buy the store. I can use this for a down payment, if it's okay with you. I'll pay you back, plus."

Sadie fussed with the love knot, working at keeping her voice calm. "If you want to buy the store, why talk with Thomas?"

"What if I told you the hundred bucks could be kind of an early wedding present?"

"What if I told you, don't tell me!"

"Great idea!" Yivvy jumped to her feet. "I coulda told Pa, if he was here. But listen"—reaching across the table, wagging her finger under Sadie's nose—"I'm a big girl, and I'm gonna earn my own livin' in a big way, 'n Thomas is gonna be a Sergeant." She inhaled a gust of air. "And then we're gonna get married, 'n that's that. You don't get to pick out my life."

Sadie blinked against furious tears, swiping at them with the love knot. *No and no and no!*

"Ma, you hear me? I said, you picked out your own life; you can't pick out mine."

⚜   ⚜   ⚜

"No," Ike said that evening, over tea and lemon cake, he didn't remember the dance contest was almost here. But they'd be ready, more than. He'd suggest they push hard on the tango. Let those other *yussels* hop around in a polka, the cakewalks, foxtrots. The tango, that's the dance for making judges go crazy. Say, listen, how about this—he'd get the cylinder of the tango music to the musicians before, pass around a couple silver coins in the right places, they'd start up the dancing with that piece. Leave it to him.

This man had no memory. He'd arrived for rehearsing with his smile and his snappy hat, not a word about the other night, no sorry or excuse me. They tangoed for two hours, Ike leading Sadie into and out of twists and backbends, and low, slow, body-to-body slides, the two of them so close, who knew where one ended and the other began?

Pleading for time out, Sadie ran cold water over her wrists, cooled her face and neck with crushed ice wrapped in a towel, closed her eyes, imagining a bathtub filled with cool, pale-green, mint-flavored water, an enormous fan, a bottle of scented liniment oil nearby.

Ike, flinging the windows open, stuck his head out and

announced to Orchard Street, in English: "Hello, America, I feel like a million new dollar bills! Sadie"—he turned around—"who's the ugly face on the dollar bill, John Woosh, Woosh something?"

"George," she said, from the sofa, where she was rubbing her foot.

"John, George! I mix up all those not-Jewish names."

"Washington," she added, rubbing her shoulder.

"Ha, who cares on history on such a night?" He put his arms out and said, "More dancing," pulling her to her feet.

Sadie pulled away. "If you are asking, I take the history lesson, no hanky-panky, no kissing fingers."

He stepped away and, for a moment, frowning, seeming to be running her words past his brain. Then, pulling his jacket on: "Okay—my new word—I can play take-it-or-leave-it. But don't call me back when you change up your head." He moved toward the door.

"I call you up for dancing, nothing after," she called after him.

⟡　　⟡　　⟡

One, two more weeks to the dance contest. At the beginning it didn't seem crazy, inviting Herschl to see her on the dance floor. But, now that she knew him from the inside, she had to admit, it might be easier to walk barefoot through hot tar and come out with clean feet.

In the end, hope swallowed pessimism. Sadie decided to invite Herschl by not inviting him face-to-face. She'd use the mailings, which was cheap and fast, sending him one of the announcements printed by the club: *For Special Invited Friends and Guests of the Dancers, Free Admission, Free Seltzer, All You Can Drink. No RSVP Needed.*

At the bottom, in her best penmanship, she wrote: *Thought you would enjoy a high-class place to sit and sip in the company of friendly people, Jewish, and also some soothing music. Yours, Sadie Schuster.*

Sadie knew how nervous felt: sweaty, perspiration in her armpits, puddling in her cleavage, never mind that she'd danced at the Club a thousand times, that she and Ike had practiced plenty, and the musicians would start the contest with their tango. Today even her fingernail looked sweaty, like it was feeling sympathy with her, or—too much to hope for—could it be planning for some kind of special assistance? If so, the quicker, the better, but, please God, no sirens!

"Like a bouquet of roses," Ike said, when they met at the curb on the evening of the contest, twirling Sadie in a circle, so he could admire her pink chiffon shirtwaist and pleated skirt. She'd pondered, silk shawl or no silk shawl and, in the end, the heat decided for her.

"You're not too terrible yourself," she said. His skin carried the scent of something woodsy, mixed with something tangy and mysterious. His hair was *black*-black, slicked back and shiny. "Nice goods," she said, patting the sleeve of his white linen jacket.

He brushed away a dust mote. "For tonight, nothing is too good." They splurged on a taxicab. Sadie splurged. Ike said payday wasn't until next week, you know how it is, America *costs*, plus sending boat tickets home to Riga, and anyway pink chiffon on the trolley?

They were early, a good thing. The musicians—a clarinetist, a drummer, who could also shake a tambourine when necessary, a piano player and an accordionist—needed fine-tuning on tango music. "Light on the piano, heavy on the drumrolls," Ike said. "Like this." He *mmmm'd* a few bars from their cylinder, demonstrating the step-glide-step. The clarinetist yawned and scratched his crotch with his clarinet.

By seven o'clock the Social Club hall was almost filled, a nervous, electric hum of conversation floating over the drinkers and smokers, the circle of *kibitzers* clustered around the bar. Lippke's business was going strong, as if whiskey were free tonight. Sadie tried catching his eye. Looking up, he winked and made a circle of thumb and forefinger, a good sign. Lippke didn't bet on losers. Too bad he didn't know Herschl. She'd ask him to look out for his arrival, send cold seltzer water to his table, courtesy of her.

Glancing around, she saw no sign of him. The club was a thousand degrees hot, and smelled of floor wax mixed with sweat and cheap perfume. Sadie dabbed at her forehead and neck, careful not to smear her makeup, feeling relief when Hymie Popkin, the club manager, bounded to the center of the room waving a megaphone and called for the dancers to line up *right there*.

"Rule number one," he shouted, "no kicking other dancers to get out of your way. Rule number two"—he held up two fingers—"no picking a fight later with the judges." He waved the megaphone at two men and a woman seated at a table near the dance floor. "They work for no pay, please show respect."

A splatter of applause broke out, and shouts of, "Let's go already!"

"Rule number three," Hymie went on, "the ten dollar all cash prize is a once-in-a-lifetime award. No winners from other years can repeat themselves."

Ike—where'd he go? Ha—what else? In the archway, making goo-goo eyes at Lena Soskewitz, a skinny redhead not a minute older than nineteen, who taught roller skating evenings, and fixed salads in Eisler's Cafeteria by day. Pressing forward, arms braced against the wall on either side of Lena, he said something that made her laugh, then looked up and saw Sadie. Waving, he held up a finger, said something more to Lena, and came across the room.

"Why waste time with such a . . . a"—Sadie fluffed the ruffles on the front of her shirtwaist—"dumb *tsotskey*?"

Ike patted her cheek. "You couldn't be jealous?"

She pulled away. "I'm nervous, you should be here with me!"

"Relax, we're almost counting the money. Here." He held up a card on a long string, dropping it over her neck, before dropping another over his. "That's us, number sixteen."

"Bad luck." She pulled the card up so she could examine the number. "One plus six adds to seven. Seven means losing. Why didn't you get even numbers, one added to one, or one added—"

"Stop the *bubbeh meises*, numbers don't mean nothing." He ran his hand over his hair, a sure sign he was *fahrtootst*.

"Says who! I know from these things, who's the magic *mayven,* anyway?" Still no Herschl, and silence from her fingernail, plus more sweat, rivers, all the way to her belly button. Sadie poofed air down the front of her shirtwaist.

Frowning, Ike closed his eyes, counting under his breath, then opened them, snapping his fingers. "Now I got it, something didn't feel to me kosher. On the last glide, turn, then dip, I pull and you follow, not the other way." He did a few quick steps, ending in a graceful thrusting backward of one leg. "See?"

"Dancers, attention," Hymie shouted into the megaphone.

Ike grasped Sadie's arm, and they joined six other couples lining up in front of the musicians. "I pull, *you* follow," she whispered. This place was a steam bath. Where were the fans? "Like we always did."

"Don't argue, just do like I said." The couple in front of them, number fifteen, turned to stare.

The music began, a foxtrot. Ike, reaching for her hand, stopped and pulled back, eyes snapping with surprise. He swiveled to face the piano player. "Where's the tango?" he whispered. He had on his don't-fool-with-me look.

The pianist, pounding out a lively foxtrot beat, raised his shoulders and looked at the ceiling. "Orders is orders."

"Number sixteen!" Hymie shouted. "Begin, please."

The foxtrot eased into a cakewalk, then they polka'd, Ike and Sadie moving across the floor and in and out among the other dancers with the ease of a single body dancing on four legs. Please, God, Herschl should be here, she'd never moved so good. Ike thrust her into a final whirl-dip-whirl, whispering, "So far, wonderful." He directed her into a foot-forward ending. "Sixteen is good luck for us."

"Don't count your chickens without hatching," she whispered. Should she wipe away all that sweat between her shoulders or just let it drip down?

"The judges love us." Ike nudged her arm, Sadie looked. The female judge was drinking seltzer. One of the male judges was writing in his notebook. The other was tapping his fingers on the table.

"You call that *love?*"

"I read their lips. They looked at us and said, 'They're the ones.' "

Hymie Popkin jumped up and shouted into the megaphone, "And now, the final number, a romance special for all you lovers, a Jewish-Latin tango," bowed to the dancers, and shuffled off the floor.

"Aha, our song, Sadie." Ike grasped her waist. His hands felt damp through the pink chiffon. He licked his lips and clamped his jaws together. He really did look like a moving picture star; Ronald DeVon, mostly, the one with the white teeth and muscles who saved ladies from wild horses. "Ready?" he asked and, without waiting for her answer, pressed his arm the length of hers, pulling hers forward and upward into a graceful arc, and clamped his cheek against hers. "Look like what he just said," he whispered, "look Latin."

Sadie bit the insides of her cheeks, hoping they'd appear suddenly sunken, and pulled her stomach in. She never knew chiffon could feel so scratchy. No Herschl anywhere she could see, but she couldn't move her head to look around the room, Ike was holding her so tight.

The music began, mostly drums, then the high, thin wail of the clarinet. Their opening slide-turn-glide-hold didn't impress the judges, who seemed to be scrutinizing a short, pudgy redhead in green satin dancing with an equally short man, his toupee sliding back farther and farther as, knees bent, they stomped around the dance floor in fierce sweeps.

Whispering, "Keep close," Ike pulled her into a nonstop whirl of knees, hips, shoulders until, gliding past the judges, Sadie saw a flash of approval in their raised eyebrows. The other dancers were now a splatter of footsteps, a blur of color. The audience faded into a series of pale moons bobbing against the darkened walls. She was swallowed up by bliss.

A drumroll, an accordion trill, and then their final moves: slow, sweeping slides, melting into the final, deepest dip; she, backward, Ike bending over her, holding her close to the floor, barely inches above. The audience gasped. Surely, surely, she had to slip away from him.

She and Ike knew they could dare this; she'd never slipped. She wouldn't now. Except that—when Ike pulled her up and forward, then quickly backward, expecting her to follow, and she pulled back, expecting him to follow *her*—she did. Caught off guard, his hold loosened and she fell away from him, an awkward billowing plop of pink chiffon, onto the slick hardwood floor.

⁓⁓ ⁓⁓ ⁓⁓

The first thought Sadie had the next morning was, Thanks God Herschl wasn't there. The second thought she had the next morning was, Thanks *God* Herschl wasn't there.

She heard a hesitant tap on the door. *Ike*—some nerve! Come to say, *Forgive me.* Not even one tiny stab of help-me-up-off-the-floor last night, not even a never-mind-it-could-happen-to-anyone, to get her through the buzzing crowd and out the door.

The voice from outside the door: "Sadie." She rushed to the china cupboard, grabbed a wooden tray, easier to throw than glass, and no splinters to pick up after. Another knock, another "Sadie." Wait—this wasn't Ike's voice. It sounded more like—"Herschl!"

Herschl, on her doorstep, looking like a picnic: white-and-red-striped shirt, sleeves rolled to his elbows, blue wash pants, bright-red suspenders, white cap.

"I came to get you," he said, twirling his cap.

"*Get me?*" She was still holding the tray. "For what?"

"I have a surprise."

Sadie blinked. "You got my invitation for last night?"

Looking sheepish. "Today is better."

"Better for what?"

"You'll see."

She craned her neck to peer down the hall and toward the street door. Nothing.

"Where is it?"

Pointing: "Outside."

"Bring it in."

"Put on something and come look."

She looked down at her clothes: white cotton shirtwaist, pink-and-lavender cotton skirt, white boots. "This isn't what you call *something?*"

"You're comfortable?"

"Comfortable to do *what*?"

"That's the surprise." He turned toward the door.

"Okay, okay." Her fingernail looked shiny, perked up. "Ladies don't move so fast like men do, I need one minute." She went into her bedroom, brushed her hair, stopping to study her nail. The air around her throat and arms shifted, as though it had thickened, the room smelled perfumed. Wheeling around—what? She saw a speck of brilliance bouncing along the edge of her bureau and, looking down, now her nail was gleaming, a real lighting up show.

Grabbing her purse, she remembered: her new Herschl love knot. Thanks God she'd put it together just this week, scrounging around on the floor, picking up all the mashed-up bits and pieces. Now she snatched it up, tucking it into her purse.

She stepped out onto the top stoop, and there was Herschl on the sidewalk holding a red bicycle built for two: shining chrome fenders, black leather seats. Sadie froze.

"You said you love bicycles." He jingled the bell.

"I *did*?" Never in her life could she bring herself to put her leg up that high, and set herself down on the seat of a bicycle, those skinny tires holding you up, or *not* holding you up.

Herschl looked amused, enjoying her dilemma. She had to admit, for a bicycle, it was good-looking. Where it wasn't red, it was shiny metal and the tires smelled a nice rubber smell, like new, and a fancy light up front, almost like an automobile. "It's yours?"

"I rented." He patted the front seat, kicked the front tire, bending down to adjust something.

"Oh, but I—couldn't. In the summer, the heat, I faint without warning"—snapping her fingers—"just like that. We could be killed, or worse."

"Heat?" Herschl frowned. "Today is nice and cool." He slapped the rear seat. "You sit in back, me in front, that's who does the steering part. You only pedal. Easy."

Ticking items off on her fingers, she listed what he couldn't do: ride on the street, turn corners too fast, mix them up with horses, wagons, trolley cars, other bicycles, automobiles, scissors grinders, peddlers' carts. She was about to add baby buggies when he took her hands between his. "Don't worry, you leave everything up to me."

Of all times to hold her hand! She was too nervous to squeeze back, let alone enjoy. "Well . . ." Holding her hand out to Herschl for balance, leaning her weight on her left leg, Sadie raised her right leg as high as she could, swung it up and over the bicycle, grasped the handlebars, and struggled onto the rear seat. "Don't you dare to go fast."

Herschl nodded. One hand grasping the handlebars, he clamped a metal half circle onto each pants leg, and mounted the bicycle. "Ready?" he called over his shoulder. Sadie didn't nod. Even that little bit of commotion could pull her off the seat. "Here we go . . ." He twisted around to smile. Something about a bicycle, who knew what. He hadn't stopped smiling.

Before they reached the corner, Sadie had it figured out. If she pedaled quickly, grasping both handlebars, sitting in the middle of her seat like she was nailed onto it, not moving or shifting her weight to either side, she wouldn't upset their balance, and Herschl could steer them through the packs of people parting, like the Red Sea, as they approached.

At intersections, Herschl jumped down and walked the bicycle across the street, guiding it in and out among the carts and wagons and people and horses and dogs. Sadie, knees pressed together, feet dangling, knuckles bleached white from grasping, kept her eyes closed. From time to time he looked back, pumping his thumb up and down, grinning as though they were in a joyful conspiracy against everyone else milling through the streets.

She couldn't nod back, too strenuous. So. A bicycle was to him what dancing was to her, only without music, and more dangerous, like flying, announcing out loud: *World! Pay attention, today I'm not who you think I am, I'm more, I'm better, I'm special!* The important thing was, he wanted to include her. After his *too-soon* speeches, who could believe?

Twenty minutes, and Sadie felt an allover sagging. Not even if Herschl were to turn and throw her a string of kisses, could she continue to hold on to the handlebars, or keep her feet untwisted from the wheels' spokes. Spotting Nussy's Delicatessen at the corner up ahead, she hollered, "Stop, I'm dying," hoping the effort wouldn't topple her off her seat. Herschl scraped one foot along the sidewalk, slowing the bicycle.

"I'm thirsty," Sadie said. Her bottom ached, all those loose cobblestones and potholes. "Nussy's Deli," she said, pointing, "the best egg cream on the East Side, my treat."

He hesitated, then hopped down, steadying the bicycle against his leg, and offered Sadie his hand. "You did good, like you ride around all the time."

"It wasn't me," she said, holding on to his hand, "it was you, such strength. You don't find it every day, believe me!" His skin was hot and damp; he was breathing hard. What luck, standing this close to him. If she weren't so busy sweating, she'd be shivering. He looked uncomfortable, but didn't drop her hand. "You after all did the work." She slid from her seat. "I was only along for the ride, so to speak."

He leaned the bicycle against a lamppost without answering, but Sadie knew a happy look in a man's eyes when she bumped into it. She could have stood on that sidewalk holding his hand for an hour—two hours—but then he was opening the door of the delicatessen and she followed, pointing to a table near the window.

Five men were crowding around a counter at the back of the room, their attention focused on a newspaper held up by one of them. "I'll do two dollars," one man said.

"Little Lover," for certain, another man said, "two dollars, my limit."

A third man, wearing an apron, waved at Sadie and Herschl. "Just a minute folks, I'll be right there." When he brought menus, he yawned, eying them as they pondered.

"Two-cents plain seltzer, please," Herschl said.

"Seltzer!" The waiter's eyes puddled into circles of sorrow. "At Nussy's nobody drinks plain seltzer. Take my word, order the egg cream."

Herschl shook his head, "Too much on my stomach when I ride a bicycle. Only seltzer, please, a little ice."

"Egg cream for me," Sadie said, "seltzer for him."

The waiter regarded Sadie with a soulful expression before turning back to Herschl. "Listen, I'll give it for four cents, you should only taste it."

"I just said, I couldn't."

"Oh, I get it, you're tryin' for three cents!"

"Sir!" Sadie snapped her fingers. Where was the owner, anyway? "I'll take the bargain. He'll take the seltzer, or do you want we should take our extremely valuable business across the street?" She glanced at Herschl, who had the look of a man who couldn't understand what the fuss was about.

The waiter sighed, snatching Herschl's menu from the table. "I don't work on commission, whadda I care!" Walking rapidly to the counter, he hollered, "One egg cream, one two-cents plain. One aspirin for me."

"Well . . ." Sadie said, and patted her damp face.

"I know how to tell him myself," Herschl said. Sadie blinked. He leaned across the table. "No egg cream. I know how to say *no*."

Well! Now the whole thing was her fault! Where was the Herschl who just now held her hand on the sidewalk? "He didn't listen. Delicatessen men don't listen, they want what they want."

"*They* don't take no for an answer?" He drummed his fingers on the table. The muffled rat-tat-tat gave her goose bumps. She was about to ask him if he was telling her that *she* didn't take *no* for an answer, but he surprised her by grinning. His eyes puckered up good when he smiled like that. "The waiter looked like he believed you," he said, "about going across the street."

"He"—she looked up at the waiter, who was now leaning on the counter listening to two men read from their newspapers—"has a fresh mouth. And besides"—the men were slapping dollar bills onto the counter—"I think maybe they're doing some hanky-panky in the bargain."

Herschl turned around and watched the men. "None of our business."

Sadie leaned across the table and lowered her voice. "They could be breaking down the law, gambling, the police'll pile in here, we'll all go to jail, you'd like that?"

"*Fahrbrent*," he whispered. The grin was back. "You." He leaned across the table and patted her hand.

"What a surprise, my *zaide* used to call me that! 'Sadie,' he'd say to me, 'You're a *fahrbrenter*, always on fire.' Imagine! You and my grandpa, the same exact thing out of both your mouths."

She was suddenly happier than she could remember, even with those terrible aches running up and down her legs. She hoped she didn't still look sweaty or smell funny.

Herschl sat back. "Your *zaide* must have been a patient man."

"My *zaide*," she began, and got ready to pull out one of her best looks, the kind with her eyelids lowered halfway. But someone said something in Yiddish, the tall dark-haired man in a white straw hat with his back to them, the one who had been sitting, and was now standing, reaching behind the counter for a package of cigarettes.

"*Gonse knocker*," the man sang out, taking money from his pocket, laughing again, in a loud, pushy voice, just like Ike's voice. "One dollar to make a win," the man said in Yiddish.

Sadie stiffened. She'd know that broad, checkered wool back if she bumped into it in a dark room. Terrible spirits were riding on her shoulders. Her fingernail—it looked pale, ordinary—went over to the enemy. Always, *always*, when something went right in her life, everything went wrong.

"Herschl," she whispered, "all of a sudden I'm not so thirsty." She started to get up.

"You're sick?"

Just then, Ike turned and saw them, his black eyes flashing surprise, then delight. "My, my," he murmured, and hurried to their table. "Such a nice surprise," he said in Yiddish, putting one hand out to Sadie.

This man had the nerves of a Cossack. "Mr. Tabatnik," she murmured, looking at Herschl, who was staring at Ike, his face closed off, eyes guarded, "meet Mr. Diamond."

Ike removed his hat and executed a half bow. Energy puffed up from him like steam. "Any friend of Sadie's"—Ike sang her name, drew it out through his teeth and over his tongue like an I-love-you valentine—"is my friend, too." Herschl's eyes were still on Ike, but told her nothing. Turning to Sadie, Ike asked, "So, what do you do in this place?"

"The same as you do," Sadie said, "or maybe not," as she glanced at the men at the counter.

"Ha, Sadie, you always know where is the dead dog buried." Rubbing his hands together, Ike shuffled a few fast steps. *He's going to start dancing!* But he grabbed a chair from the next table and, turning it backwards, pulled it up next to Sadie, and sat down, tipping forward. "A few boys from the neighborhood having fun, nothing to hurt anyone." Turning to Herschl. "That's what I love about Sadie, you can't pull nothing over her eyes."

Herschl cleared his throat and coughed into his hand.

"How is your dancing?" she asked. That should get him out of here! Looking at Herschl: "Mr. Tabatnik was my contest dancing partner."

Herschl nodded, but his eyes showed no interest. She couldn't say Mr. Diamond used to dance, too touchy a subject. Sadie did a silent, hurried run through of possible subjects connected to dance, and came up with nothing. Ike opened his mouth, but the waiter appeared, still acting injured. He murmured, "Drink up in good health," and slipped the check under the sugar bowl. "Tip not mentioned in the bill."

Ike opened his mouth, and Sadie interrupted: "A shame you have to go," she said, stirring her drink with her straw, "good-bye."

Herschl's eyes, fixed on her, practically shouted: *Rude, rude, rude!* Too bad. Ike Tabatnik was the president of rude, he invented rude, even if he couldn't spell it.

Ike seemed unsure of what to do next. Finally, he stood, clapping his hat onto his head. "Well," he said in English, "very nice to make your hello." Sadie kept her eyes on her egg cream, as he flicked two fingers against the brim of his hat, a snappy *ta-ta* sound, then bent down to pinch her cheek. "I'll see you around sometime, so long."

When Sadie looked up, Ike was gone, and Herschl was making wet circles on the table with his glass. Jealous would be wonderful, but she couldn't be sure she wasn't seeing annoyance. Should she say: *Good riddance, such a pest*, or, *How's your seltzer?* No. She'd just act like a normal person having a normal conversation in a delicatessen. "You are so right," she began, "fresh air, exercise"— she stretched—"you feel like one million dollars."

Herschl's mouth pursed into a tight, unhappy look. "Sadie."

She sat very still.

"You don't have to talk just to talk. Sometimes saying nothing is all right."

"Huh!" She sat back. Anger—okay. Annoyance—also okay. But this quiet, pained look, she'd never seen that look, even on Fivel's face. His lonely sadness, like he'd been betrayed, shot her full of guilt, a guilt that shook its finger and said, *Sadie, shame, shame.*

Herschl continued fiddling with his glass. "That man"—he flicked his head—"he made you so upset, you, you—I don't know what. But"—he held one hand up—"I don't ask questions, I got no right, who am I?"

"*Who!*" She was shouting again. "You're *you*, that's who, my good friend. Ask me questions, anything!"

He pushed his chair back and stood up. Then she saw it again. Not the sweet, sad, hurt look that put a crack in her heart, but the closed-up face she hated. "Ike Tabatnik is my tenant," she blurted out, "my cleanup man."

"I'm not asking."

"My dancing partner." He sat down again. "Only for the dancing contest, and only because, if not him"—should she say it? She sat up straighter. "No one else danced so good."

"You won this contest?" That voice, so sad he could have been asking who died.

"Almost."

"We should go." He glanced at his watch. "The bicycle rental time is almost over."

"You don't want to hear why I say to you *almost?*"

"Please, I must be back with the bicycle."

"*Klugizmir!*" Sadie snatched at the check and clattered a handful of coins onto the table. Herschl, waiting at the door, touched her elbow lightly as they left the delicatessen. Then he clipped his trouser legs, kicked the bicycle's tires and looked up and down the street. With his wonderful, strong shoulders set in that obstinate way, he steadied the bicycle while she climbed onto the rear seat, then got onto the front seat without saying a word. Silence, like a hammer, like a knife at her throat.

When they reached Orchard Street, after a brush with a German Shepherd that followed them for six blocks, nipping and barking and slobbering on Sadie's skirt, Herschl's mouth was still wrinkled up like a prune, his eyes cold and sour. On the sidewalk Sadie held on to his hand, pumping it up and down, doing her best to keep her smile from slipping. A headache announced its arrival.

"Nevertheless," she said, and studied Herschl's face for a sign he might be softening. He looked puzzled, as though wondering: *what now?* She shrugged. For her, *nevertheless* described them perfectly at that moment: him pulling away, her holding on. She waved toward her building. "Can I ask you to come in?"

He shook his head and pointed to his watch.

"We must do this again," she said lightly, keeping her voice breathy. "Soon."

Herschl gestured with his cap, a motion that could mean yes or no, or not on your life.

If she could just get him back to that wonderful moment on the sidewalk in front of Nussy's. "I'm surprised I did so good, after starting out such a baby. Aren't you—surprised?"

He was, yes, surprised. He didn't say, as she hoped, that he was happy. Maybe happy would come later, when he'd forgotten about meeting Ike. Avoiding her eyes, he mounted the bicycle, and rode away. At the corner, he half turned to look back—that was *something* at least—but didn't wave.

ꙮ   ꙮ   ꙮ

The next morning, she wrote a note to make sure Ike didn't get the idea that he could come sniveling around. *Out of town*, she wrote, *to put out a family emergency. Will be gone for weeks.* She slipped it under his door.

Thirty minutes later he pounded at her door. "Sadie, open up!"

"Break up my building," she hollered, "I'll whistle for the police!"

"You're not even here, you wrote you went out of town, you're a terrible liar!"

"And you're an insulter besides everything else!"

"You're acting crazy, I didn't do nothing! Tell me, just tell me, who did I give an insult?"

"Mr. Diamond, that's who."

"That old fart!" She heard labored breathing. "How old is he, fifty, sixty maybe, old enough to be your *zaide!*"

"Ha! There, that proves, insults fall from your tongue like spit, that man is only"—furiously counting on her fingers, ignoring the

141

fact, which nevertheless was flattering, that Ike didn't count her to be forty—"five years more than me, six, not a minute more."

"Who is he? What business you have in Nussy's, tell me that!"

"I tell you nothing, my business is none of your business. Go do a tango with someone who likes being dropped in front of all her friends." She heard silence. His black eyes must be snapping up pretty good this minute, his cheeks puffing with fury.

"A terrible thing, a person gets accused and don't have no chance to show he's innocent, what kinda American are you?"

"Who was it pushed instead of pulling, who was it walked away over my dead body *fahrschprayt* all over the club floor, everyone laughing. Who was it?"

"All right, enough already. Your fault, too. I told you, follow me, but no! Sadie Schuster knows better than anyone." Then, softer, wheedling: "I miss you." Silence. "Sadie, you heard that?"

"Go, find for yourself another partner, a lady who takes from you, do *this*, don't do *that*."

"Okay, okay, I know a good-bye when it hits on my head." She heard two doors banging, and knew he was gone.

Meanwhile, she wondered, what was her fingernail doing when she was at Nussy's? She inspected it: nothing special, an everyday-pink fingernail. Sirens it blew for the policemens. It could have peeped once or twice to warn her: *Ike is coming.* Or—she held it under the cold water faucet, drying it on her skirt—maybe it used up all its magic powers protecting Yivvy, and got worn-out, slipped back into being just a fingernail. No guarantees, no refunds on magic.

She would need more than magic to discuss with Herschl her business with the library ladies, if he was interested in discussing anything with her after bumping up against Ike. *Oh, yes, and by the way, in my spare time I march around with those lady suffragettes*, and he never mentioned the papers she'd slipped into the book of poems, like it wasn't important, just one more *mishagash*.

No way of knowing if he would say, *Sadie, Sadie, this is one thing too much, good-bye*, or, *I'm proud on you for standing up for what you believe in.* Men. A giant question mark.

Chapter Eleven

Thanks God, the following week was quiet, a good time to think up final plans for her first time organizing a march, only one week to go. How many marching ladies to make a good showing for the watchers? Free soda pop, popcorn, to keep the audience in the park for speakers at the end. Get a permit for using the streets. Would the city send policemens for just-in-case accidents?

Mrs. Pomerantz called fighting to vote a quiet revolution. Easy to say, hard to do. So far, no one was smart enough to make a revolution to explode up the old way of doing things without someone—*lots of someones*—getting bumped up.

Sadie made a list: *print up banners, papers for handing out*—people should know why women were being cheated, don't blame George Washington—*find drums or trombones or some noisy marching music, find chairs for speeches at the end, balloons, confetti, clean cloths, bandages, aspirin.*

The march being important business, Sadie wrote notes in ink on her best business paper, telling the ladies in her library group they would begin at East River Park, go down Broome Street, and finish in Union Square. Two miles away, was it? Maybe a touch more, good exercise. No boots with high heels, no tight corsets, better comfortable than thin. A friendly tip: no tea, no coffee for breakfast. Clean public bathrooms don't grow on trees. After, stay to hear the speakers, two lady writers just now out of the Canal Street Jail. Bring clean underwear and pajamas, in case of an emergency overnight stay in jail. Jail fine, maybe ten dollars, to be paid by the New York City Women's Suffrage League.

The sheet to hand out to spectators took special thinking. Sadie rejected a long message—people didn't have reading time—or an accusing message. Something angry could close up minds before they even opened. In the end, she decided on pointing out a short history. Printed inside a rectangle edged in black, a few simple lines in bold, italic letters, a message Sadie had not fully understood when she'd first read it, but now believed when explained by Mrs. Pomerantz. *We hold these truths to be self-evident*—meaning, everyone can understand how true these words are—*that all men and women are created equal.*

Mrs. Pomerantz told her that these words were written when America was being born, in a paper called the Declaration of Independence, by a man named Jefferson, his first name, Thomas, like Yivvy's friend. Only he didn't include *women*. That word was added when the first brave ladies began demanding the vote.

☙ ☙ ☙

The weather on the day of the march was what Sadie called, *beshert*. Meant to be. Enough, but not too much sun, and no threat of rain. Timmy Hogan and two friends, each boy bribed with ten cents and two bags of Sadie's homemade chocolate toffee, a cherry baked into the top, wheeled the banners and paper handouts from Orchard Street in their wagons, along with the popcorn, soda pop, bandages.

All the marching ladies arrived on time, excited and wary. Sadie counted fifty-four, everyone carrying small bags packed with underwear, pajamas, water bottles, smelling salts; and, in some cases, peppermint candies for sucking.

Lining them up, she put two women in the front row: Hattie

Milligan, mostly young, red hair, a *punim* populated with freckles, with a strong voice like a streetcar conductor, new to America from Ireland. Hattie had brought her flute and wanted to play "Yankee Doodle" as they marched. "An American song," she said, "to show we're patriotic." Sadie shrugged and thought, flute, trombone, what's the difference? They both make look-at-me noises. She'd had a special affection for Hattie since the girl told her she'd heard God telling her to keep fighting:

"Your God talks in Irish?"

"Yeah, and even Jewish, if you know how to listen."

Next to Hattie, Sadie put soft, round Fagele "Frances" Rabinow-itz—mother of six boys—with her oldest son's drum, who explained, "I don't know about reading notes, but for sure I'll get us plenty of attention." When Sadie had met Fagele, she told her, "Call me Frances, we're in America now."

Sadie, congratulating herself for not having one minute of thinking who was and who wasn't a good prospect for buying a love knot, passed out white satin banners emblazoned: "New York City Women's Suffrage Association." She lined up the women side by side, eight in a row, with every fifth row carrying signs reading, "Women for the Vote" on some and "Women Marching for Women's Rights" on others.

At two minutes past ten o'clock, Sadie blew a whistle, hand in the air, and shouted, "Ready, set, going," stepping out of the way to let the women pass. She brought up the rear waving an enormous American flag, thinking first, thanks God Fivel can't see, then, what if Herschl is watching? But she let that worry melt before it took hold. Too bad, this is me, blame it on too many books, too much thinking. Blame how I hate—more than I hate the Cossacks—anything that says, Sadie, you are not one thousand percent a good enough person.

After the first block, the crowds on the sidewalks grew thicker, toddlers waving, women calling out to them, dogs barking, a few men booing. *So far*, Sadie thought, *so good*. In her first march, two, two and a half years ago, nobody clapped or waved or hollered, "Hurrah for you!" Today she felt a faint whiff of: *We're in this together, keep on.* Or was she imagining?

The street intersections were the hardest. The women, tangled up with cars and buses and taxis and dogs; the police, directing everyone to slow down or hurry up or get out of the way, blowing their whistles, until somehow the marchers made it to the opposite side, regrouped, and moved on. For several blocks, a small clutch of boys, twelve, thirteen, fourteen years old, tagged alongside, shouting, "Go home, do the dishes, your kids are calling you."

Sadie, moving, always moving, front to back, then back to front, shouting, "Don't look, don't touch, don't talk back, make like they aren't there, keep up, march, march." Close to Union Square, Fagele began walking backwards, beating her drum, then broke into, "My country 'tis of thee / Sweet land of liberty," until the women sang along, waving their hands, their signs, hesitantly at first, then louder, louder, then on to "O say can you see," until they arrived at Union Square, gathering a crowd of men, women, and children eating ice cream cones and drinking soda pop.

Everything was in place: folding chairs; several young girls borrowed from the high school handing out soda and popcorn; and, at the front, the two speakers: Olga Kitzoff, and Maggie Riley, schoolteachers, fresh out of the New York City Workhouse, where they'd been sent for chaining themselves to the fence around City Hall while carrying placards demanding votes for women. For ten days, they'd eaten oatmeal and soup crawling with worms, then refused to eat, were force fed, and put into solitary confinement.

When the crowd was seated, Sadie clapped for attention, and introduced Olga and Maggie, adding where they'd been, why they were there, and how they'd been treated. The young women spoke about how the warden and guards at the Work House treated them like they were criminals—worse than—and brought in other prisoners to beat them. A husky man in the front row—straw hat, handlebar moustache, holding a bottle of beer—called out, "Stay home, where you belong, you won't get beaten up." As though pinched, the young woman sitting beside him jumped up, a small child clinging to her hip and, stopping long enough to make *humphing* sounds at him, turned, pulling her now howling child, and left.

For a moment, silence, as though everyone had been struck dumb. Then an older man sitting at the back, stood up. "Whatta you expect, lady, going to jail? You *are* a criminal," followed by angry shouts from the crowd, for and against. A rabbi, sitting in front in a *keepa*, called out, "Ladies, ladies, if God wanted women to vote, He'd have written it in the Ten Commandments."

A young woman in a red straw sailor hat and polka-dotted jacket stood up and hollered, "Sell your religious stories somewhere else, grandpa!"

Sadie, standing at the back, felt a strong taste of trouble about to happen, and hurried to the front, where, summoning a smile she didn't feel, she thanked the speakers, thanked everybody for coming, and invited them to mingle, talk out their ideas, that's what's good about America, have more popcorn, plenty of soda pop left.

The crowd was leaving the park slowly, as though expecting a final act that hadn't been played out, trailing empty bottles and candy wrappers. Sadie heard a loud noise, like firecrackers, then saw the men. Ten—no, more, maybe twenty—coming up fast, from God knows where, carrying paper bags.

The man in front, tall and strong looking, like a fireman, maybe a policemens, but no uniform, was beating on a drum, rat-ta-tat-tat, not music, exactly, more like noise. The men mingled with the dispersing crowd, then surrounded it, and turned into a wall of men looking angry, everyone with a bag. "*Gott im Himmel*, what is?" Sadie asked nobody, everybody. She got her answer when a skinny man in a yellow vest opened his bag, shook it, put his hand in and pulled out a handful of what looked like garbage, which he threw, then did it again, until all the men were pitching coffee grounds, soggy lettuce, rotten tomatoes, empty tin cans and milk bottles, at the ground, into the air, and then at the people who had broken away from the circle, and were now screaming, running, pulling small children behind them.

"Garbage, for the garbage you just heard," the drumming man hollered after them.

Sadie stood to one side, watching, stunned. Fivel, for sure, would say, "Sadie, you asked for trouble, marching around, for what, to vote? Who voted in Luvel?" *And Herschl would say—*

"Stand to one side, lady." The drummer was talking to her, scattering leftover popcorn over the foul mix littering the ground.

As far as Sadie could see, the grass was in ruins, folding chairs flung everywhere, empty bottles, so many bottles. A garbage can smell seemed to be rising from the ground like a foul fog. This man was one time someone's little boy, loved, played with, and could be now someone's husband, even a father to girls. Why did he hate so much, to make him get dressed in maybe a nice bathroom in a nice flat, eat his breakfast, kiss his wife, his children good-bye, and come down here to spill trouble? "Mister, mister . . ." He stopped, looking back at her.

"Yeah?"

"Why do you have to do this, *this* . . ." Empty hands gesturing to the rubble, blinking back tears. "We gotta be telling the truth, you're so afraid from us."

Chapter
Twelve

Mrs. Pomerantz was, and wasn't, a help when, two days later, Sadie met with her at the library.

"All in a day's work," she said, when Sadie described the men, the garbage, the stink. They were in her small office, surrounded by shelves of books, so many books. Sadie couldn't believe anyone had time to read them all, plus a typing machine, newspapers, everything looking like important business was going on here.

"Maybe for you. For me, I could wring the necks of those kindsa men." Mrs. Pomerantz smiled. Sadie loved her smile: patient, but not patient-weak. This lady was patient-strong, something Sadie couldn't practice. She wanted to ask her: Why did ladies who speak English so good and went to college, absolutely refuse to get angry out loud in public?

"Sadie, Sadie . . ." Mrs. Pomerantz got up and came from behind her desk, taking Sadie's hand. "Nobody thought, when we began this crusade, because that's what it is, that it would be easy."

"Easy, I could live without. Nothing since I came to America is easy." Should she ask her what perfume she's wearing? It smelled expensive. "But a little bit respect for opinions you don't like—"

"What we're asking is to change the world. Think about it, Sadie," she went back to her desk chair. "When the abolitionists wanted to fight slavery, we went to war over it. Our Civil War. Our soldiers are women, so it's a kinder, gentler war."

"I know, I read, Abraham Lincoln. He got shot-up for his ideas." A sudden thought pushed through her pessimism: *Abraham.* Her face lit up. *Is it possible, it sounds crazy, but could he maybe be Jewish?*

꩜   ꩜   ꩜

That week, the first in August, was a series of scorchers that left Sadie irritable by noon each day. No sign of Ike, thanks God. No sign of Herschl, again. Nothing from Fivel either. Enough quiet time to take care of the love knots, and plan another suffragette march, but not before September and some cooler air. *Suffragettes.* She loved the way the word came out with that tiny sizzle at the ending, the *gettes*, like a surprise.

She was returning from a love knot delivery on Baxter Street—twins, only nineteen years old, and who could believe, they wanted to marry twin brothers—when fantasies of chilled beet *borscht* spiced with flicks of diced cucumbers, enough to fill her bathtub, enough to pour over her heated head, took Sadie on a detour to Delancey Street to browse among the fruit and vegetable pushcarts, to maybe pick up a scarf, a paper flower to pin on from one of the pushcarts.

A perfect day for blintzes: delicate, golden pancakes, rolled over a creamy filling of sweetened cottage cheese, then layered with dollops of rich sour cream. Herschl loved blintzes, she hoped. Walking, Sadie imagined him seated at her table, his face heavy with the pleasure of eating her food.

At the corner of Broome Street she paused to watch the crowds: housewives, children, peddlers, dogs, shoe polishers, singers, and dancers. In summertime, the East Side streets were everyone's front parlor—the street was the sidewalk; the sidewalk the street. Sadie loved the confusion and the noise soothed her, reminding her she didn't have to be alone. On a good day, she could pick up more news while moving among the pushcarts than she could from reading *The Daily Forward.*

"Sadie." She turned. Her neighbor: Hannah Bernstein, a tall woman about her age, sad, pulled-down eyes, two chins. "Congratulations. Your love knot customer, my niece, Bessie Grubstein, it worked! Obby Rappaport. A vegetable peddler's daughter, and an almost-rabbi. Surprised?"

Surprised? *Astonished.* Never did Sadie think, when Bessie bought the love knot, this one would work. A mama's boy who was almost a rabbi, a mother who thought he was the Messiah, marrying a poor girl with a so-so face, and funny eyes.

Sadie summoned a smile. "Everyone knows my love knots are magic." Craning her neck toward the Grubstein's pushcart, she saw Bessie's mother, Rifke, wrapping vegetables for a customer. "Excuse, please, I must congratulate the bride's happy family."

Rifke Grubstein signaled, *Just a minute.* Sadie circled the pushcart, inhaling the fragrance of oranges and strawberries, fondling eggplants, rubbing the rind of a grapefruit. She sniffed a melon, one fruit that grew closed-up tight, not a hint on the outside what goes on inside. She held it to her ear and jiggled. Herschl was a cantaloupe. Fivel was a lemon. You bit it, it bit back.

Sadie handed her beets to Rifke, along with her congratulations. "I love weddings, and not only because I'm in the business."

"I love weddings," Rifke said. "To go to, not pay for."

An idea sifted through the afternoon heat. Her fingernail looked pinker, puffier. "Is it possible my friend, Herschl Diamond is invited?"

"Never met him."

Sadie scratched her ear. Her fingernail was making hissing sounds. "A pity, you'd like him. Everyone likes him."

"Everyone who knows him maybe likes him. That includes me out." Rifke handed the wrapped beets to Sadie. "Twelve cents."

Sadie pulled a dollar from her pocket, pointing out that she never bragged, but, without her magic, Rifke wouldn't have the pleasure of seeing her daughter so happy.

"Here's news you wouldn't believe, but I'll tell anyhow. You know my husband?" She pointed to a short man with sad-looking eyes and a scruffy moustache sitting at the curb, reading a newspaper.

Sadie looked. "A smart-looking man."

"*Smart*? *Just* ask him! I married a man too good to get his hands dirty, except"—Rifke grunted—"where the ink off the newspaper rubs on his skin. Here's *my* news. For me the world wouldn't end if Bessie got married later. She has a good job, she pays her bills, she stays out of trouble."

Sadie watched Rifke's husband's hand wander to his crotch, lie there, then scratch. "One rotten apple," she said.

"One for me is too many," Rifke said. "How many apples do I get to pick? I told Bessie a rabbi is important on *Shabbas*, not so important in the kitchen, and terrible in the bedroom."

Sadie reached for a cabbage, felt the heft of it, smelled it. "Weigh me this." She noticed that her nail was twice its normal size. "And this." She added a second, bigger one. "I'll cook up a triple big pot of my famous stuffed cabbage for the wedding reception, my present to you."

Rifke wrapped the cabbages in brown paper. "I'll say yes to the cabbages, and I'll invite Herschl what's-his-name. Don't tell me why you want, and don't bother to thank."

Sadie took the paper packages from Rifke, noticing how her nail was puffing down, but quivering. Quivering was good.

What luck! Herschl Diamond and a three-piece band in the same room, and not just any room. A room with a wedding, with romance floating around, catching, like chicken pox. If you wait long enough, opportunity comes knocking in the shape of a skinny girl with a bad eye and yellow curls. This wasn't called the Promised Land for nothing.

First, she'd write a note to Herschl, a few words to explain. He didn't know the Grubsteins, he might think the invitation was a joke, a mistake. More important, after the Nussy Delicatessen scene, and especially if he'd read the marching handout, and thought, this Sadie Schuster is too much for me, a note would be a good second beginning.

She brought a pen and expensive pink stationery to the kitchen table and thought, what special reason could she give to make him say yes? Ha, of course—*ice*. The Grubstein's would need lots for the wedding reception. What better person to buy it from than Herschl?

Dear Herschl, she wrote, *I met today with a wonderful business opportunity for you, which could also turn into a lovely evening*, and went on to explain that he could deliver the ice to the downstairs kitchen at the New Hennington Hall, clean himself up, then come upstairs to join her for the ceremony and supper.

She closed with: *No need to jump to any answer right away. Your invitation is on its way. In the hope that you will find it possible to conclude this important business arrangement, and also join me in a happy occasion with dear friends, I am yours, with sincere thoughts, Sadie Schuster.*

She mailed it, along with a note to Rifke Grubstein, telling her about Herschl's beautiful ice, good prices, and marvelous service, and a note to Yivvy: *Congratulations, I suppose. The policemens examination should come out with a happy ending, even if one person's happy is another person's not-so.*

cᏚᎧ   cᏚᎧ   cᏚᎧ

Saturday night wasn't hot, a good time to go back to the Irving Street Club and tell Lippke how Ike had dropped her on purpose. He'd spread the news. She'd dress up, maybe her pink chiffon. Head up, stomach in. She dressed slowly, enjoying the shimmery caress of pink chiffon on her skin, patting gardenia toilet water behind her ears, down her cleavage, behind the knees. Mitzi's trick. It could be a quiet night at the club, with no one there worth five cents for a dance ticket, but tonight wasn't for dancing. She'd tell Lippke her story, stay a while, *schmooze*, catch up on gossip about new babies, new greenhorns, which boarder climbed into which landlady's bed while her husband was out.

Sadie knew they made a strange-looking couple, she and Semke
Leiberman, but he'd pestered her to dance, looking like he'd cry if
she refused; looking, like always, soft around the edges, and young,
not a minute older than sixteen, with leftover baby fat around his
face and smooth skin that looked like, why bother to shave?

She'd stood at Lippke's bar through the first, second, the third
dance, explaining. The crowd was thin; none of the regulars. That
left a lot of space for Lippke to listen, toothpick drooping from the
corner of his mouth, *uh-huh'ing* from time to time, polishing the
bar, looking up, finally, to say: "You got mixed up with a *kniver*."

Cleared, declared not guilty! Sadie could have kissed him, but
first she had to know: Ike, had he been around? Lippke shook his
head and poured a shot of whiskey, sliding it across the bar to
Sadie. She was about to reach for it when Semke, who had been
standing to the side, shook her arm and gestured toward the dance
floor. She hesitated until Lippke urged her to go on, give the kid
a break.

"You look beautiful tonight," Semke said. Then, without waiting
for an answer, he grasped her hand and plunged into a bouncy
cakewalk. He led pretty good for a boy. His hand pressed against
her back felt like he knew what's what. Sadie pulled away for a
closer look at him. Sweat rolled down his round face, over his
dimpled chin, onto his wide neck. His chocolate-brown eyes were
serious, bordering on sad.

"How old?" she asked. "Twenty-two, -three?" Patches of sweat
stained his yellow-and-black checkered jacket. "Don't work so
hard, you'll melt." The band broke into a polka. Pulling her into
a frantic whirl, Semke held up three fingers. "A good age." Eyes
closed, Semke's face creased in a look of pure joy. He seemed to
be feeling the music as she did, such a sweet boy. A little too *zaftik*,
maybe, someone should tell him it's better a dancer stays thin.

The polka faded into a tango, setting off alarm bells. Sadie
glanced around the room. No sign of Ike. Semke pulled her into a
fancy twirl, dip, bend, moving so fast, she felt a sudden stab, *there*,
in her back, and stopped mid-twirl to fan herself with her hand.

"We'll sit a while," she said, "cool down with a sip of something."

Shrugging his disappointment, he followed her to a table in the next room. Over cold seltzer, Sadie studied his turned-down eyes, the droop to his mouth. Familiar signs. He suffered from a bad case of lonely. Dancing with a woman forty years old, a waste. Did he have a girl, she asked, someone he kept company with?

"Naaaah," Semke blew toot-toot noises through his straw.

"I know a couple nice girls—"

"You're jokin'."

"I look like a comedian?"

"Yeah, well"—Semke stared at the wall behind her—"those girls, none of 'em would like me."

"That's not your business, that's *my* business. Look at me." Semke sat up straighter. "You need a love knot. Pick out a nice girl, healthy, smart, from work, or a neighbor, even a distant cousin, if nobody has a disease and the families don't fight. Or"—patting his cheek—"take one of the sweet girls I know, fifty cents."

"For me it won't work."

"You telling Sadie Schuster she's a liar? Two weeks, you'll have yourself a sweetheart." Semke looked miserable. "Or your money back, and I never give money back."

"Why do you even care?"

"A boy like you, sitting single. No such thing as being single and happy, it's not natural. Also, it's bad for my business."

In the next room, the band was starting up a ragtime. Sadie gasped. "My favorite music in the world! You don't know this song, you're too young, but I love it." She sang a few words, snapping her fingers. "We'll dance, I'll pay." Rummaging in her purse, she held up two tickets.

"Lady"—from behind her, a male voice speaking Yiddish—"can I have this dance?" A hand on her shoulder turned her around, and she was looking into Ike's snapping black eyes. He was wearing a white suit, white shirt, black knit bow tie, smiling a sure-of-himself smile. "Please," he said.

Sadie hummed a soft *"Hmmmph"* that, she hoped, told Ike he could go now, and beckoned to Semke. Slowly, she told herself, walk away nicely, with dignity, no need to run.

Semke started to stand up.

"Sit!" Ike said, pressing him back into his chair.

"Stand!" Sadie said, reaching for Semke, who was frozen in place, blinking.

"Our music, Sadie." Ike executed a graceful step-glide-step around the table. A couple at the next table looked up to watch.

"What are you looking at?" Sadie asked, turning to them. "You never seen a man make a fool of himself before?"

"Terrific," Ike said in English, and reached for her hand.

"Terrific?" She pulled away. "Somebody teaches you to talk American?"

"Moishe Pipik's," he said, still smiling, smoothing his tie, his hair.

"Moishe Pipik's!" She had to admit, but never to him, not even that moving picture star, that what's-his-name, looked this beautiful in his all-white suit.

"Moishe Pipik's Cafe," Ike said, in Yiddish, "on Broadway and—"

"I know where is Moishe Pipik's, thank you very much, Mister New York." She hoped her hair still looked good; she needed a *schpritz* of perfume, a little something to gargle.

"I go sometimes, sit, listen to gypsy music." Ike tapped the side of his head. "You'd like it there, Sadie. Lively people, dressed up, everybody talking American. Your kind of place."

"Now you're a *mayven* on what I like!"

"I forgive you, you forgive me."

"*Unbelievable!*" She was talking too loud. He always made her forget to act like a lady.

"Sadie, he's bothering you?" Semke stood up, struggling to square his shoulders.

"Here." Ike took a coin out of his pocket and held it out. "Go buy an ice cream cone."

"Say, mister!" Semke slapped the coin out of Ike's hand. They watched it roll under a nearby table.

"Look what you done." Sadie accused Ike.

"Aaaaah, to hell with five cents," Ike said, waving it away, "I got plenty more."

"Somebody died and left you rich? Maybe you should pay rent."

"Sadie, he's bothering you, let me know." Semke doubled his fists. His nose was running. He wiped it with his sleeve.

"Sadie, a wonderful idea!" Ike threw his arms around her. "We'll go to Moishe Pipik's, a glass of tea, a piece strudel—"

She pulled away. "Not on your life!"

"Keep off your hands," Semke warned, stepping towards Ike.

"Okay, *pitsele*, call up your mama, tell her come get you."

Semke struggled to come up with a glare, but bit his lip instead.

"Don't be such a *gonse knocker*," Sadie said, "he's here with me." Pushing past Ike, she put her arm around Semke. "This is not your problem," she whispered to him and patted his cheek. "Better you should go now"—smoothing his hair—"I had a good time dancing with you."

Semke looked at Ike, then shrugged, and moved toward the other room.

"Now we can go?" Ike flicked his cigar onto the floor.

"Not so fast, Mr. Tabatnik," she said, and called after Semke. "Don't forget, darling, one first-class love knot, half-price, the offer good for one week." Semke nodded, and kept walking. "For you, two weeks," she added. Turning back to Ike: "And you, go sell your stories in the five-and-dime, I'm not talking to you."

He reached for her hand. "Don't talk. I'll talk, you listen. Only a cup of tea, a piece strudel"—he raised one hand—"so help me God." She pulled away. "I like to be with you. No one I've met since coming to America is so, so . . ." He frowned. "Hah! I'll say it in American, a new word—is so *interesting*!" He looked triumphant. "I said the word right?"

"Hold onto your high horses." She sat down, took out her compact, and peered into the tiny mirror, arguing with herself: What harm? She'd look like a real lady sitting in the middle of all those potted palms and pleated lace curtains on the big windows facing Broadway. So, Herschl didn't like Ike. This minute Herschl didn't like her.

She stood up. "I'll go if I have absolute say-so."

"All right, all right," he said, "throw it up already."

Friends, they were friends, nothing more. In fact, they were distant acquaintances—two new vocabulary words she never thought she'd string together in one sentence. She'd go, have a little supper, some chitchat, then back home early, goodnight, and—finished.

Moving across the screen of Sadie's mind, Herschl went to Moishe Pipik's with them. He was balancing an enormous cake of ice on one shoulder, looking at her with his sweet, patient look. Herschl on the bicycle, smiling, signaling: *thumbs up.* Herschl saying: "I didn't know that being alone was such a lonely thing to be." She saw and heard him as clearly as she saw and heard Ike as they walked along Allen Street onto Canal and over to Broadway, as Ike took her arm, told her he was about to ask his boss for a raise, just let him say *no.* Then he laughed his this-city-belongs-to-me laugh and Herschl's face went *fahrkrimpt.* His eyes, that could be soft, blue and gray at the same time, were cold, sour, disapproving.

Standing behind Ike in the cafe's foyer, Sadie inhaled the fragrant air. She felt lightheaded. Not dizzy, but full of expecting good things to happen. Balalaika music floated across the smoky rooms, in, out, and around the loud talking, the laughing, the smell of strong coffee, cinnamon, roasting chickens.

Ike pointed to an empty table in the middle of the room. "We'll sit there," he said to a waiter in a tuxedo and hairpiece. The waiter glanced down at his ledger on a wooden stand, then up at Ike, and arranged his face into a look of sorrow. "Sorry, sorry, sorry, sir, full up. Saturday night, nothing until ten o'clock." He scratched his head; his hairpiece slipped slightly.

"Please"—Ike, looking around the room, taking in the diners, the gypsy violinist in the black velvet suit, white shirt, red sequined tie—"there is nothing to be sorry."

This man, Sadie thought, moves into America like he has a hundred-year lease. Then she saw him fold two dollar bills, palm them and, smiling his I-love-you smile, smoothly transfer the money to the waiter's hand. The waiter whispered, "Follow me," and led them to the table up front, among the *machers*. Finished. Done. The waiter left them with menus and the suggestion, repeated twice, once in English, once in Yiddish: "The schmaltz herring, don't miss it, but order fast, we run out early."

Sadie took a deep breath. Moishe Pipik's from this location smelled the way she felt when she settled into a long perfumed soak, buried to her chin in lilac bath salts, expensive talcum powder for dusting off later.

Lots of pretty ladies, all right, dressed up in bright silks and chiffons, one woman with a red peony blooming on her white straw hat, like she was celebrating something wonderful. A very young, very blonde woman, sitting with a man Sadie was sure could be her father, had an expensive—it had to be—black-and-white-striped silk cape thrown across her shoulders; so careless, you'd think she had four more just as fancy at home in her closet.

Sadie smoothed the front of her dress, happy she'd worn the pink chiffon, shook her head, and heard her crystal earrings ping. She glanced at Ike, who was smirking in the direction of the blonde in the cape. Some profile he had. He tilted his chair back, onto its rear legs, and snipped the tip of his cigar with a tiny pearl-handled scissors that must have cost plenty.

"Tell me," she said, "what you learned, six weeks in America."

"Seven." Flicking ashes into an ashtray, he looked around, "I enjoy this place, it's lively, good music, nice food."

"When we leave, ask the waiter. They got postcards with a picture on it. You can write home to your wife and children, Dear, dear . . ." She frowned. "Excuse me, I forgot your wife's name, maybe you remember."

Ike crushed his cigar into the ashtray. "I'm all of a sudden hungry." He opened his menu. "*Gefilte* fish with horseradish," he read, "blintzes with sour cream—"

"Write her what a nice place you found in New York."

"That's what I want," he said, snapping the menu closed. "Blintzes, a sprinkle cinnamon, a dish sour cream on the side."

"She'll be happy you're happy."

"Bertha." Sadie looked confused. "My wife," Ike said, "Bertha, that's her name, and you're a *nudnik*. That's Yiddish for pest."

"I know what is a *nudnik*, I was married to one."

"Why, tell me why"—he snipped the end from a second cigar—"you want to all the time talk about my wife!"

"Tell me, Mister Big Shot, why you want to *not* talk about your wife?"

Two young women approached their table. The first one walked into the back room, but the second—a plump blonde in a bright-blue shirtwaist—glanced at Ike and stopped. "Ike Tabatnik!" Her voice was soft, musical. Pressing herself close to the table, she lowered her face until she brushed his cheek, then dropped her purse, a white silk pouch next to his plate.

"Miss, Miss . . ." Ike jumped up, looking to Sadie like he'd been caught shoplifting.

The young woman put her hand out. "Clara," she said, "Rubinoff, last week . . ."

He shook her hand, dropped it, shook it again.

"Rubinoff, yes," Ike said, "I remember." He released her hand and, looking into the distance as though expecting someone, picked up a glass of water and emptied it in a single gulp. "At the union meeting, yes, yes . . ." He put his head back and raised his glass to his lips. Then, realizing the glass was empty, said, "Oh."

"The union?" Sadie said. "What a nice thing, you're a lady butcher. Only in America."

"Oh, excuse . . ." Ike turned to Sadie. "This is—"

"Sadie Schuster," Sadie said, "Mr. Tabatnik's landlady."

"Yeah?" Clara said. "How sweet."

"Sweet?" Sadie said.

"I mean"—Clara shrugged—"I don't know, eating supper with your landlady."

Ike said, "Well." Sadie and Clara waited. He was still standing, still holding his empty water glass.

"Drink," Sadie said, "water is good for your digestion." To Clara, she said, "I take good care of his health, I promised his wife when he came to America."

Clara looked at Ike. "Wife?"

"Bertha," Sadie said.

"Who?"

"That's her name," Sadie said, "his wife, Bertha."

Ike snapped his fingers. "Waiter." He tapped his empty glass. "They act like water costs money."

"Yeah, well"—Clara cleared her throat—"my friend's waiting." She looked toward the back room. "Pleased I met you."

Ike grabbed Clara's hand and pumped it up and down. "Any time."

She turned away.

"Your purse," Sadie said, "don't forget."

Clara snatched the white silk pouch from the table, mumbled something, and left.

Ike made himself busy with a box of matches. "A pretty girl," Sadie said, "especially for a lady who works as a butcher, but she should be more careful with her purse."

Ike mumbled something about *terrible service* and, twisting in his chair, called out, "Waiter!"

"Ike Tabatnik, you're a terrible liar. You're so crooked, your name should be Mister Pretzel."

"A person could starve before—"

"What kind of *cockamamie* union meeting?"

"Why should I talk lies about union meetings, am I crazy?" He balled up his napkin, and tossed it on the floor.

"And don't make dirt, Moishe Pipik's is a fancy place."

"Listen," he hissed, stretching forward until his face was close to hers, "you're not my rabbi, don't push me too far. So, I talked with a pretty girl. Is that a crime? Put me away in jail!"

"Happy you mentioned that. In America jail is where men go when they play *pishy-pashy* with pretty girls and they have already a wife." The waiter was watching. Any minute he'd come back and insist: Hurry up, order the schmaltz herring. "Don't turn everything on its head. You, Mister Tabatnik . . ." The waiter again, clearing his throat. Sadie ignored him, whispering, "You are a one hundred percent cheater. I hate cheaters." The waiter said something about the kitchen closing. "I feel pity for your wife."

"Don't waste your pity, my wife is a happy woman." He smiled at the waiter, who was looking at the ceiling. "Blintzes all around," he said. Turning to Sadie: "Anyway, my treat, I invited you."

"*Anyway*? You use my word!"

"*Your* word? An American word, anyone can say it."

"Anyone who talks American!"

"That includes me. Anyway, always, after, aunt," he recited, ticking each word off on his fingers. "And that's only words with *a*."

"Save up *b* for your lady butcher." She started to get up.

He caught her wrist as the waiter held up his pencil, obliging her to sit again, then ordered a bottle of wine. Tonight was a celebration. Sadie looked around: the fancy room, the music, the laughing people. Ten o'clock. Where would she find a taxi this hour? Promising herself that tomorrow she'd tell Ike a final good-bye, she sat back and said nothing, trying to look not happy about staying. Ten minutes later, their glasses filled, Ike raised his. "A celebration, a toasting to talking American in America."

Sadie sipped, welcoming the warm sweet wine with her tongue, letting it help her pretend. A celebration, yes. She deserved one, all the troubles she'd had lately.

Chapter Thirteen

Turning one-thousandth of an inch was torture. Wrapping herself in her quilt, Sadie shuffled to the icebox, chipped chunks of ice, swaddled them in a towel and, returning to bed, burrowed deep into her covers and pressed the icy towel to her forehead. From now on, no more wine! How could something that tasted so sweet, and went down so nice, smack you in the head? Thanks God, the cold dulled the ache between her eyes, but there was still that knot in her stomach, and the feeling of hot, then freezing, then hot. Fivel always said one drink was two too many.

Ice water trickled down her forehead, over her nose, onto her chest. She sat up. Louie Finkelstein, her new tenant, third floor, rear. She'd promised him he could have a love knot today—free. Louie was an emergency case. A widower, good-looking, if you liked sad eyes, skinny everything else. Not a minute past thirty years old, fresh from Romania, carrying his fiddle, leading three daughters with red hair and enormous freckles. He found a job working evenings at the Chemnovsky Banquet Hall on Avenue B. But who would take care of his children?

Sadie's answer: get married, suggesting shy, skinny Leah

Applebaum, more or less in her late thirties, never married, who gave piano lessons and lived with her mother on South Street in a big flat with empty bedrooms left behind by dead boarders. She was a smart talker, also pretty enough, if you liked genuine blonde curls, a peppy walk.

Louie had shrugged. "Why not?"

Happy to have somebody else's troubles to focus upon, she pulled on her robe, doused her face with cold water, did a few hurried things to her hair, and sat down at the kitchen table. Fingering the bits and pieces: a scrap of violin music, one of Louie's shoelaces, a hairpin Sadie bought for a couple of pennies from Leah's haircutter.

She sniffed. The Slivovitz' Sunday dinner from two doors down, burning again, like always. Through the open window, a child whining, a monkey grinder, an accordion. Ike had two small children, and *that* reawakened her headache.

She decided on a square of red-and-black cotton *schmattah* to wrap the love knot. Working fast, she tucked everything—including a crumb of *halvah* saved from a visit to Leah's flat—into the fabric, then tied the plump bundle with a strand of gold silk ribbon Yivvy had saved from a box of chocolates. Sadie fondled the love knot, murmuring soft, soothing sounds, a mix of Polish, Russian, Yiddish, and English, the chant falling from her lips like droplets of sweet cream.

This love knot was a special tricky situation. Always, one member of the couple picked out the other. Now she had a he who needed a mama for his babies as much as a wife for himself, and the she in this case knew nothing about anything. The spirits had to make Leah think marriage one-two-three, on her first looking at Louie, an event that would take place when Sadie dropped into Leah's house for a quick hello, with news of her new boarder, who just happened to need for special performances, a lady who played the piano. Exit Sadie, who just happens to turn careless, dropping the love knot on her way out.

Now Sadie held the love knot aloft, chanting, "Make this knot—*powerful!*" Twirling, she caught one foot in the hem of her robe, flung the garment off and thrust herself upward, naked, flushed. She hoped her spirits didn't have rules: what was, what wasn't decent.

A hot wind blew into the flat, soothing her clammy skin. "*Ahhhh!*" So soon—wonderful! A good omen. A split-second how-do-you-do meant a special good luck, a signal that Louie Finkelstein's love knot would work immediately.

So! While she was calling up the spirits for Louie, why not, at a time when she needed special help with Herschl after what she called the "Nussy Delicatessen Drama," slip in a me-too plea? She sang out, "Spirits!" The faintest rush of wings, unheard by most ears, but familiar music to Sadie's. She felt surrounded by vibrations. There was no going back—*ask!* Rising on tiptoes, Sadie sucked the heavy air into her lungs and whispered: "*I need you!*"

Huh! She caught her breath. Spirits, hundreds, thousands! Whirling in a circle of light, pluming upward, brushing the ceiling, spiraling downward, *shooshing* past her, trailing a dizzying scent. The spirits loved hearing her plead, they'd give her anything if she begged.

"Spirits," a whisper, barely parting the air with her breath, she shouldn't bruise a spirit. "Time is slipping, my face is slipping. I need you." She hurried into the bedroom for her Herschl love knot, returning to hear a faint chorus. Was it possible? Applause, the unmistakable gossamer tap-tapping of wings. "Is it too much to ask, happiness in my soon-coming-up old age?"

She didn't have to wait long. A weight no heavier than an eyelash caressed her lips, a barely audible *puh*, and it was gone. Sadie knew what it meant: *yes, yes, yes.* Settled. Both she and Louie were about to have special happenings.

Monday's mail brought the letter:

Dear Sadie, I thank you for thinking on me, and especially after our last meeting, in regard to ice for the Grubstein wedding. It is not everyday I get such a big business. Also in the same mail with your letter came the invitation for the wedding, a nice kindness, since I am not acquainted with the bride's family, and the cost of weddings being no small thing.

If all goes well I'll see you upstairs at the New Hennington Hall Sunday, August 26th at 5 p.m. after putting 100 pounds of ice, washed off, in perfect condition, into the icebox in the banquet hall kitchen downstairs.

I look forward and thank you again for making it possible for me to profit from your friend's happy occasion.
Yours with complete sincerity,
Herschl Emanuel Diamond.

Folding the letter, she caught sight of several lines scrawled across the back:

P.S. I want you should know how much I enjoyed sharing my bicycle with you on a recent day, in spite of our interruption at Nussy's. Not many ladies are willing to push into New York traffic on wheels. Also, I have a new (second hand) poetry book to talk over. Signed, H.E.D.

Chapter Fourteen

Only this week and next, and a thousand things to do before the wedding, including—and especially—making sure she didn't see Ike. Before she'd heated her breakfast tea, she left a note for Louie Finkelstein outside his door, wrapped in a swirl of purple tissue paper tied with red tassels: *Get ready for a wedding.*

Then she went down to the basement flat and slipped a note under Ike's door announcing a crisis, her daughter, something serious, but not fatal. Details later. She signed, *Sincerest.*

Returning to her flat, water boiling for tea, she pulled out a slip of paper and listed: *Cook up double big pot of stuffed cabbage, deliver to Rifke Grubstein. Ask Mitzi's say-so on the red lace dress from Klein's.*

Which raised the question: that man she'd seen going up the stairs yesterday, with all that forehead and the pasty face with freckles. Was he the same one Mitzi got into a taxi with weeks ago? *That* day he wore a policemens uniform. Yesterday he was in people's clothes. Why was he here? Mitzi wouldn't spill what she wanted unspilled, but maybe running upstairs with the red lace dress would loosen her tongue.

A few evenings later, as she was chopping meat and onions and boiling cabbages, Semke knocked on her door. For one minute, she couldn't think why he was there, looking so embarrassed, why he thrust a crumpled paper bag at her, then fifty cents.

"Here," he mumbled, "Not that it will work." Turning, he almost ran down the hall, stopping at the street door to shake his head when Sadie called after him, "Who's the girl?"

⌁ ⌁ ⌁

Fifteen minutes past four o'clock on the day of the wedding, Sadie stepped outside, walking on tiptoe to avoid soiling her white patent leather boots. Thank heaven, no rain. She was already sweating with worry, where would she get a taxi on a Sunday, when one turned the corner. Ah, of course, the spirits were close, supervising the details. She yoo-hooed it to a stop. Trying to imitate Mitzi's way of gracefully leaning into the open window of an automobile, she ducked her head, bumping it, and told the driver, "The New Hennington Hall, please, and drive careful. You have in your taxi today a big tipper."

⌁ ⌁ ⌁

The New Hennington Hall was all yellow brick and promise, columns supporting a dark-green canvas awning that announced in Yiddish above and English below, "At the New Hennington All Your Affairs Can be Catered." The vestibule opened into an enormous room with a polished wooden floor and, at the far end, a low platform on which was set an electrified *chupah*, the first marriage canopy in New York City to light up.

The taxi ride had been fast and cheap, six blocks up and three blocks over in six minutes. Sadie adjusted the silk shawl over her arm. What a strain, trying to stay beautiful in this weather. She was already too late to be early, almost every seat on both sides of the aisle—taken.

Such a crazy business. Did these people think the Grubstein's

168

gave out door prizes to early birds? Such clothes, a roomful of peacocks! Flowered silks and pale, crushed linens; bright chiffons; hats like in synagogue for the High Holidays: plumes and flowers and birds perched, looking ready to fly away or sing or lay an egg.

Wasn't that—Sadie squinted—sitting up front on the bride's side: Morty Jacobson, the shoemaker with the damp hands, a good dancer, but stains all over her clothes every place he touches? And right next, she'd know that mustache anywhere, waxed and sticking out like spikes on a fence: Sy Sirotksy. No wonder he doesn't have a wife (or does he?) back in Kiev.

There, in front of Morty, Lena Gerwitz. *Gevalt*! How did she know the Grubsteins, to get invited? Cousins, maybe. Cousins you got to invite. How about that hat on her—*feh*! Black taffeta roses, or are those ugly *chochkeys* fake carnations? Across the aisle, on the groom's side, Sadie saw only strangers, everyone *tsk-tsk'ing* over that old man with sad eyes and a long, white straggly beard, who must be—who else—Rabbi what's-his-name, the teacher to today's groom, the one everyone called *Rebbe*; he's so holy.

No Herschl. Sadie peered at her watch. Twenty-five minutes until five o'clock. She shook it. Fivel's birthday present, who could be sure it wasn't lying? *Keep yourself cool, Herschl's downstairs in the kitchen wrestling with a fifty-pound piece of ice, water spots dripping down his good pants, all over his white shirt.*

She took one final look around the hall: the pots of flowers adorning the balcony, the gleaming satin bridal path running down the middle of the room to the platform. *Such a fancy place, so many happy people, and all because of me, the spirits and me. We did it. Not bad for only fifty cents.*

Sadie started toward the front of the hall, stopping to shake hands, nodding yes, yes, a wonderful occasion, such lovely young people, a marriage made for sure in heaven, all the while thinking: *Red lace, it shows off every pound, especially from behind, I've got some nerve*; excusing her way to two empty seats in the third row, smiling at everyone who smiled at her, as she folded her shawl and lay it across the second seat, to save it for Herschl.

Her minute-by-minute schedule wasn't going well, men don't know from being on time. Twenty minutes until five o'clock. She would watch for Herschl and yoo-hoo him to her side. Later at dinner, after he'd been softened up by a little *schnapps*, she'd suggest they dance. He'd refuse, but you go ahead, he'd insist. She would. Maybe with Morty or Sy, they looked good on the dance floor, they made her look good.

Fifteen minutes until five. A violinist, clutching his instrument, stepped onto the balcony, acknowledging a faint ripple of applause. He put bow to violin and coaxed the trains of a soulful Hebrew melody. A little girl pulled away from her parents and danced in the aisle.

Sadie felt a pang of uneasiness. Herschl wouldn't be a no-show? Impossible! The food would spoil without him, she'd spoil without him. She inspected herself in her hand mirror. No damage yet, but in this heat, anything could happen. She checked her watch. Ten minutes until five.

The music stopped, Sadie looked up. A short, heavy woman wearing black silk and a tightly curled marriage wig was speaking to the violinist, who produced a sorrowful look. Abruptly, the woman turned and left the balcony, the violinist gathered up his instrument and music. A minute later the woman entered the hall through a door at the front, walked up the steps to the platform and stood under the *chupah*, facing the guests.

An anxious silence swallowed the noise. The woman fingered her black silk skirt.

Someone behind Sadie whispered, "The *rebbetzin*, Rabbi Macchik's wife, he does the wedding today."

The rabbi's wife coughed into her hand. "I have a sad duty," she said, and repeated "sad," rocking back and forth. Murmurs, like vapor, rose above the crowd. She cleared her throat. "The rabbi sends me to say"—her mouth sagged in disappointment—"the wedding is delayed."

An explosion of voices rocked the hall. The little girl, still dancing, was pulled onto her mother's lap where, screaming to be released, she was slapped, then kissed. The lady in purple silk in front of Sadie stood up, calling out, "Some nerve, I gave up two parties to come here today, I—"

Her husband tugged at her skirt and asked her to please shut up.

"I mean," the rabbi's wife continued, "the wedding is canceled." She braided and unbraided her fingers, adjusting her wig, sniffing hard, as though warding off a sneeze.

Two women at the rear of the hall cried, *"Vey!"* and the man sitting next to the *rebbe* demanded an immediate and full explanation.

The rabbi's wife smiled a sour smile. "You'll be quiet, I'll explain. Obby Rappaport, who is, as you know, the groom and, as you also know"—she gestured toward the *rebbe*—"a student of the revered and honored Rabbi Chaim Levovnik."

Applause broke out, a ripple throughout the hall. Rabbi Levovnik struggled to his feet, waved and nodded, then sank back down.

"Hurry up, it's a hundred degrees in here," a voice called. A woman *shushed* him and said some people didn't know when to shut up and let other people speak.

"The groom," the *rebbetzin* went on, "a brilliant young man, like I said, from a lovely family, is sadly not well." She rotated one hand in apology. "Who can say, maybe later he'll recover." Laughter; soft, then louder. "Meanwhile, the bride's family invites you to stay, eat supper"—a sweep of her hands—"so much food." She walked down the steps, then hurried out through a side door.

Sadie rushed after her, calling, "Wait—what happened!" The *rebbetzin* turned. "I'm the reason for the wedding in the first place," Sadie said. Now she was for-sure sweating, not a good thing in red lace. "Schuster, Sadie, professional full-time *schadchen*," she said, putting her hand out.

"Well"—the *rebbetzin* ignored Sadie's hand—"next time you'll maybe be more careful."

"Of what?"

"Next time talk also to the groom's mother."

So, Sophie Rappaport! Sadie had smelled that one's evil eye from the beginning. "Where's Bessie?"

"Downstairs, crying out her heart." She pointed to a staircase at the end of the hall. "Hymie Grubstein's going crazy, what else?"

Sadie hurried toward the stairs, reaching them as a voice behind her shouted, "Sadie, Sadie—don't go!" She turned to see Semke, flushed and beaming, rushing at her. *"I-yi-yi!"* Seizing both her hands, he held onto them, wringing them until, wincing, she pulled away. "Such a wonderful thing," he exclaimed, "I'm so happy, who could believe!"

"Later Semke, later." She started down the stairs.

Semke pounded after her. "Wait!" he exclaimed, pulling at her shoulder. "You don't know!"

A sweet boy, but a problem, a whiner, she'd talk to him, tell him grow up, Semke, girls don't like crybabies.

"Bessie! Her things are in my love knot, I love her!"

Sadie stopped, wheeling around, her face fierce with surprise. Semke pulled back. "*You* did this," she shouted, "you mixed up the spirits! I told them, Obby, Obby, Obby; you told them, Semke, Semke, Semke!" Her heart was thumping like ten drums. "You tricked me!" Time to quit this business, she couldn't fight up the world. If Semke did this, who else could do God knows what? She'd treated him like a son. "Monster!" She cried, sinking onto the bottom step.

The young man pulled off his tie. "I didn't trick anything! You said, who did I love and I loved—love—Bessie. I've always loved her, since fourth grade, so I bought a love knot." He rummaged in his pocket, holding up the bright-yellow satin love knot Sadie had delivered the week before.

Sadie eyed the knot. "All the snick-snacks you gave me to put in your knot, the pencil, the eraser—hers?"

"You said"—his voice broke—"I should buy some hope for fifty cents, so I did."

Sadie felt a stab of remorse. What was she hollering on him, a sweet boy, an innocent. Maybe it was the spirits, they had a hard day, *they* mixed everything up. She patted his hand. "Shhh, let me think." Herschl was God knows where, they wouldn't dance, twelve dollars for a dress to sweat in. Once the spirits said, *no wedding*, you could spit up blood, they wouldn't change.

"Maybe Bessie will marry *me*," Semke said, brightening.

"You're crazy!"

"You talk about crazy! What about your *cockamamie* spirits, who's crazy? But I said, all right, if you say so, here's fifty cents. I trusted you!"

Sadie had never seen him this way. Anger made him taller, even when he was sitting down; thinner, cockier, a regular man-of-the-world. That glazed look was gone from his eyes. He looked like a somebody.

"Listen," he said, grasping Sadie's hand. He had a plan. Sadie should tell her spirits to make Bessie love him, why should they care which groom was which? Sadie's mind seesawed from *crazy*, to *possible*, He maybe had a point. The wedding would go on, Hymie Grubstein would be a happy man, she would dance with Herschl. But—one problem: "Does Bessie know who you are, even?"

"Yes . . . and no," he said, thoughtfully, ducking his head. "I never said anything to her, I was too scared."

A high, thin wail floated down the hall from behind one of the closed doors. Semke jumped up. "I'm going in there!"

"All right, but let me talk first, whose spirits are they?" She started down the hall, stopping at every door, listening until, at the end of the hall, they heard the high, thin wail of a woman. Sadie knocked.

"Go away." Bessie's weepy voice.

Rifke Grubstein pulled the door open. "*You*! Your poison love knots, I can't stand to look on you."

"I'm in already." Sadie pushed past her, followed by Semke. Hymie Grubstein, crumpled in a chair, shook his finger at her.

Bessie was lying on a cot, sending up moaning sounds. Sadie sat down next to her, patting her hair, her dress, tsk-tsking, until Bessie sat up, and began to hiccup. "Never mind," Sadie said, "he's not worth your little toe, a nothing, a puffed-up mama's boy."

"His mother hated me."

"It was me she hated." Rifke flicked her chin at her husband. "She wasn't too crazy about him, either."

"*Who*?" Bessie pointed at Semke.

"Bessie . . ." Leaning down, he stroked her arm.

"Who is *this*?" Rifke squeezed herself between Semke and Bessie, pulling at his hand. "Don't touch her!"

"Rifke Grubstein, meet Semke Leiberman," Sadie said, trying to sound calm, but how was that possible when she felt covered with sweat and her hairpins were falling onto the floor?

Bessie, eyeing Semke with suspicion, then curiosity, hiccoughed louder, and managed to sit up.

"Bessie," he said, his eyes shining, "marry me!"

"*Veyez mir, meshuga*!" Rifke Grubstein cried. She rushed to the door, opened it and pointed down the hall. "Out!"

Semke, kneeling now, grasped Bessie's hand. "Ask Sadie, I bought a love knot with your tooth, a piece of eraser from your desk I got from the janitor who cleans up in your office."

"Again with her love knots! Arrest her!" Rifke rattled the doorknob furiously.

Sniffling, Bessie squinted at Semke through swollen eyes. "Semke?" she whispered, and rubbed her eyes with the heel of her hand. "Semke Leiberman?"

"She knows me!" Semke jumped up, grasping Sadie's sleeve.

"Careful," Sadie said, stepping back, "the lace costs."

Rifke put her head out the door, "Police!"

"At school I loved you from the first day," Semke said to Bessie, who was now peering up at him with baffled interest, "from six years old. You wore brown stockings and galoshes, red rubber galoshes with metal buckles that clinked when you walked." He imitated a clinking sound. Bessie smiled, then buried her face in her hands. "I was *L* and you were *G*," he went on. "I could see your braids from the back every time I looked at the blackboard."

"You could?" Bessie accepted the handkerchief he took from his pocket.

"That's what I liked best, that narrow white line down the back of your head. It made you look so—" He blew his nose. "Like if anyone touched you, they would hurt you," he blurted out.

"And my ribbons," Bessie said, looking almost happy, "you forgot my ribbons. Those were satin."

"I almost forgot! Every day another one to match your dress, a new color every day!" Semke squatted next to Bessie again, laughing, rubbing his hands together, until she laughed.

"Where did he come from?" Rifke demanded, closing the door. "Who is he?"

"Wait, let him talk," Sadie said. "He loves her."

"*Loves*!" Rifke glared at Semke, then at Sadie, reminding her she didn't care if Bessie never got married, they were a laughingstock, the whole family, everybody they knew upstairs taking them apart with their tongues.

"How good did you know your husband before?" Sadie asked.

"Too good," Rifke said. Her husband was counting under his breath, ticking something off on his fingers.

"You could do worse," Sadie said, turning to Bessie, "a boy like Semke, a kind person, crazy in love with you." Semke nodded. "He's honest, he's smart, hardworking."

Rifke Grubstein looked at Semke with mild interest. "What does he do for a living?"

Semke sprang to his feet, and squared his shoulders. "Buttons," he said.

"Your Bessie will want for nothing," Sadie said.

"Buttons on what?" Rifke asked.

"Buttons and linings," Semke said, "my uncle's business, on Cherry Street."

"So, your uncle has a business," Rifke said, "it's *his* business."

"Not true," Sadie said, hoping she was getting the facts straight. Did she hear Semke's uncle was rich, or was it the uncle of that girl who bought a love knot last week, the one from Brooklyn with the crossed eyes? Everyone was looking at her. "Soon the whole business will be his!" She pointed at Semke who, thanks God, looked at that minute like she was talking the truth.

"You don't say so?" Rifke closed her eyes, teetering back and forth, then opened them. "Hymie, wake up, he has a big business."

"Excuse me," Bessie said, snapping her fingers.

"Also," Sadie said, "he's an orphan."

Semke, beaming, looked from Rifke to Bessie to Hymie.

"Don't I get to say anything?" Bessie said.

"No mother-in-law," Sadie said. "That alone makes the whole thing wonderful. Think of it as an arranged marriage after they met."

"Two hundred chickens," Hymie said, pointing a finger toward the ceiling, "fifty calves' livers, two hundred pounds of beef, sugar and honey cakes, fruitcakes, tortes with hazelnuts on top—"

"What are you," Rifke Grubstein said, "some kind of catering company?"

"I'm adding up," he said, "all the food I have to pay, two hundred people sitting down to dinner, drinking my *schnapps*."

"I loved him," Bessie said, her mouth trembling.

Sadie spit into her cupped hand, "*Ptooey, ptooey, ptooey*! He didn't appreciate; he's a terrible person."

"Throwing you out like water from a bathtub," Semke added.

"He does this before, think how he'd treat you after," Rifke said.

"You're lucky you got out now," Sadie added.

Bessie opened her mouth, then closed it. "Speak up," her mother demanded, "all of a sudden you're a mumbler?"

"I won't be passed around like a prize in a box of candy," Bessie said, "what will people say?"

"*Say!*" A vein pulsed on her father's forehead. Jumping up, he stood over her. "They'll say, 'When do we eat?' "

Sadie leaned down to Bessie. "Think about this, darling: left waiting under the *chupah*. That means from now on, plain talk, you're marked-down merchandise." She brushed the palm of one hand over the other. "*Finished.*"

Bessie picked at a seam on her dress.

"But," Sadie continued, "you can get even, better than even. Make it look like *you* changed your mind."

"No!" Semke shouted, startling everyone. "Make it look like *I* changed your mind. Sadie." He pulled her aside. "Do it now, you know, with the spirits." He took the love knot out of his pocket, and pushed it into her hand.

Sadie looked at the knot, hesitating. Was today a good day or a bad day to ask the spirits a favor? They already had their hands full getting Herschl to the wedding; and, after, making sure he loved her dancing; and, after *that*, making sure he took her home. Maybe taking out Obby and dropping in Semke would be too much, they'd get worn-out, annoyed. This was, after all, their busiest season.

She patted the knot. It vibrated. Semke was watching her, his dark eyes so sorrowful, she could fall into them. Everyone was watching her: Rifke, stiff with suspicion; Bessie, flashing out calm looks of skepticism; Hymie still counting to himself.

The love knot hummed. *Maybe!* Sadie shivered. A tightening in her chest, nothing much, enough to make her hope it was a message, and not a heart attack. Her feet were killing her. She rubbed her eyes. Colored pinwheels shot across the screen of her eyelids, then rockets, followed by shooting stars. An announcing from the other side? Or, possibly, eye problems.

Excusing herself, she had business to take care of. She went into the far corner and, crouching, squeezed her eyes shut, buried her face in her hands and swayed side to side, murmuring a string of barely recognizable sounds. Nuzzling the silky love knot against her lips, she suddenly felt stronger. Talking to the spirits did that. Too bad Herschl wasn't here to see.

"Sadie Schuster," Rifke said, but Sadie went on chanting. "Stop that," Rifke insisted, "you take me for a *nar*; I'm no fool to believe such *mishagas!*"

"All right," Sadie said, opening her eyes. "*Done!*"

"I decided." Bessie hiccoughed again.

"Sadie, you did it!" Semke jiggled with excitement.

"If I never get married, that will be"—Bessie looked down at her hands—"all right."

"*Now* you say!" Hymie jabbed his finger at the ceiling. "Upstairs is an army of people waiting to eat supper."

"It's my life, it's my say-so," Bessie said.

"What happened to your spirits?" Semke asked Sadie.

"Be careful how you talk to a father," Hymie said.

"We never should let you decide the first time," Rifke said, "such an important thing like a husband, a girl only twenty."

"Twenty-one," Bessie said.

"Next month," Rifke said to Semke. "This month she's still twenty, a young girl."

"Don't cut away your nose because your face is angry. It's a lonely life, no one next to you in bed." Sadie pulled Semke to her. "Boys like this don't grow on every tree on the East Side. In my business, I see a lot of fellas. Junk"—she pinched his cheek—"compared to this jewel." Herschl, by this time, was probably out the door and back on his wagon, halfway home.

Bessie shook her head.

"Some magic-maker you are!" Semke pulled away from Sadie.

"Who wouldn't believe you woke up this morning and hollered *Gevalt?*" Sadie went on, "Help, I made a big mistake. Good-bye, Mr. Rappaport; hello, Mr. Leiberman, the last laugh is Bessie Grubstein's." Her feet were throbbing, dancing was out.

"All right, all right, I need some quiet," Bessie said. She covered her face with the handkerchief.

Semke paced, cracking his knuckles, finally sinking into a chair. Sadie tried to decide if the itching she felt along her right arm was the spirits or prickly heat. The bright-red polish on her special fingernail was peeling.

Bessie looked up and, flicking the handkerchief aside, whispered, "Yes."

"Hurry up." Sadie pushed Semke toward the door. "Run, catch the rabbi."

Chapter Fifteen

S adie returned to the main floor to find the guests gathered
in anxious knots: should they go or stay, what went wrong,
who walked away from who, was the bride's father serious,
there would be food anyway, and dancing?

Scanning the crowd, she searched for that one sweet face she
needed to calm her jangled-up nerves. Nothing. No Herschl seated
up front, no sign of him in the aisles or—standing on tiptoes—at
the back of the hall. He had come, maybe, but he had definitely
gone. Semke got Bessie and *she* got nothing. She'd stay to see them
married, then go home and cry.

The *rebbetzin* stepped onto the balcony and, peering over the
railing into the faces below, cleared her throat.

"*Say something already,*" a woman's voice called out. A man in
the front row applauded and stamped his feet.

Holding herself erect, the *rebbetzin* explained that the ceremony
was about to happen, so please, everyone, sit down. "Only"—
dabbing at her lips—"we have, there is one . . ." She paused,
blinked several times and sighed. "The bride is still Bessie
Grubstein, but the groom is not—"

A wave of laughter rolled through the hall.

The *rebbetzin* wagged her finger. "The groom is not Obby

Rappaport, he's Semke Leiberman, who some will recognize from around the neighborhood."

"Why?" a man shouted.

"Why not?" another man called out.

"Who cares?" his wife said, and a chorus of applause broke out.

The *rebbetzin* put her hands out to her sides, palms up: *these things happen.*

Sadie excused her way back to her seat, hoping she wouldn't get weepy and embarrass herself during the ceremony. Weddings did that to her, especially on days when she felt as lonely—as sad, as cheated—as she did this minute. Violin strains floated across the hall. She glanced down. The fiery-red lace of her dress burned her eyes.

Beaming, Semke bounded out of the foyer and down the aisle, walking so fast the *rebbetzin*, behind the foyer curtain, called, "Slow, it's not a race." Still beaming, he stopped at the foot of the platform. Bessie, pale, her smile wavering, emerged from the foyer between Rifke and Hymie.

Sadie watched the trio move toward the front of the hall. Here, anyway, was a new beginning, fresh hope. Then: *Gevalt!* Sadie jumped up, then sat down when the man behind her poked her shoulder and hissed: "Sit, lady." Semke couldn't marry Bessie; they didn't have a marriage license.

The rabbi, short, spectacled, solemn, in his white silk robe and skullcap, was raising his hand in benediction over Bessie's and Semke's lowered heads. Rifke stood to one side, weeping, but smiling. Hymie, looking like a man adding a column of figures, stood, distracted, next to her.

Now she'd done it, *really* done it, broken the American law. A United States citizen, she'd go to jail just the same. That's what America did, you fool around with not buying a license. Even for peddling, Fivel went, paid two dollars in City Hall for a piece of paper. Nobody got away.

Semke stamped his foot, once, twice, bringing his weight down on a tiny object wrapped in a white cloth. The sound of splintering glass, then applause, *Mazel Tov, Mazel Tov,* and whistling from the front row.

The rabbi pronounced Semke and Bessie man and wife, signaling, *Kiss the bride*, and Semke did, a kiss that landed on her left ear, because she'd turned to look at Rifke. Then he hugged her so hard, he lifted her off the ground, forcing her to squeal and grasp his lapels with both hands.

"All right, already," a man called from behind Sadie. "Play later!" Laughter ripped the silence, and everyone stood up, calling out congratulations, as Bessie and Semke hurried down the aisle and disappeared behind the foyer curtains.

Sadie excused her way across three people, and rushed up the aisle. Bessie and Semke were standing against the far wall of the reception room, looking like they were waiting to be rescued. "Don't do nothing," she called out, then, closer, whispered: "A terrible thing, you aren't married. No license!"

She should say something comforting, like not having a license is only a small wrinkle to iron out, but her heart was pressing against her chest, and the pressure behind her eyes had ballooned to a fifty-pound weight. She needed a chair, a sip of cold seltzer, she wouldn't live to wake up tomorrow.

Then the rabbi and his wife were there and Bessie repeated Sadie's terrible news. Everyone was talking at the same time, only it sounded like they were arguing, until Bessie, her bridal headpiece tipped over one eye, lipstick smears across her cheek and chin, said that Sadie must be joking—she certainly did have a license. "Ma, you saw it," she said. Sadie replied: yes, a license for her and Obby; not her and Semke. Semke, looking dazed, cracked his knuckles.

The rabbi hollered at the *rebbetzin*, who should have known, how could she let him do something so unholy, commit a sin, a terrible sin! The *rebbetzin* pressed her thin lips together and patted her *shaytl* which, to Sadie, looked like stiff waves pressed into pale-brown straw. Ugly, and nobody deserved it more than she did.

Now Sadie felt less guilty. Maybe the rabbi would go to jail or—even better—the *rebbetzin*, and she'd be excused. "*I'm only a matchmaker*," she'd tell the judge. "I start things up; it's not my business to finish off." He'd have pity, a woman alone. How much profit did she make on fifty cents?

"Nothing to holler about," Semke assured everyone, looking

suddenly confident. "I'll buy a license tomorrow." His voice was a Semke voice Sadie didn't know; deep, strong, the old trembling gone. Married ten minutes, and no more *schlemiel*.

"Tomorrow!" Rifke, reaching around Semke, pulled at Bessie's skirt. "Then today, please, don't touch my Bessie!"

"Maaa," Bessie wailed.

"Where were you, you didn't ask about a license?" Hymie Grubstein asked his wife.

"*Me*? When did I get married in America, I should know?"

"Will everyone please stay calm, please," Semke said, still gripping Bessie's hand. "A small mistake, nothing important."

"*Small!*" Hymie's no-nonsense eyes bulged. "You call two hundred chickens a small thing? Beef brisket, kosher, first-cut, at today's prices!"

"Pa, your blood pressure," Bessie warned.

"Take a pill," Rifke said. "Someone bring him a glass of water." No one moved. "Sadie, you're the marriage *mayven*, you let her marry against the law!"

"I'm not the president of licenses," Sadie said. "My customers do their own papers. Hundreds, thousands of weddings I made happen, and not once did I break the law."

"Never would I have ordered brisket, had I'd known she wouldn't marry two people on the same day," Hymie grumbled. "A little sponge cake, a glass of wine . . ." He wiped one hand with the other. "Plenty!"

"Nevertheless," Sadie interrupted. It was time to bring in some long English words. "We have here an easy complication." Four syllables. She pronounced each one separately. For a moment no one spoke, waiting for her to continue, even the rabbi, who had been rocking back and forth. "We'll keep it our little secret." She liked the respect she saw on their faces. Talking fancy American words, it never failed. Rifke opened her mouth. "I mean, tonight," Sadie said, "Then tomorrow—"

"Then tonight she comes home with us," Rifke said.

Semke looked miserable, tears slid down Bessie's cheeks.

"Settled," Sadie said.

"Wait," Rifke said. "Rabbi?"

Everyone turned to stare at him.

"In the *Talmud*," the rabbi began, eyes closed, "it says . . ." He hesitated, massaging his eyelids. "Let me think, it says—"

"Well"—Hymie rubbed his hands together—"if it says so in the *Talmud*, then it's good enough for me." He looked around for agreement.

Sadie kissed the air around Bessie's face, and started out the door, where she bumped into a group of guests who were, they said, looking for the happy couple. Sadie pointed. "Ready to be kissed."

She hurried downstairs to the banquet hall. Herschl, not knowing of the license complication, maybe had gone down there in search of her after the ceremony upstairs. A few guests were gathered at a long table against one wall, on which Lippke had set out two liquor bottles, seltzer, and ice. She hurried to her friend and, stepping behind the table, whispered, "You seen Herschl Diamond anywhere? I'll make any information worth your while."

Lippke sucked his toothpick and, not taking his eyes from his work, whispered: "A short, healthy-looking man, lots of hair, sells ice from a wagon around here?"

"That's him."

Lippke wiped his hands on a towel. "Ten, fifteen minutes ago, right there." His chin pointed to the far corner to the room. "Talkin' with your dancer friend."

"No!"

"Ike—"

She held her hand up. "Stop, don't finish, I know the story."

"—Tabatnik. He looked, Diamond I mean, may I tell you, not happy."

"They went—where?"

"Not together. First Diamond went, then the other one."

"I'll kill him."

"I'll help."

Sadie found a taxi at the curb, waiting, the driver said, for someone named Idelowitz. "That's me," she said, and got in. "Minnie Idelowitz, take me home to Orchard Street, fast." Her curls were wilting, the red lace had lost its sizzle. A lifetime of delivering happiness to other people, look what it brought. Dust in the mouth, ruin, emptiness running into emptiness for a future.

"Lady, how do I know?" The driver swiveled around and looked at her.

"Know what?"

"You're who you say you are. I gotta wait for the person what called me."

"Would I say my name is Idelowitz if it wasn't?" The driver pondered the question. "Would you, would anyone?" His eyes leaked uncertainty. "I see you're a man who recognizes an honest person when he sees her. Ten eighteen Orchard, second brown building from the corner of Delancey. Hurry."

Sunday night on the Lower East Side meant no traffic—except tonight. As soon as the taxi pulled away from the curb, an ambulance wagon, siren clanging, turned the corner and the taxi trailed behind for two blocks, before beeping its way around it. When Sadie stepped onto the curb in front of her building a few minutes later, the ambulance was parked there. Two uniformed men were running up the stairs carrying a stretcher.

Sadie threw three dollars at the driver, hollered, "Mail me the change," and ran up the stairs behind the men, remembering to hold up the red lace skirt, demanding to know *who, why*. Lila was at the door, pointing the men up the stairwell. Seeing Sadie, she seized her hands and broke into shrieks, interspersed with something that sounded like, "He's dyin', Lordy, he's dyin'."

Grasping the girl's wrists, Sadie pulled her up the stairs to Mitzi's. The door to the flat flew open and a tall blonde Sadie had never seen before—in a purple satin something or other, orange feathers flying from her disheveled hair—pushed her way past them, followed by another girl, shorter, wider, what Sadie called *zaftik*, in black-and-cream tulle, a white fur cape thrown across her bare shoulders.

Ike—*Ike!*—paced in the foyer, collar unbuttoned, tie askew; two things Sadie had never seen. But when had she seen his face stiff with terror? He told the men carrying the stretcher, "There, *there!*" pointing down the hall; then murmured, "Sadie, Sadie," more plea then greeting, pulling her to him, holding on, his face buried in her shoulder. If she didn't know it was impossible, she'd swear he was crying.

"What is?" His shoulders shook, but he didn't answer.

Mitzi, a flash of red velvet, something plumed and black pinned in her upswept hair, was everywhere; in the kitchen ordering Lila to bring ice—no, hot water—clean towels, acknowledging Sadie's arrival with, "You, *now?*" before dialing the hall telephone. She hollered at whoever answered that the doctor was supposed to be here thirty minutes ago, Jeezus all-to-hell, someone was dying.

Ike was still holding onto Sadie. Those *were* tears, she felt them on her shoulder. If she didn't want to kill him, she'd feel sorry. But first she had to see what-was-what in that bedroom and, gently pushing him away, walked around Mitzi and pulled the bedroom door open.

A skinny, pasty-faced man was lying on the bed, eyes closed, bald head rolled to the side. The men with the stretcher seemed to fill the room, standing at the foot of the bed, looking down at him, at Sadie. "You want him outta here, lady? Someone gotta tell us what to do."

"*Gott im Himmel*, dead?" Sadie backed out of the room and into Mitzi.

"Close, thanks to him." She pointed to Ike, who was running his hands through his hair, looking around as though trying to figure out how he'd gotten there.

The next ten minutes were a confusion of arriving doctor and departing stretcher, the bald-headed man moaning, when he wasn't cursing. By then, three more young girls—in underclothes, trailing elaborate dresses, furs, shoes, feather boas, cosmetic cases, one brushing her hair—clambered down the hall and out the door, followed by two men who were buttoning and straightening their clothes. Tenants in night clothes, carrying crying infants, crowded the stairwell, demanding to know what the hell's going on?

Someone pounded on Mitzi's door, hollering, "Open up, you're breaking the law in there, I'm callin' the cops!"

Mitzi signaled for everyone to *shush*, especially Ike, who had regained his voice and was insisting to Sadie that he should be pitied, not blamed. He should drop dead if he meant anyone harm. She clicked the double lock into place. Then she explained to Sadie, who, too weak to stand, had flung herself on the parlor love seat. "Gin," Mitzi said. She eyed Ike. "His."

"Let me." Ike took Sadie's hands. "I learned from my friend,

Izzy, from Budapest. Bathtub gin, made cheap."

"Sold expensive," Mitzi said.

"The man just now, he drank?" Sadie asked.

"He drank," Mitzi said.

"Excuse me, but don't I know him?" Sadie said.

Mitzi nodded. He was her contact with what she called "the boys downtown," a big shot, big enough to play the killer fish swallowing the little fish, taking care of annoying details, so she could do business as usual. "He took his fee out in trade, twice a week, sometimes a little extra squeezed in, with Tessie, that tall blonde who flew outta here."

Sadie sprang to her feet. "Enough emergencies for one Sunday. I'm late for my bed."

"I'll take you," Ike said, "I'm passing right by your door, my way down."

Mitzi walked Sadie and Ike to the door. "Stay in touch, pal, we're both cooked geese if somethin' bad happens to my friend."

Stopping outside her flat, Sadie told Ike, "Don't see me in, I want to fall into bed and sleep until next week." Her brain felt fried, her feet throbbed. She needed aloneness.

"I've got just the cure for your troubles, invite me inside, please."

Please? Peering at him as closely as the gloom permitted, Sadie couldn't see his eyes, certainly not well enough to decide what kind of monkey business was going on. She hesitated. Who knew how quick his anger would shoot up, how much noise he'd make? The Capronis, the Hogans, after what happened at Mitzi's, they could hear him, call the police. She slid her key into the lock. "At my age, I belong sleeping by now, all this excitement."

"Your age!" He did a fast shuffle. "Don't talk crazy, you're younger than anyone. Listen." He grasped her arm. "I have something to tell. Life is short, you saw upstairs, we got to grab at every chance."

"Five minutes." One sip of wine, she'd send him home.

He trailed his finger across the back of her neck. "You won't be sorry."

"I'm sorry already." She threw her shawl onto the sofa and settled in a chair, glancing at her watch, then at Ike, who had flung himself onto the sofa as though he belonged there, her shawl across his lap.

Grinning, electric sparks practically shooting out of his eyes, he said, "I have for you a wonderful surprise. But"—he jumped up—"first, some wine to celebrate."

"*Celebrate*, there's something to be happy for, you didn't see a man almost die, maybe did die?" She wanted to say: *My life is ruined, also, thanks to you*, but settled for: "More of your tricks?"

"Don't get up, I know where things are." Hurrying to the china cupboard, then the icebox, he brought two glasses and an opened bottle of wine and set them down on the small table. "There!" He stood back as though admiring the arrangement. "Now." Reaching into his jacket pocket, he held out a creased sepia photograph.

Sadie saw a woman and two children, the photograph he'd shown her that first night. She looked up, "So."

Grinning, he came over to her and kneeled, grasping her hands, crushing the photograph. "I want you to meet my sister, Bertha Livinoff of Riga, Latvia, and her two little children."

Sadie smoothed the photograph, and stared at the woman's face. "Sister? I don't see no family look-alike. She looks kind."

"Sadie, Sadie, she's not my wife! I don't have a wife. I made it all up."

"No wife? *Gott im Himmel*! You're evil, worse than evil, all the time playing tricks, you should be locked up."

"Sadie, listen to me what I say." Ike pulled at her hand. "I got no wife in Riga, so now I can have one in America."

"Congratulations! I'm happy for you, but who would marry such a criminal?"

"*Who*?" Standing now, he ran his hand over his pompadour, fixing her with his everybody-loves-me look. "You! I want to marry you!"

"*Me!*" Surprise, as shocking as a jolt of electricity, rocked her. "Your idea of a joke; another trick!"

"Okay, okay." Leaning down, he reached for her hand. "I made too big a surprise, and you didn't expect. Only this is not a joke for me. I love you." Now his eyes were serious. She opened her mouth, and closed it again. "Ha, Sadie! For once nothing to say, I love it!"

Nudging her aside, he thrust himself onto the arm of her chair. "Listen, if I knew I would—how do they say in English?—*fall in love*, I didn't dream, nothing."

Her heart—this whole night was too much! She breathed slowly: in-out, in-out.

"So, some surprise, huh?" He blew a soft *puh* into her ear.

For sure, no goose bumps. She sat very still, trying not to breathe.

"I told you that you wouldn't be sorry I came in."

Sadie pushed herself out of the chair. "You're not"—pacing now, not looking at him—"for getting married, there are women everywhere." She circled to the other side of the room, close to Fivel's photograph, standing, looking down on Ike. It was always better to look down on Ike Tabatnik. "Blonde ones"—ticking her words off on her fingers—"red-haired ones, skinny ones." He was breathing hard, his chest going up-down, up-down. She hoped he had a healthy heart; she didn't need more trouble with doctors and ambulances. "Round ones . . ." She trailed off.

"Yes, yes, I admit, but"—he gestured *finished* with a flick of one hand—"no one else, none of the other ladies I met are so, so . . ." He looked past her shoulder, as though hoping to find the right word floating across the far wall. "I don't know." He smiled, looking suddenly boyish. "I only know, since I came to America I have had Sadie Schuster on the brain. How do you like that for talking American, what a pair we make!"

"*Oy*" She excused herself and rushed to the sink, filling a glass with cold water. Words. She needed some American night school words. Nothing made sense here: *Marry Ike! She couldn't.*

"Sadie, what's going on, something smells not so good to me. I thought you'd be jumping into your skin with happiness."

"*Out of* my skin," she corrected, "jumping *out*!" She sipped, refilled the glass and drank again. Nobody would believe it; *she* didn't believe it. This was her chance, finally, to live with passion, a whole lifetime of being *tsehitst*. She knew enough words, but she didn't know how to say this: the passion part wasn't enough. Not enough to marry on, even if she never in her lifetime saw Herschl again.

Ike was waiting.

"Nothing's going on, only"—she drank more water—"I can't marry you." She was ice cold, burning up. Now she'd die a lonely old woman. She felt strong. She felt frightened.

"Am I hearing you right?" Even shock looked good on that beautiful face. "Come on, come on," he said, gesturing impatiently, "spill everything."

"Nothing to spill, only the truth."

"What kinda *cockamamie* talk!" He was pacing. "That crazy business just now, at Mitzi's?"

Sadie shook her head.

"Oh, hoo-ha! That's where the dead dog is buried! That old fart, what's-his-name, that Diamond! Don't talk to me about other ladies."

"Leave him out, he's nothing to me," she said. A tight black line burned behind her eyes. "And for sure I'm nothing to him."

"I don't ask twice something like this, Sadie. That's one thing about me, I'm a proud man." Pushing the glasses and wine bottle aside, he sat down on a corner of the table and faced her, his fisted hands on his knees.

"You should be, you got a lot to be proud."

Chapter Sixteen

Another week until September and, after that, the Jewish new year beginning. And didn't the city air crisp up after so much heat, and didn't the sky turn bright royal blue, and no rain, hardly? Then why, this year, did everything feel to Sadie like it was ending?

Two days after the wedding, Mitzi, dolled up in fuchsia embroidered silk, came to say good-bye, smelling like a two-hundred-dollar bouquet of roses. If asked twenty minutes earlier, Sadie would have said, uh-uh, who, her *cry*, if Mitzi Beuhler went away? But now her tenant was hugging her and patting her cheek and talking about keeping in touch, and how Sadie couldn't guess how much she meant to her. Sadie felt the surprise of tears slipping down her face: too moved to turn away and pretend she had something in her eye; too sad to think one minute about losing so much rent money.

"Why are you going?" Sadie asked.

"My benefactor. A great word, write it down."

"He died?"

"No, too tough, that bird. But plenty mad, so *ta-ta* to all that. It ain't safe, I'll keep on movin' for a while."

"Where you'll be?"

"I ain't decided, but you're not done with me. I'll set up shop close by, kiddo." She crossed the room to the china cupboard. "This your old man?" She scrutinized Fivel's photograph. "Kinda cute, the way he's so friendly with his horse."

"I appreciate, you know, everything, all what you did for me, the beauty tricks, good advice," Sadie said. "Not that I came out so good, but it's nobody's fault. Just bad luck."

Sadie walked to the street door with Mitzi, and was waving her off when Timmy Hogan ran up the stairs, shouting: "Phone call, Mrs. Schuster." He jerked his thumb over his shoulder. "Patinkin's Candy Store." He rubbed his shirt sleeve across his nose. "Worth a nickel?"

Yivvy. She'd just heard about the crisis at Mitzi's, and wanted to know, was Sadie okay?

"Yes and no." The phone line felt dead, she jiggled the hook. "Thomas?"

"A new Sergeant. The swearing in on Labor Day, only I can't go. I might bump into some'a the guys who hustled my store."

"This means you'll"—Sadie cleared her throat—"marry with him?"

"Well, yeah, I suppose you could say so. Anyway"—Sadie heard Yivvy sniff—"he and I said yeah."

"*Oy!*"

"You happy for me, or not?"

"You want me to be happy for you?"

"Who said wants? I *need* you to be!"

Both women laughed, and Sadie said something that could have been, *Congratulaions,* and Yivvy told her to say it like she meant it.

"This costs a lot of money, we'll talk when it's free."

"Ma—I can afford it."

Sadie held the receiver against her chest. She felt like she'd swallowed three glasses of wine too fast, plus *Tante* Zippke's homemade beer.

"Ma, you there?"

Sadie nodded. *Fivel, I wish I could call you up on one of these for a real heart-to-hearts.*

"Ma, say something."

"You said it already: you get to choose what you want for your own life."

"We want you there. We wouldn't get married without you."

"I wouldn't miss it." Sadie sighed. "I got just the red lace dress for the occasion."

The letter Sadie never expected from Herschl arrived the next day: "Dear Sadie," she read aloud, "I am not a person to go back over things—"

"Says who?" she asked the paper.

"—being a firm believer that whatever happened, happened for a reason, my own personal brand of religion, put together from one part-Jewish, one part my father." She glanced down the page to see the letter's length. It covered one side of the paper, which she was pleased to see, was pale blue and—sniffing it—expensive. Not the stiff white paper you pick up for three cents at the corner candy store.

Although it was early afternoon, the light splashing through the windows like a fine golden net, she turned on the gas lamp above the kitchen table, holding the letter up to its illumination, admiring the paper's delicate transparency, and continued reading. "I am, not necessary to say, not happy—"

Hoo-ha! Herschl unhappy because of her. *That* made Sadie very happy.

"—about the sad circumstances of not meeting you at the wedding, and meeting our friend, Mr. Tabatnik instead. I am therefore willing—"

Therefore! Reading does that, she thought, spreads your English out in such nice sounding ways.

"—to meet with you—"

Now he was sounding like a banker, like a precinct captain.

"—for some honest talking."

Not on your life, Mister Diamond. Talking always got her into hot water with him. No more talking. They needed more doing.

In the final paragraph, Herschl said he was open to any ideas she might have about the where and when and how of their future meeting, closing: "With kindest thoughts for your good health, plus hopes for a quick answer, your friend, Herschl Emmanuel Diamond."

Think! Sadie slipped the letter between the pages of *The New Yiddish Poetry*, just out that month, three dollars. A lot of money, but it had been put together by someone famous, a Professor Kaufikoff, someone-or-other. She'd bought the book on Second Avenue the day before, prodded by the hope that the spirits knew about the terrible doings at the wedding, were working full-time on her problem, and she'd see Herschl soon. At first, she'd resisted the price: three dollars! Enough for a used chair. *Almost* enough for a dotted fake leopard jacket, used, but only a few times.

Leafing through its silky, fragrant pages, she'd felt the book vibrate in her hands and heard, as clearly as she heard the street noises rumbling outside the shop, a faint shoo-shushing. Wings, probably, or her fingernail sighing, and then a humming that sounded enough like *Sadie, buy me*. She did. Now she knew why.

Not more talking, Mr. Herschl Diamond, but *what*?

Filling the tea kettle, she was aware of music floating through the open windows, a lively, dum-ta-dee-dum, an up-and-down carnival tune, music she could always dance to. She put her head out the window, and watched a circle of children crowded around a dancing monkey, a short man wearing a red bolero jacket and black pants blowing on a harmonica and pushing on an accordion at the same time. *Yoo-hooing*, she fished out a penny and threw it down. The monkey snatched the coin from the sidewalk, looked up at her, offering first, a salute, then a loud kiss.

That music—Sadie tap-tapped her fingers on the window sill—it had to be another message from the spirits. Somewhere this week she'd seen a photograph that looked the way this music sounded: crowds of people in holiday clothes strolling and laughing, some clutching enormous stuffed animals, some trailing vivid-colored balloons. But *where*?

The accordionist swung into a polka. Sadie closed her eyes. The Rotogravure section of *The Daily Forward* flashed across her mind. The boardwalk at Coney Island. On one side: the Atlantic Ocean; on the other: Ferris wheels cartwheeling against a royal-blue sky; a tattooed lady in tights singing to a snake; cotton candy on sticks; Kewpie dolls, and sticky-faced children. What could be more American! What could be more doing without the talking!

She'd write to Herschl, let's have a picnic on Coney Island, then ride the mechanical horses, see the two-headed man, maybe fly around a little on the double roller coaster. And what about that new ride everyone was talking about, the Bumpsy Boops, where you walk in over a *schpritz* of hot air and the ladies' dresses go flying up over their heads?

Just the two of them alone together for a whole, entire day. Anything could happen. Maybe even a few foxtrots down at the pier where the three-piece band sets itself up. Could be—moving back into the kitchen now, getting out her best writing paper, a new pen and her inkstand—just being out there with all those happy people, he'd do a kind of softening up, like a pear ripening in the sun.

Don't sound anxious or pushy or timid. Don't apologize. *Dear Herschl*, she began the letter, *I have your sweet—*

She crumpled the paper, took a fresh sheet, replacing *sweet* with *kind*.

—letter, and was very happy—

Beginning a third time, she used *pleased* instead of *happy . . . Yes, by all means, we should meet, such a wonderful idea—*

She thought for one quick moment, then started over again, using *nice* instead of *wonderful*. What about the upcoming Labor Day, wouldn't it be good not to get hard-boiled in the city on a hot holiday? She suggested a picnic on Coney Island, a short ride if they caught the new fast trolley over the Brooklyn Bridge. She closed the letter by asking him to stop by during the coming week to tell her *Yes*, capitalizing it, hoping to make it look important, impossible to resist.

By four o'clock that afternoon the letter was in the mailbox on the corner; pricey, considering the cost of postage but, under the circumstances, slipping it under his door, or trusting it to his landlady didn't seem elegant enough.

The letter should be settled into his mailbox by the following day, Thursday.

That gave him twenty-four up to forty-eight hours to consider.
He should be at her door by Friday. Saturday, the latest.

He was.

～～　～～　～～

At six o'clock on Friday evening, Sadie—about to sit down to a
supper of cold spinach soup and leftover salmon loaf, an old copy
of *The Daily Forward* to keep her company—opened her door to
a hesitant Herschl, in a white shirt and creased pants, red suspenders, holding a blue-and-white-striped cap. She waved him into the
flat, hoping she looked welcoming, but not grateful.

No, he wouldn't sit down to supper, he'd already had a bite at
home, and no, his hand raised against her insistence, he didn't
want a glass of something cold and fizzy or hot and lemony.
Thanks all the same.

He put his cap on, then took it off again, avoiding her eyes.
He certainly was a good-looking man—*solid*. A good thing to
be, solid, responsible. She felt a ping of pleasure, wishing there
was time to run into the bedroom, pull a comb through her hair,
schpritz on some of that lilac cologne she got at Klein's on special.

Herschl twirled his cap. "You are"—looking over her shoulder—"by yourself?"

A good question, a jealous question. He was here to say yes to
the picnic, a forgive-and-forget, let's start over. "Who else would
be here?"

Herschl's mouth sagged into a maybe-I-believe-you-maybe-I-
don't expression.

Sadie sat down on the sofa. Her face felt oily. Thanks God, no
prickly heat today. "Please sit," she said as she patted the sofa.

He continued to stand. Sadie drummed her fingers on her knee,
and hummed. Herschl coughed twice into his fist, and sat down.

"Well," she said.

Now looking directly at her: "Well, Sadie—"

"I didn't think I'd see you again, after you not waiting for me
at the wedding." *There.* Out in the open, no playing pishy-pashy.
"I'm happy you came."

"Well"—was that a blushing she saw?—"I made up my mind about . . . about"—he rocked back and forth, twirling his cap.

"*About*?" she prodded.

"Tell me about your friend, Mr. Tabatnik."

Careful, she told herself. "Mr. Tabatnik is no friend of mine. In fact, heavily to the contrary." He waited for her to go on, his eyes serious, but not accusing. A good sign. "How could you doubt?" she continued and, reaching across the distance separating them, tapped his knee. A little pushy, maybe, but sometimes a little pushy was a good thing. He startled—she was right!—as though her touch had jolted him.

"Every time I see him," Herschl said, "and that's two times"—holding up two fingers—"I more and more know that I like him less and less."

"My feelings exactly," she said, making a circle of thumb and forefinger. The picnic, that's where she'd give him the book, ask him to read to her. His reading aloud always sounded like a love letter.

"That's for sure," he added.

"For me, too," she said, jiggling her leg enthusiastically.

"Just think how much I'll hate him if I bump into him the third time," he said. Now his eyes had a mischievous sparkle, and the corners of that sweet mouth were turned up. A grin was about to break out.

"God forbid you see him five times, or six." *Show him she knew how to go along with a joke.* "Now, about our picnic—"

"Except," he said, wagging his finger.

Trying to hide her irritation: "Except?"

"This business with Mr. Tabatnik is not something for joking."

"Business?" Straightening, she sat up as tall as she could. "There's no *business*."

"How good did you know Mr. Tabatnik?"

Sadie blinked. "So-so."

"So-so?"

"That's less than very-good and more than not-at-all."

He seemed to be thinking about what she'd said. "How long?"

Trying to keep her voice light, ignoring the sweat puddling up in her cleavage: "I already answered your questions, my turn to ask." She smiled what she hoped was her best moving picture smile. Even if he didn't like moving pictures, he might like snappy-looking smiling. "Like I said, how about our picnic?"

"I'm not finished."

"You can finish up at the picnic."

He hesitated, then shrugged. "What do I got to lose?"

"Nothing to lose. In fact, the opposite." She went to the china cupboard, and rummaged in a drawer for a pencil and notebook. "I'll write down a list, what you like to eat sitting on a blanket under the hot sun. Special order, just for you." She wrote: *potato salad, hot dogs, pickles.* Looking up: "Lemonade, ice tea, or, maybe my special recipe root beer, guaranteed for picking you up on a hot day?"

"I let you do the choosing," He put his hat on.

"Wonderful." Thinking, how could she get him to stay, have a bite supper? "Maybe you would welcome a small bite supper, very small, with a taste of this special root beer, which I happen to have this minute in my icebox?"

He took his hat off. "Sadie, Sadie, did anyone say you are hard to take no for an answer?"

Sadie stood up. "Never," she said, "until now."

∽〰〇   ∽〰〇   ∽〰〇

Ike would move, of course, but where, and with what commotion? Finding his note thumbtacked to her door the day before the Labor Day picnic gave Sadie sweaty palms.

"Sadie, good-bye," she read. "I wish you luck, wish for me the same. I'm going to my friend, Nathan Perelwitz, the fish person on Spring Street, until I get my own place, which, to judge from my fast success in America, should be soon.

"I still say we were good together. Anyway, don't feel for me sorry, I'm still the Dance King, and don't forget it. Ike Tabatnik."

Sadie carried the letter to the sink and, striking a match, held the flame to one edge of the paper. Everyone knew Sadie Schuster wasn't some cry baby, so why did she feel like doing that now?

Chapter
Seventeen

On Monday morning, Labor Day, Sadie stepped onto her front stoop at eight o'clock carrying a large wicker basket, a blue-and-white-striped parasol and a red string bag from Klein's Emporium, in which she'd packed her new navy-blue serge bathing suit, red bathing cap and rubber shoes, in case Herschl said yes to a cooling off in the Atlantic Ocean.

Who knew if he'd relax and dunk in the water? He'd maybe sulk, or pull out a roll of white paper and read off one hundred new Ike Tabatnik questions. He had made up his mind, he said, started to say, but about *what*? Finished, his mouth zipped closed. So sue him.

Earlier that morning, after her bath, she'd dusted her love knot with a sprinkling of crushed, scented rose petals and, after chanting a just-thought-up, half-English, half-Polish chant, sent up a two-part urgent message to the spirits: *No more questions*, and *Hurry*! Coney Island was a perfect spot for romance. She could think up the place and deliver the man, but she couldn't get a happy ending on her own.

Wait! All that rushing, *did she*—plunging her hand to the bottom of the food basket—*yes*! Her rose-scented love knot and the new poetry book, wrapped in white tissue paper, nestled among the beet *borscht*, potato salad, fried chicken, salmon patties, *zizel* bread, chilled cucumbers, double chocolate brownies, and raspberry-lemon cookies.

She inhaled. Orchard Street, for a change, smelled sweet. Cool, but the newspaper report promised plenty of sunshine, maybe a breeze later, in time for dancing. All that was missing was Herschl. Setting her bundles down, Sadie poked around in her purse and, taking out her hand mirror, scrutinized her face. Not bad. A peck pale—puckering up her lips, pinching her cheeks—but a little sunshine, a little dancing, would rosy her up.

She flicked a speck of dust from her sleeve, humming a few bars of "Daisy Bell." She had no regrets, none, about spending so much money on new clothes for this outing. Wetting her handkerchief with the tip of her tongue, she wiped grease from the heel of her boot.

Everything she wore was red or white or blue, or all three: red linen shirtwaist; navy-blue pleated skirt; white straw hat bound with red grosgrain ribbon; red-and-blue straw purse; red patent leather boots with white tips and heels. Wasn't this an American holiday, wasn't she a full citizen since 1906, and proud of it? Wasn't red her best color, except when it was lace and jinxed by Ike's evil eye?

Twelve past eight. Sadie went down the front steps and peered around the corner of the building into the alley. No Herschl. She returned to the front stoop. He couldn't—*no, he wouldn't*—sit her down. Was that the right way to say it in American?

She strained to remember a conversation with Lippke at the Irving Street Social Club about someone who'd invited his lady friend to supper, and failed to appear. *Stood her up!* That was what Lippke had called it. Better it should be called *knock her down.* Be honest, Herschl could have a medal in stood-her-up. Why did she think today was a holiday from doing that?

She hummed "Alexander's Ragtime Band," watching two small boys sail clothespin boats in the gutter. It was nice, watching children when they weren't crying or dripping with ice cream or saying, "Quick, where's the bathroom, my pee is coming." The bigger boy, the one with dark curls, and already, under that thin shirt, strong-looking shoulders, made her wonder how Herschl looked when he was six, seven years old. Then she saw him coming toward her, a not-really-tall, not-really-short man in a white shirt, dark pants, sporty-looking blue suspenders, and a cap, carrying a paper bag, crossing Delancey Street. Looking up, he saw her and, taking his cap off, waved it.

She felt heady, short of breath, but not in the way that said she needed a doctor. The spirits were for sure in the neighborhood. Picking up her parcels and humming, Sadie started toward him. Life felt good.

⟋⟋⟍   ⟋⟋⟍   ⟋⟋⟍

"Imagine!" Sadie peered down at the Atlantic Ocean from the Coney Island Boardwalk, gesturing at the hundreds of noisy bathers scattered over miles of wide, smooth sand, and then at the brilliant bleached sky, the blue-green water. "You got . . . you got—"

"A beach," Herschl said, swiping at the perspiration beading on his forehead.

"Not only just a beach, you got a wonderful thing! Look: so much healthy enjoyment!" Sadie inhaled, exhaling in a noisy, joyful burst of air. "Water, something about it makes me feel so—so free!"

Herschl grunted.

"What's wrong, you don't like the ocean?" Before he could answer: "Ooooh!" and she was pointing to a spot just below them, where three muscular young men in bathing costumes were dumping sand atop a blonde, skinny, young woman, stretched out, faceup, in a bright-pink bathing costume. "Doesn't that look like fun?" Sadie squirmed. "Sand all over your skin"—her eyes closed in imagined ecstasy—"like having an up-and-down, allover massage!"

"Me," Herschl said, "I like the shade!"

"Okay, okay, we'll find a quick cooling off." She turned from the beach, looking to her right and, with a gasp of happiness, saw the jumble of carnival scenes she'd seen in the newspaper photograph:

a forest of white towers and minarets stretching into the horizon; screeching tilt-a-whirl cars careening close to loop-the-loops that threaded in and out among the roller coasters and parachute jumps.

On the far horizon, a man exploding out of a cannon shot across a backdrop of enormous signs and billboards pulsing with electricity as, beyond that, a leering face beckoned everyone to enter The Dreamland Amusement Park.

No quiet to be found there. Shading her eyes with her hands, Sadie spotted, directly ahead, a grove of trees fringing the crest of a grassy slope. "There," she said and, grasping one basket, hurried toward the hill, followed by Herschl, carrying the other.

Midway up the slope she found an empty patch of grass surrounded by an army of noisy families lounging on blankets and quilts. Not exactly private. Nearby, a knot of small boys tossed a baseball back and forth. To one side, three men drinking beer played horseshoes. But it was a million degrees cooler than the blistering boardwalk and, for now, anyway, none of the babies was crying.

Herschl, looking relieved, said, "Sure, sure, anywhere."

Spreading a table cloth, Sadie stretched and lifted her face toward the sun: *Shoulders back, chin thrust forward to make the neck look longer,* all the things Mitzi said to do when a man is watching. "Such a pleasure, just being out of the city!"

Herschl set his basket down and shook a book out of his brown paper bag, holding it out to her. "Gruenfeld."

"Wait!" She rummaged through her basket, pulling out the book she'd bought for him. "Here."

Herschl stared at it, at her, that almost-holy-looking gleam on his face she'd seen before, in the park, when he talked about his poetry books, what they meant to him. "What?" he asked, taking the book, cupping it in both hands.

"A surprise, I bought it for you this week."

He lowered himself onto the grass, knees braced together to support the book.

"*The New Yiddish Poetry,*" he read, "Collected by Professor Sol Kaufikoff, Columbia University, New York City." He held the book to his face and closed his eyes. "It smells new."

He should only say *Sadie* with that much feeling, and pat her in the tender way he was patting that book. "The last time I gave you a used book, Komaroff. I wanted this one to be new, your eyes the first to drink it in."

He looked happy, all right. "Where?"

"I have my places for special things."

"I heard about this, but didn't . . ." His voice trailed off, his interest snagged by something behind her.

Wheeling around, Sadie saw a young couple lying face-to-face on the next blanket, arms clasped around one another's waists.

Herschl, clearing his throat, opened the book and lowered his head over the title page. "Aha," he said, "look!"

"Shhh." Sadie pointed to the young couple.

"I see poems in here by Gruenfeld."

Sadie nodded, but didn't answer, absorbed by the couple, now kissing, then wiggling and caressing one another. Loud, lip-smacking sounds floated toward her, and one of the kissers sent out hoarse, gurgling noises. "Hmmm, nice," she said, to no one in particular, "friendly. Also, very healthy."

Paging through the book, Herschl said something that sounded like *Phhooom*.

Now the girl, nuzzling the boy's ear, giggled a soft, fuzzy purr, but more than a purr.

Glands! Sadie thought. What if they were catching, like the everyday cold or whooping cough? You just happen to sit down on the grass next to two people with full-time healthy glands who are going about their business and, pop! The next thing you know, you end up with a full-blown case of not-so-bad glands of your own.

Sadie glanced at Herschl. He was reading, pretending to, but his eyes were only half-opened and he leaned slightly in the direction of the couple, as though refusing to look, while not being entirely unhappy about listening. Her own glands worked good, better than good, that was for sure. The big question here was *him*.

"Hungry?" She asked.

He shifted his knees, still turning pages. "After."

"After?" Sadie's eyebrows shot up. "After *what*?"

He pointed to a page. "I'll read out loud. Gruenfeld, he's a genius with poems about flowers and sky and, and . . ." Looking into the distance, as though he'd forgotten the lovers, or even about her, his eyes held that dreamy look she loved, more like a poet himself than an ice peddler. A thrill, a tiny bubble building up and getting close to bursting, began somewhere deep in her chest.

Too bad she'd miss what might happen next with the couple. Two good things always showed up at the same time. "I'm a big nature person myself," she said, and unlaced her boots, kicking them off. "Begin."

She agreed with him. Gruenfeld's poems sounded the way paintings looked, only he used words instead of watercolors or oils: "The sea erased the sun, Berries bleed sweet on my tongue," Herschl read, seeming not to notice that Sadie, intent upon the pleasure of listening, shivered from time to time.

The sound of his voice soaked into her skin. Who would know Herschl could read poetry like a regular college professor, with a deep, strong voice that went up and down exactly where the words needed?

Herschl read, "Spring, with its passion of—"

Sadie sat up, as though jolted by electricity. *That* word she knew! "Hold it, repeat that, please." Just the word to maybe get them to the subject of glands.

"Repeat?"

"That word you just now read, *passion.*"

His eyes announced: *annoyed.* "You just now said it, why repeat?"

"I can't believe. Once my horoscope in *The Daily Forward*—"

"Sadie, please, don't interrupt for one word, it breaks apart the whole, the whole—"

"What's so terrible if you stop to repeat one word? Mr. Gruenfeld doesn't blow away, don't be such an *ockshen!*"

"So," he said, then clamped his mouth shut, breathing hard through his nose—a sure sign of anger. "*I'm* stubborn!"

A temper, *hoo-ha*! Something she'd never seen on him. Not as hot as Ike's, no banging on the table, but *still*. Good to get these things out in the open.

"And you," he went on, shaking the book and closing it, then hugging it to his chest, as though they'd damaged it by arguing, "you're being a *nudnik!*"

Spoiled, this beautiful day gone, over nothing. They were

fighting, their first fight—only, *wait!* This didn't happen between strangers, people you can take or leave. You got to care about someone to get this angry. "Herschl," she said, "do you know what's happening here?"

"Something I don't like," he said warily, still embracing the book, "that's for sure."

"No, listen." Sadie put her hand out, reaching for his arm, as he pulled away. "We hurt each other's feelings, so—"

"*So?*" His face was still *fahrkrimpt.*

"—that means we got to be good friends." He looked skeptical. "Because," she hurried on, "did you ever fight with someone when you thought, hello, who are you to me, who needs this aggravation, you're not even worth my time of day?"

He was about to say something, but changed his mind and laughed instead, until, shaking his head, he took his handkerchief out of his pocket and wiped his eyes. "Sadie, Sadie, what makes you so . . . so"—he chuckled, still wiping his eyes—"*different?*"

What a compliment. "I don't do nothing special," she said, blushing, setting out the parcels of food. "I just go along, paying attention"—a lovely word, one she'd never used with him before—"to my own business. How's for some *borscht?*" He nodded. "But thank you for saying so. I appreciate it."

He accepted the soup but, instead of sipping, sighed, staring into its depths. Maybe she should slip her love knot out of the basket and under her plate, the closer the better. All that poetry, especially the one about passion, could get the spirits juiced up and ready to strike. Her fingernail looked nicely rounded and shiny. She poured *borscht* into a bowl for herself and, reaching for the basket, stopped midway when she saw a look cross Herschl's face that she recognized as *unhappy-thoughtful,* with a sprinkling of *doubtful* on top.

Putting his spoon down, he cleared his throat. "On the subject"—it was his I-have-questions-about-Ike voice—"at your place, I asked a few things about Mr. Tabatnik but, as I recall correctly, you didn't answer." He sniffed. Not a my-nose-is-running sniff, but a disapproval sniff, a sniff about knowing all the answers even before trying out all the questions. "Nothing," he added, accenting both syllables.

"It's simple," Sadie said, watching the boy and girl on the next blanket gather their things. This was no time to holler out good-bye and good luck. "There's nothing to tell."

"Oh?"

"It's a quick story in two parts." Avoiding his eyes. "Part one: before, I knew him." She snapped her fingers. "Part two: after, I don't." She sipped her soup, good idea to look calm, innocent.

"Before?" he repeated. "And after, after what?"

"After Herschl Emmanuel Diamond."

Silence. Then: "Sometimes," he said, looking at her, then away, "I think I know what I'm ready to say, down to the last, final comma. Then you say something and, all of a sudden"—he snapped his fingers—"I can't remember my words."

Stretching past him, Sadie reached into the basket, and felt the love knot nestled at the bottom. Her fingernail was a nice shade of warm. The spirits were paying attention. Pretending to fuss with her napkin, she brushed the love knot across her fingernail, then slipped it under her plate. "I'll tell you what I think," she said, sitting back.

He looked wary.

"What I think is," she said, glancing up, then away, "anyone who reads from a poetry book as wonderful as you"—waving her spoon—"is *enough*! More than enough, without worrying so much about talking out your own extra words." She stirred her soup, trying to look smart and adorable at the same time, a lady who for sure knows how much talking is good, how much is too much, and *fahrtik*, the end.

For a moment, neither of them said anything, the only sound, Sadie's spoon clinking against the bowl. Then: music! Was she imagining? Sadie jumped up. No, she heard music all right: a clarinet, a saxophone, drumrolls. Mumbling a hurried *I'll-be-right-back*, she excused her way down the slope and around blankets, chairs, until she reached the boardwalk where—pushing her way through the throngs—she stood at the railing overlooking the beach.

Three musicians, who had set themselves up at the water's edge, were beating out a ragtime, the kind of ta-ta-dum-dum music that made her blood race. And not just musicians, dancers also. A human chain of men and women, twenty—no, more—wearing bright woolen bathing costumes—the women's with puffed up sleeves, ribbon collars, embroidery hugging their waists, then falling over rounded hips to the soft zigzag of ruffled knees; the men's with tank tops cut to show off their muscles, narrow elastic belts and tight legs stopping just above the knees—and everyone holding on to one another hard, arms thrust forward, hands grasping each other's shoulders, waists, hips; frenzied, moving like one enormous wiggling animal, in and out of the water, across the sand, back to the water; kicking, singing, hooting, shimmying.

Sadie *felt* the music, inhaled it. A miracle. When did you see dancers shaking up and down on the beach, to say nothing of splashing into a state of delicious soaked, and nobody stopping them, nobody hollering, "Too much noise, too much wildness!"

She rushed back up the slope, breathless with the ecstasy of such, such—she couldn't say what, her mind racing: Where do I change my clothes? He'll say no; stay calm, don't chew his head off.

Herschl said, "Fine by me, you go, I'll watch." But his eyes said otherwise. She knew a look in the eyes when she saw it on a man, especially a look that talked louder than the mouth. His eyes said: *Go, but I won't be happy.*

What now? Careful what you say, zip up your mouth until you have the right words. *Oy!* Her love knot, there, on the blanket, tossed aside when she'd jumped up to follow the music. What a foolish! Worse than foolish, leaving the knot out to cook up. The spirits hated the sun, heat made them cranky. They liked dark, cool, secret places, places like the cemetery, swarming without being seen. What if they punished, disappeared even, and never came back!

She snuck a look at Herschl. He was still busy admiring his new book, like she'd never said a word about dancing or music. Thanks God. Mister Relaxed, Mister Why-Get-Excited. Mumbling something about looking for her dropped-out hairpins, Sadie crouched, snatched up the knot, concealed it in her hand, before swiveling to check closely for any signs of damage.

Was she imagining? The knot was moving, puffing up—she spread her fingers to give it more room—then shrinking down again, almost a *breathing* motion, like something was pushing at it from inside. Sadie puckered her lips and blew, *puh*, at the soft, round, plump snippet of pink satin *schmattah*, hoping to soothe it. She waited. Nothing. Too much sun, all that excitement on the beach.

Now the musicians were pumping out a march, people shrieking, a happy kind of roaring, and then applause floated up from the water, tapping at her brain, heating up the heat even higher. A party was happening, so many happy people. She wanted to go.

Twisting around to look at Herschl, who was this minute watching her with suddenly sweet, peaceful eyes, Sadie saw a blinking on, a blinking off, a message, as plain as if it was written out in bright-red letters across his calm forehead.

Thrusting the knot into her pocket—*hoo!*—that was no imagination playing tricks, *something* had just quivered the faintest quiver against her fingertips, like that time when the spirits tap-tapped at the bridge of her nose, and that other time, when a single spirit whooshed in and out of her eyelashes, trailing puffs of perfumed air.

"So . . ." Jumping up, Sadie brushed dirt and grass from her hands and knees. "A *schmooze* up the boardwalk, you said."

ᵕ⁄⁄ᵒ   ᵕ⁄⁄ᵒ   ᵕ⁄⁄ᵒ

Sadie heard them first: women, a lot of women, and singing, then a flute, drums, a trombone, or was it a saxophone? Then she saw them, just past the hot dog stand, up that small hill. A parade, at least fifty women—no, there were more—wearing red banners across their white dresses, carrying flags and signs: "Votes for Women. Now." Dropped down smack into their picnic day, out of nowhere. Perfect.

Nothing from Herschl about the voting announcement she'd slipped into the poetry book. A good time now to spill out to him what voting meant to her. A good time for him to say, "Nice," or, "*Gevalt.*"

She walked faster, almost running. He followed and, by the

time he caught up with her, she was clapping, singing "The Star-Spangled Banner" along with the marchers. Turning to him, so excited, she was almost trembling, she grasped his hand. "Don't you love this song?"

"Not to sing out loud, in public," he said. His face didn't tell her the story she had to know: women voting, yes; or, women voting, no.

The marchers passing them that minute held up a sign, "Women of the Upper West Side, New York, for the Vote." Sadie waved, hollering, "Yes, yes, me too!" One woman waved back; two others turned, raising their fists, a kind of salute.

"Sadie." Herschl leaned closer. "Not so loud."

"Why not loud? Nobody hears if you whisper."

"People come here to have a good time."

"I'm having a special good time."

"You work so hard at everything," he said, patting her shoulder. Well, *something*, a patting, but not enough to satisfy. "You're going to maybe wear yourself out."

"This isn't work to me, Herschl. This is saying"—*should she push this, what if he says, 'Sorry, the end, too much mishagash already, good-bye'?*—"women"—*how to say this so it wouldn't sound angry?*—"we're Americans, too."

"Who says no?"

"*Who?* The Constitution is who." Four syllables. Mrs. Pomerantz worked so hard teaching her how to say that word, the *t-u-t* coming out like *s-h*, and not like a *tu tu tu*. "And George Washington, he's who. He forgot about us when he put the country together."

A smile. Not exactly sweet, but, still, a smile. "Do you want to know what I think?" Now, the end of the parade, a tall, thin man in a red, white, and blue costume, juggling red, white, and blue balls and playing "Yankee Doodle" on a harmonica.

"Tell me first, then I'll know if I want to know."

"If I know you, Sadie"—he took a deep breath—"and excuse me, if I say I know a little bit."

What kind of serious talking was he doing to her? "So, say it already."

Shading his eyes with his hand, he looked at the receding parade, shrugged, and looked at her. "Who knows? Soon, maybe even next year, what with all these women, you'll be doing all the voting you want."

"From your mouth to God's ear!" She could hug him right here, but that kind of fuss could maybe be too much for him out in public. "Thank you"—she was working to keep her voice soft—"for saying so."

The crowd was scattering. Sadie took Herschl's arm and felt—*thought* she felt—a tiny shifting of his arm to make more room for hers. Strolling, they threaded through the crush of people, baby buggies, dogs, past the vendors hawking peanuts, hot dogs, cotton candy, taffy apples.

Farther up, the gateway to Dreamland Amusement Park beckoned, gates thrown open wide enough for them to squint down the midway at golden-roofed minarets rising like mirages, glinting against the royal-blue sky. Sadie read from the billboard posted outside the box office: "A whole town of Eskimos, a train ride over the Swiss Alps Mountains, a genuine romantic gondola ride." She asked, "I know romantic, but what does gondola mean?"

Herschl frowned. "I think . . ." He trailed off uncertainly, then smiled. "Some book I read, *hoo*, years ago, said it's like an Italian streetcar or trolley, only on water instead of land." He looked at the billboard, then at Sadie. "Should we?"

⌁ﬗ⌁   ⌁ﬗ⌁   ⌁ﬗ⌁

Afterward, Sadie said it was her second favorite thing, even when she counted the show with one hundred dancing and singing midgets, and the one where six fire engines acted out a fake, four-alarm blaze. Her first favorite? The roulette wheel that spun her—lying scrunched up next to a dozen people—in a whirlwind of circles, finally flinging her, dizzy and doubled up with laughter, into the arms of an astonished Herschl.

"No more doing dangerous things," he said, brushing her off. "Let's win some souvenirs," and they pushed and pulled themselves in and out of the crowds wandering through the shooting galleries.

Stopping at one booth, Herschl put five pennies down for five darts, piercing a row of colored balloons, and the fat barker with the moustache, tan derby, checkered vest, gave them an alarm clock with a pink-and-white-striped face that played "Yankee Doodle" when they turned the small hand to twelve and the big hand to six. But Sadie's cotton candy cone melted, dripping sugar all over the alarm bell, turning it a mottled green.

"Give me, please, another prize," Sadie said, pushing the damaged clock across the counter toward the barker. He yawned, waving her away: *nothing doin'.*

"It turned all funny, here," she said, pointing to the discolored metal.

"Whaddya expect for a nickel, lady, the crown jewels?" He turned away. The sound Sadie uttered was somewhere between a squawk and a shriek, but failed to get his attention. Stepping up to the counter, Herschl signaled, *let me*, snapping his fingers at the barker, who half turned with an annoyed scowl.

Herschl explained how disappointed they were, the clock was ruined, no fault due to them, of course, cheap metal. Please, what other prize, like one of those, pointing to the rows of dolls and stuffed animals on shelves behind the counter.

"Look!" Sadie pointed to a brilliant green-and-yellow parrot with a red-and-white checkered kerchief tied around its neck. "Holy Spirit." Never in her life had such an absolutely unmistakable sign of good luck been *kerplunked* into her life. Only, this time it wouldn't fly away. She'd die before she left here without that bird.

"*That*," Sadie said, pointing to the parrot, pushing the clock across the counter.

"No new prize, and that's final," the barker said, cracking his knuckles. "Now why doncha just—"

"Then maybe I'll just whistle for the police," she said, twisting around to peer into the crowd.

"You can whistle, lady, until your lips fall off," the barker said, and popped a toothpick into his mouth.

"Sir," Herschl said, "no use being—"

Sadie, tugging at Herschl's arm, whispered into his ear. "Go on," she insisted, "tell him."

Herschl took a deep breath. "In our building at home we have a lawyer—"

Our! Just hearing him use the word sent a ping of pleasure up and down Sadie's skin.

"—who is happy to take care of swindlers for his customers."

"Say, listen you old coot," the barker growled. "Threaten me 'n I'll—"

Sadie, pounding on the counter, hollered, "Careful who you call—"

She couldn't remember who did what next, or if that shrill whistling sound was her fingernail; or if a real-live policemens, seeing the ruckus, was trying to break it up. By the time Herschl, his eyes bulging, had stepped back, fisted hands waving in the air, and the barker had, in one grunting leap, jumped over the counter and was punching his dirty forefinger into Herschl's collarbone, she'd scurried around the counter, plucked the parrot from the shelf, thrust it into her straw purse, and was grabbing Herschl's arm.

By then he seemed to be doing a funny hop-hop, ducking the barker's jabs, and she had to grab at him harder, noticing a trickle of blood running down his face. There was no time to wipe it up, they were running down the midway, knocking into so many angry, surprised people, that they couldn't holler, "Excuse me," to all of them.

Then they were outside the entrance to Dreamland Park and back on the Boardwalk, where they could no longer hear the barker yelling, "Stop, thieves!" They weren't running, only walking fast, weaving in and out of the crowd, trying to blend in, looking over their shoulders, not stopping until they found an empty bench hidden by bushes.

"What did we do?" Herschl swiped at his face with his handkerchief.

"My heart!" Sadie pressed her hand against her chest. Then, looking at him closely: "Let me . . ." and, pulling his hand away, she squinted at the dark-red streak between his nose and upper lip. "I'm sorry to report blood." Seeing a water fountain nearby, she rushed over, returning with a dripping handkerchief, which she pressed to his face. "You cut your face"—she was glancing over her shoulder as she tended to him—"anyone asks, with your razor."

Wincing, he said, "For me this was a first, breaking the law."

"You think I go around stealing parrots every day of the week?"

She giggled, pulling the parrot from her purse and pressing it against her mouth.

When she looked up, Herschl was laughing, too, shaking his head, dabbing at his face. "I got to admit, I gave him a couple good jabs." His eyes turned serious. "These crazy things always happen when I'm with you. Why?"

"Maybe it's because"—she removed the wet cloth from his face—"when you're with me, I'm also with you, and we make a good team." *There!* She said it, so sue her! "All cured." She sat back, scrutinizing her nails. *Say something! Say I made up my mind; say I'm finished with mourning—something!*

For a moment, he seemed about to say something, but then—the sudden crackling of fireworks, colored pinwheels skyrocketing in the distance, followed by a lively rush of music floating toward them from the beach.

"Imagine," Sadie said, her voice too eager, too loud, "still dancing!" She climbed onto the bench, standing very still, listening. A polka, for sure, and was that someone playing an accordion? "Let's dance!" she said.

Herschl's head snapped back, he looked up at her, raising his hand against her insistence. "You—"

She clambered down, trying to be graceful, knowing she wasn't. "*Us!*"

"I couldn't," he protested; again, that unhappy look from the walk by the East River plastered on his face: his Gittel look.

"*Wouldn't.* You liked to dance, you danced good, you told me."

"That was before—"

"Before Gittel died." It slipped out. She wanted, and didn't want, to stop herself.

He looked startled: "Yes." A faint murmur.

"*You* didn't die, and *I'm* alive!"

He pulled in his breath, a sharp hiss, as though he'd been struck.

"Well," she went on, and waited. But he was half-turned away, she couldn't see his eyes. "Me, I'm a dancer."

"I know."

"And"—her voice faltering a little—"I'm also a fighter for women voting"—better to assert that now rather than putting it off—"sooner, not later. I don't wait so good. We waited long enough for this." Everything tied into a neat package, all at once, take her, or leave her, she was who she was. She stood up. He sat, shoulders sagging, almost as though the air had been pumped out of him, looking down at his clasped hands. "Better to say all these things now," she said, turning to go.

She thought she heard him say, "I'm sorry," but he didn't try to stop her from walking away.

Getting ready to swim took a while. She retrieved her bathing costume, cap, shoes, from her picnic basket, then found one of those wooden box dressing rooms that weren't big enough to turn around in, so how could she do a good job of struggling out of and into clothes?

She hoped her new blue serge bathing costume looked as good here as it had in the Klein dressing room. She pulled on the ruffled bloomers, tied a wide, red silk ribbon around her hair—not a sliver of a mirror, anywhere!—and, last, slipped her love knot, still all-puffed-out and warm and fragrant-smelling, down her cleavage, not that it mattered anymore. Not even magic could make her turn into who she wasn't, whether she loved him or not. Then she gathered her clothes, purse, and boots, into a bundle, thinking: *Oy, our food, my baskets, up there with Herschl;* knowing, even as she gasped: leaving those behind was only a tiny, baby-sized part of what she was losing.

A ten-minute walk—it felt like sixty—down the beach to where the musicians were now playing something hard, fast, loud. She stuffed her rolled-up bundle under a bench, and walked straight into the thump-thump beat, squealing with terror, with ecstasy, as it pulled her into the water, hurling her—sandwiched in the dance chain between two fat blonde women, twins, the same face twice, in leopard skin bathing suits—into water up to her hips and out again, bumping and kicking across the sand, moving so fast she tripped and found herself sitting down. Suddenly she was pulled to her feet, and thrown back into the lineup by a bearded man in a black derby, smoking a smelly cigar.

Now a tall, skinny woman in a peppermint-striped bathing costume—a crying baby propped on her hip—squeezed into line in front of her, swung around and, dancing backward, hollered, "Hold on, hard, honey, but don't pinch my baby, gotta go to the ladies, be right back," and pushed the infant at an astonished Sadie, before abruptly leaving. Another whip-around, sand-water-sand, people forming a bridge of clasped hands, and everyone else snaking underneath. A tricky business with a wiggling baby cradled in the crook of her arm.

When she looked up, Herschl was standing among the crowd at the railing on the precipice, looking down, a not-here, not-there look on his face. Then he waved, looking quizzical, hesitated, and held up a hand.

He's *leaving*!

Now her free hand was grasped by a muscular young man with a drooping handlebar moustache, who swung her around, a fast two-step that ended in the crest of an enormous wave, delivering them, giggling, onto shore, and the screaming baby into her mother's eager hands.

Struggling to her feet, Sadie looked up again, but Herschl was gone, and the chain was snapping past, eager hands reaching out to pluck her back into line. Now the music was a polka, hard on her knees and hips, but she kept up, managing to plunge one hand down the front of her suit to check on her love knot.

Water, skin, salt, air, but no love knot—*nothing*! That last splash-down in the water probably shook it into the ocean, and out of her life. Her fingernail looked soggy, the tip broken off in a jagged slope.

One more fast whip-around, someone patting her bottom in time to the music, someone pinching her shoulder hard. *Now what?* Soaking wet and on her own, the um-pa-pa beat giving way to music she'd swear was the hot-pepper stuff Ike loved so much. She needed a minute to catch her breath, but someone behind her pulled her out of line and up toward the cresting, hard-packed sand.

"Hey, mister!" She wheeled around, trying to pull free, one hand flung back so hard it glanced off of Herschl's chin.

"A waltz, I think, Sadie," he said, holding his arms out and smiling his sweet, calm smile, his eyes for sure more blue than gray, thanks to the Atlantic Ocean. There he was, looking, in his wool bathing costume—especially with those beautiful shoulder muscles—like he was born to go to the beach.

The musicians were deep into a tango, all right, she'd know that music anywhere, except for no castanets, and no tambourines or flute. "Certainly," she said, grasping Herschl's hand, her other hand resting lightly on his bare shoulder, moving closer into the circle of his arms. "Who doesn't love a waltz?"

GLOSSARY

babushka: Head scarf

bar mitzvah: The coming-of-age religious ceremony for Jewish boys at age thirteen

beshert: Meant to be, fated, usually used romantically

"Bintele Brief": A story, usually sad, often published in *The Daily Forward*, a newspaper published in Yiddish on the Lower East Side

borscht: A soup made primarily of beets and served hot or cold often with sour cream

bubeh meises: Grandmother stories, old wives' tales, usually associated with gossip

challah: Traditional long twisted bread, usually eaten on the Sabbath and holidays

chochkas: Small, interesting, ornamental, often valuable items, such as jewelry, vases, perfume vials

chupah: The four-cornered arrangement—floral, satin, embroidered or woven cloth—under which Jewish marriages are consecrated *chutzpah*: Excessive self-promotion, guaranteed to annoy

cockamamie: Outlandish, unusual, of no value, even inflammatory

fahrbrent: Burning with an emotional response to any situation, on fire to do something

fahrkrimpt: Wrinkled, unattractive, a response of disapproval

fahrputzt: Very dressed up, elegant, fashionable

fahrschprayt: Spread out, fallen, even collapsed

fahrtik: Expressing, often with annoyance, a wish to be finished with the discussion

fahrtootst: Annoyed, even outraged

feh: An expression used to reject something—an object, an opinion—considered as having no value

gefilte fish: Stuffed fish

gevalt: An emotional outburst in response to a surprise or threat

gezuntheit: A wish for good health, spoken when someone sneezes

gimnazye: A European secondary school that prepares students for the university

goniff: A thief, anyone who cheats or swindles

gonse knocker: One who has an exalted sense of self

Gott im Himmel: An emotional response to danger or surprise or threat; literally, God in heaven

halva: A sweet confection of ground sesame seeds and honey *holdupnik*: An idiomatic expression accusing one of being a thief or cheat

hotsy-totsy: Slang that compliments anyone who is well-dressed or coiffed

kerplunk: To make a thudding or thunking sound

kibitzer: Joker, a comedian, one who makes small talk that evokes laughter

kishkey: Slang for innards, used to indicate that an emotional or dire situation has affected one to his/her very center

klugizmir: Spontaneous outcry when facing a difficult or frightening situation

klutz: One who is clumsy, awkward

kniver: One who is likely to cheat or suggest investing in an unsavory enterprise

macher: A person of importance in social, political or business affairs: a leader

mayven: An expert, one who is especially knowledgeable in an admirable pursuit

mazel: Good luck

mazel tov: A congratulation, expressed for a marriage, birth, engagement, graduation

mensch: Male or female who has admirable qualities, is seen as being fully human

meshuga: Crazy, foolish, fails to make sense, applicable to human beings as well as situations *mishagash*: A foolish or dangerous attitude or situation

mishmash: A mix-up, a mess

nafke: Prostitute

nar: A fool

nudgy: To pester someone

nudnik: A pest

ockshen: One who is excessively stubborn

pisher: Slang for one who is too young or inexperienced for whatever he/she is attempting

pishy-pashy: Slang for "fooling around," failing to take the situation seriously

pitsele: A small piece or person

punim: Face

putz: To spend time in an aimless or idle manner, usually *putz* around

rebbe: Rabbi

rebbetzin: The wife of a rabbi

schadchen: Matchmaker, especially to bring two unmarried individuals together to promote a marriage

schlemiel: A male deficient in physical, as well as intellectual qualities, a loser *schlep*: To proceed or move especially slowly, tediously, awkwardly, or carelessly

schmaltz: Chicken fat

schmattah: A small piece of fabric or, idiomatically, a description of an ugly garment

schmooze: Chitchatting with friends or family, or even strangers

schnapps: Any of various liquors of high alcoholic content

schpritz: A small touch, a dab

Shabbas: Friday evening and Saturday, holy days to Orthodox Jews

shah: Please be quiet

shammus: An employee of a synagogue

shaytel: A marriage wig required for Orthodox Jewish women, usually stiff, unattractive

shtetl: A small Jewish town or village formerly found in Eastern Europe

Talmud: A collection of sixty-three books containing commentaries upon commentaries, studied by Orthodox Jews

tante: Aunt

tsehitst: Passion

tsotskey: A female who wears too much makeup or provocative clothing, often considered a criticism

ungeblozen: A pout, a show of dissatisfaction

veyez mir: A spontaneous utterance of disappointment, or even despair

yenta: A woman of vulgar manners, a shrew, a rumormonger

yussel: Idiomatic expression for someone who is far short of being competent

zaftik: Having a full, rounded figure, usually descriptive of females

zaide: Grandfather, but can be used derogatively to describe a young man whose mannerisms are those of an old man

zizel: A bread sold in Jewish food stores, has a delicious crust and brown seeds

zoompah: An expression of excitement, happiness

CPSIA information can be obtained
at www.ICGtesting.com
Printed in the USA
FFHW01n1919070818
47665196-51277FF